ASSASSIN'S CAPTIVE

Elite 6 Assassins - Book One

KAT CARRINGTON

Published by Blushing Books
An Imprint of
ABCD Graphics and Design, Inc.
A Virginia Corporation
977 Seminole Trail #233
Charlottesville, VA 22901

Kat Carrington
Assassin's Captive

Print ISBN: 978-1-63954-007-5
v1

Chapter 1

Chloe stood on the sidewalk, dusk settling around her, and gazed doubtfully at the nondescript building in front of her. She peered at the address on the piece of paper she held; it was indeed the correct address, but everything about it seemed wrong. The place was dark and foreboding, just like the neighborhood in which it stood. The skin crawled on the back of her neck and every instinct was clamoring for her to get out while she could. And yet, if she could just hand the envelope she held to the right person, her job would be done and she could pay the rent for another month. Hesitantly, she stepped forward, her hand raised to knock on the door. Before she could carry out the motion, the door burst open and a burly, rough looking man grabbed her wrist and yanked her inside. She opened her mouth to scream and he clapped a hand over it, dragging her deeper inside, to a room deep in shadows. There were some other men in the room, though she couldn't get a clear look at any of them.

"What the fuck?"

The man holding her said, "She was about to knock on the door."

"Son of a bitch. What the hell is she doing here?" The voice came from the other side of the room.

Chloe was frozen in terror, wondering what she had walked into and wishing desperately that she had never taken this job.

"Put her in a chair while we figure out what's going on."

She was propelled across the room to a chair and pushed down into it. The man who had grabbed her secured her arms and legs to the chair with zip ties and silenced her by pressing a piece of tape over her mouth. Then he joined the others in the shadows, where they talked quietly, too quietly for her to make out what they were saying. They had the envelope she had brought with her and they wasted no time in opening it and examining the paperwork inside. The tension in the room increased as they looked over the paper, and one of them swore fervently.

"Get the boss."

Another man walked out and a minute later, a man, clearly one of authority, strode into the room, followed by the man who had gone to get him. "Turn on a light," he said irritably. "It's too late to hide your faces now."

Chloe blinked as the lights came on and she could clearly see the half dozen men who were gathered together. The man who had just joined them walked over to her and studied her closely.

"I'm going to take this tape off your mouth and you're not going to do anything stupid, like scream. Understood?"

Chloe nodded and he jerked the tape off her face, causing her to let out a little yelp.

"Who are you?" he asked brusquely.

"I-I'm just a messenger. I was to deliver an envelope to this address, that's all."

"Do you know what was in the envelope?"

"No, of course not. Like I said, I'm just a messenger." Her

eyes traveled over him and she registered the fact that he looked fit and tough, with dark, tousled hair and flinty gray eyes.

"You made a bad mistake by coming here," he said diffidently. "Name?"

"Yes, that's been clear for a few minutes now," she retorted sarcastically. "I-I am Chloe."

He raised an eyebrow at her and seemed to really look at her for the first time. His gaze travelled over her thick, auburn hair, pulled back into a heavy tail, and her snapping green eyes. When he took his time looking over her voluptuous curves, she couldn't stop the wave of heat that swept through her groin, triggering a trickle of moisture between her legs. Her face flushed and he looked at her mockingly, as if he knew exactly what her reaction had been.

"If you'll just let me out of this chair, I'll be out of here and you'll never see me again."

He was shaking his head slowly. "That's not going to happen, little girl. You were set up, I'm sure, but it's too late now. You can't leave here."

"Want me to take care of her, boss?" asked one of the other men.

His eyes had never left her. He was silent for a long moment and then he reached out and cupped her chin in his hand, raising her face to his. He rubbed his thumb over her lips and she was shocked when her nerve endings prickled in response to his touch on her full, lower lip; her belly crawled with heat and she shuddered as goosebumps covered her skin. Finally, he said, "No. She's mine. I'll take care of her punishment and nobody else will touch her. Clear?"

The others murmured their understanding, although there were a few surreptitious glances exchanged. But they knew better than to question him. Chloe was still trying to understand the words he had said. Punishment? What the hell was he talking about? Who the hell were they and what had she walked into? And what had he meant when he said she'd been set up? She looked at the other men and realized that all of them were fit and tough looking.

Plucking up her courage, she asked, "Who are you? What is this place?"

He stared at her coolly and said, "Those are questions you don't want to know the answers to. I'm Jax. That's all you need to know. You belong to me now and you're going to do as you're told."

His words were outrageous. "I don't *belong* to anybody! What the hell are you talking about?"

When he spoke again, his voice was level and deadly calm. "You need to understand the gravity of what you've done. When you came here, you made a very big mistake, one that can't be undone. The life you lived up until this point is over now. You are mine and the sooner you accept that, the better for you. You have to be punished for what you've done and I will be the one to punish you."

She felt surreal, as if she was in the middle of a nightmare that she couldn't wake up from. "Please. Just let me go. I'll never speak of any of this to anyone. I just want to go home and forget it."

"Not going to happen, so just get that out of your head. There is no going back." He pulled a knife out of his pocket and her eyes widened in horror. He let out a mirthless chuckle and said, "I don't cut women. I have more enjoyable ways to deal with you." He cut the zip ties that were holding her and pulled her to her feet, holding her arm firmly. "You're going with me."

Chloe stumbled along with him, her mind racing, looking for a solution to her predicament. As frightened as she was, the heat of his hand on her arm was distracting. He led her down a hallway and into another room, one that looked like the front room of an apartment, and he locked the door behind them. He let go of her arm and stood looking at her, examining her from head to toe. His cock twitched as he looked her over and he felt that sense of recognition again, the same one he'd felt when he first laid eyes on her. He'd wanted her immediately, he knew he had to have her, and he was going to have her. But, first, she had to be punished. She had to know that to intrude into their world was something that could never go unpunished. She had to understand that from here on out, she would obey him without question. Her obedience was the only thing that would keep her alive.

He said, "This place is private. Nobody knows about it or about us. You committed the ultimate violation when you came here. Anyone else would be dead by now. I've decided to keep you for myself. Now you have to learn that you must obey me at all times. You must obey without argument or question. And you must be punished for what you've done."

"What do you mean?" She was struggling to make sense of what he said.

"I mean that I'm going to punish you now. I'm going to spank you and then I'm going to strip you naked and give you a taste of my belt. And then I'm going to take you. I'm going to fuck you like you've never been fucked before. You're going to scream for mercy and then you're going to beg for more."

"You're crazy! You can't do that to me! Who the hell do you think you are?" She was shocked and outraged at the things he said to her.

"I'm the man who owns you now. You're mine and I will do what I please with you."

She was speechless until he reached for her and then she went crazy, swinging her fists, clawing, kicking, trying to bite. He lifted her easily off the floor, pinning her arms against her sides and grunting when she connected with her flailing feet. He carried her into the kitchen and bent her forward over the table, holding her firmly at the small of her back, and he began peppering her bottom with hard smacks. Her struggles intensified and she shouted curses at him while he continued to spank her, setting her backside afire. When he lost patience with her struggling, he reached around her and unfastened her pants, jerking them down over her hips.

When the next brutally hard smack fell on her bare ass, she shrieked in protest. "No! Stop it, you can't do this!"

He spanked her harder, each blow leaving a deep red handprint on her creamy skin. She wailed at the pain and he mercilessly smacked the tender spot at the top of her thighs. The heat in her backside grew and she dimly realized that heat was growing between her thighs as well. The moisture trickled down and her pussy felt hypersensitive, swollen and aching with need. Jax could see her arousal and he grinned in satisfaction. She was raising her butt to meet his smacks and his member was iron hard, aching to be buried deep inside her. But punishment had to come first.

It took her a moment to realize the spanking had stopped and Chloe felt a sharp pang of disappointment. But then Jax unbuckled his belt and pulled it out of his pants with a swish and she struggled to understand what he was doing. She felt a moment of deep dread when he brushed her reddened cheeks with the supple strip of leather. Then the belt cracked across her ass and she sucked in a shocked breath, letting out a wail of pain when the second stripe was laid across her tender skin. The pain was tremendous and she felt a gush of moisture between her legs as the leather bit her again and again. Her arousal grew, along with the pain, until pleasure and pain and need all became one. Jax finally dropped the belt and laid a hand on her flaming cheeks, marked with the stripes of his punishment. Chloe let out a sob of pain and frustration and when she felt his cock probe between her thighs, her legs fell open in welcome.

Jax buried his shaft in her swollen, tight depths with one deep, brutal thrust and she screamed with the pleasure of it. He fucked her hard and fast and drove her to a screaming, sobbing orgasm, shuddering and jerking with the force of her climax. He kept thrusting until he emptied himself into her with a savage growl of triumph. He had taken possession of her and her training had begun. Chloe's head was swimming as she tried to accept what had happened. He had spanked her, used his belt on her, and it had aroused her beyond belief, so much that she had begged for him to fuck her, to use her, to make her come. It was beyond her comprehension and she knew that if he did it again, her body would react exactly the same way.

Jax pulled away from her, his eyes feasting on her, half naked, marked by her punishment and weak from the intensity of the orgasm he had brought to her.

She was sore and wet and she looked dazed when she finally raised her head. "I want to go home," she said.

"You didn't listen to me very well. This is your home now. The life you had before is over."

"No. No, you've inflicted your punishment on me. It's over. Now let me go." There was panic in her voice.

"Understand this. It's not over. You're not going anywhere. Your life is here now. When you came here, it created a danger for all of us. We can't afford to let you leave. And besides that, you're mine now and I have no intention of ever giving you up."

She stared at him in disbelief and began to understand that he really meant it. If she ever got out of there, she would have to escape. He could see the thoughts churning in her head.

"Chloe, listen to me. If you run, I will catch you. If you try to run, you will be punished. You are going to learn to obey me without question. If you do not learn, then you will be punished until you do. Your body told me all I need to know. Your body accepted me, welcomed me. Your mind and your soul will come next. You can make it as easy or as hard as you want."

She stared at him and she realized that he really meant every word of what he said. What kind of monster was he? What had he meant when he said that her presence put them in danger? What kind of evil had she walked into? And what the hell was wrong with her? Because he was right, her body *had* welcomed him.

"Now, follow me," Jax said. "I'll show you around your new home."

Chloe looked down at herself and said, "Please. Can I at least get dressed?"

"Go ahead," he said gruffly and then stood and watched her pull her panties and jeans on.

Her face flamed with humiliation but it was better to be covered up, even though pulling the jeans up over her flaming bottom and thighs made her gasp with pain. He showed her around the small apartment, simply a living room, kitchen, one bedroom and a bathroom with a large walk-in shower. It was comfortable enough, but she couldn't believe he was going to keep her there. She was suddenly eager for him to finish showing her around and to leave her there so she could try to sort out her thoughts and come up with some kind of a plan.

"I want you to write down your clothing sizes and what you need and I'll see that you have it. There's writing material in the desk drawer. For tonight, I'll give you a t-shirt to put on."

"And where do you stay?" Chloe asked.

He looked hard at her and laughed suddenly. "I don't think you understand. This is my quarters. You will be staying here with me."

Her mouth fell open. "B-but there's only one bedroom."

"That's right. The bed is big enough for both of us."

"You can't just keep me prisoner here!"

"Of course, I can. I'm going to enjoy teaching you obedience and acceptance. You have a lot to learn."

She stood staring at him, unable to think straight. None of this could really be happening; she must be having a nightmare. "I need to use the bathroom," she mumbled and fled. She took her time in there, trying to make some sense out of the past couple of hours. He had said she'd been set up. What did he mean by that? She was going to have to talk to him. She had to make him see reason.

When she walked out of the bathroom, Jax was in the kitchen, stirring a pot on the stove and for the first time, she realized that the smell of something cooking was in the air. It smelled good and she suddenly realized that she was hungry, although she didn't really understand how she could be at such a crazy time as this. But when he ladled out two bowls of a thick, savory stew, her stomach growled. He put the bowls on the table, where he already had bread and butter waiting, and motioned her toward the meal.

"Sit down. I'm having a beer. Would you like one? It's that or water until I get supplies."

"Yes. Please." She eased herself gingerly onto the chair and inhaled the aroma of the stew. "Did you cook this?"

"Yes. It's necessary to be able to cook for myself, so I learned." He set the beers on the table and seated himself.

Chloe tasted the stew and found it to be delicious. Surprised, she said, "It's good."

He smiled faintly and said, "I believe if you're going to do something, you should do it well."

She followed his example, taking a thick slice of bread and spreading butter on it. "Do all those men have quarters like this here in this building?"

"Yes. This is where we're based between missions."

She thought that over. "What kind of missions?"

"That's more than you need to know."

Chloe ate in silence for a minute or two and then said, "You said that I'd been set up. What does that mean?"

"Whoever sent you here with that envelope did it on purpose, knowing we wouldn't be able to let you go. They probably assumed that they were sending you to your death."

"Why would anybody do that? I don't have any enemies."

Jax said, "You weren't the target; we were. You were just collateral damage."

"What was in the envelope?" Chloe was still shocked at what he was telling her.

"Again, that's more than you need to know. It's enough for you to know that my taking you for my own is the only reason that you're still alive right now. The men were prepared to take you out. You should be grateful for my protection."

It was too much. "I should be *grateful?* You're holding me prisoner, you're telling me I can never go back to my own life, you *beat* me, for God's sake, and then you violated me. What should I be grateful for?"

He actually laughed at her. "I didn't beat you, I spanked you, and you had it coming. And I sure didn't seem to be violating you when you were begging for more."

Her face flamed with embarrassment. "I didn't... I didn't beg."

"Oh, honey, you certainly did. Let me ask you something. Was that or was that not the most powerful orgasm you've ever had?"

She refused to say another word. After they finished eating, Jax said, "I cooked; you can do the dishes. I've got to speak to my men for a few minutes. I'll be back soon." And he left the apartment. She distinctly heard the door lock behind him.

"I can't believe any of this," Chloe muttered, trying the

door even though she'd heard him lock it. Sure enough, she was locked in. She rinsed the dishes and put them in the dishwasher, then wiped off the table and the counters. She inspected the kitchen quickly, noting that it was stocked with basic utensils, including a set of knives. When she heard him unlocking the door, she closed the drawer quickly and watched him come in.

Jax went to the bedroom and returned with a clean t-shirt. "You can sleep in this tonight. I'm going to take a shower. When I'm finished, the bathroom is all yours."

So, she found herself in the shower, gingerly washing her sore body and taking as long as possible to do it. She pulled on the clean t-shirt; it reached to the middle of her thighs. Unable to delay any longer, she walked out of the bathroom and found him watching the news with the volume turned down low.

"I need those sizes," Jax said. "Someone will go get what you need tomorrow."

Chloe wrote down her sizes and a list and then handed it to him without a word.

"I'm going to bed," he announced. "I've got a lot of work to do tomorrow." He rose and took her by the hand, pulling her along with him.

Her heart pounding, Chloe said, "I'm not sleepy yet."

"You will be. Get in."

She got into bed and perched on the very edge of it, turning her back to him. He got in and stretched out on his back with a heavy sigh, turning off the lamp beside the bed and plunging them into darkness. She hadn't thought that she would sleep, but the day caught up with her when the lights went out, and she was sound asleep within minutes.

Chapter 2

Chloe came awake slowly, snuggling deeper under the covers and thinking she'd sleep for a little while longer. It was still dark, after all. She lay there for a full minute until her memory of the night before came flooding suddenly back and her eyes flew open. The bed was empty and the room was, indeed, dark. A few seconds later, she realized that she could smell coffee brewing and bacon frying. When she moved, she felt her still tender butt and thighs and knew it was no dream. She wanted to simply go back to sleep and wake later in her own bed, but she knew it wasn't going to happen. She finally forced herself to get out of the bed and crept to the bathroom.

Chloe stood in the kitchen doorway, watching her captor work efficiently at the stove. Without turning around to face her, he pointed to the coffeemaker and said, "Coffee's on, help yourself. Cups are right above it."

She couldn't deny that the aroma of coffee was drawing her in. She poured herself a cup and took a tiny sip of the rich, fragrant brew. In just a couple of minutes, breakfast was on the table and she found herself seated across from Jax. He piled his plate with eggs and bacon and a couple of slices of toast and gestured at her to do the same. Chloe nibbled at a strip of bacon and watched him eat just as efficiently as he had cooked. His face was strong and rugged and there wasn't an ounce of fat on him. He was lean and finely muscled and she could imagine the feel of the rough stubble along his jaw rubbing against the soft skin of her breasts, or even better, her inner thighs. Her face flamed when she realized where her thoughts had strayed and she was shocked at her reaction to him. Her nipples were hard and her groin crawled with a ripple of heat as she desperately forked eggs into her mouth.

Jax seemed not to notice and she surreptitiously continued to assess him while she ate. He was wearing a pair of jeans that were unbuttoned at the waist and a white shirt, sleeves rolled up and buttons undone. The hard muscles of his chest and belly made her want to run her hands down them, to feel the muscles tense under her fingers. His dark hair was messy and a little long and she wondered if it would be as soft as it looked if she twined her fingers into it. His eyes were hard and she found herself staring at his big hands, hard, calloused, and strong. She had a vivid flash of them coming down on her bare bottom with sharp, stinging smacks and she had to look away quickly. Once again, she found herself wondering how it had been possible for her to end up where she was right now.

Jax said, "I'll be working this morning but I'll be back around noon for a little while with some supplies. There are some bags over there on the couch for you. That should do for now and we can get more of what you need later."

Chloe said, "But it's only eight in the morning. How did you get all that so early in the day?"

"I told you I'd send someone for what you needed. We have our connections."

When he finished eating, he went off to the bedroom and when he came back, he was fully dressed, shirt buttoned and tucked in and wearing boots. He had combed his hair, but it was already tousled again and when Chloe saw him impatiently run his hand through it, she understood why it seemed to always be that way. He poured himself a travel mug of coffee and then looked her over for a long moment.

"I'll be gone for several hours. You can make yourself at home. There's a good supply of movies on the bookshelves and there's a good selection of books too. You'll be making dinner tonight and my right-hand man, Finn, will be joining us. Like I said, I'll be bringing supplies around noon."

Chloe stared at him. "What... what am I supposed to make?"

He shrugged. "Suit yourself. None of us are picky, we'll eat just about anything. It's nice if it tastes good, though. Sometimes we don't have the luxury of real food that actually tastes good, so we enjoy it when we can. You *can* cook, can't you?"

She said tartly, "I can cook well enough. In real life, I enjoy cooking."

He came close to her and put his hand under her chin, tilting her head up. "Make no mistake, Chloe, this *is* real life now. I've taken you for my own and I will protect you with my own life, but you will follow my rules. Take it seriously; it's the only way for you to stay alive and safe."

And he left the apartment, leaving her staring after him in complete confusion at his dire warning. She sank down on a chair and stared around her, trying to make sense of the whole situation and finally giving up. She blew out a breath and said out loud, "Just stop trying to figure it out. You're going to need a lot more information before you can figure out what to do, so pay attention and learn all you can."

She sipped a little more coffee and then tidied up the kitchen and turned on the dishwasher. Then she turned her attention to the shopping bags that were piled on the couch. She carried them into the bedroom and dumped them on the bed, which Jax had made neatly before he left. She found jeans and sweaters, pajamas and lingerie, socks and sneakers and a pair of boots of soft, supple leather. Everything was exactly the right size and it was all good quality. There was another bag of toiletries, hair dryer, brushes and combs and a curling iron. Again, the products were good quality and she wondered who on earth had done the shopping. She found several empty drawers and discovered that he had left half of the closet empty of everything except hangers, so she put all the clothing away and looked through the things he had hanging there.

Chloe was soon dressed in soft, comfortable jeans and a lightweight sweater. She couldn't resist putting on the boots, and everything fit perfectly. She brushed her hair to a sheen and pulled it up into a thick tail that fell to the nape of her neck. She spent the next hour going through the apartment, trying to get a read on what kind of person Jax was. She looked through his clothing, his books, his movies, even the contents of the pantry. When she sat down at the desk, she found that all the drawers except one were locked. The unlocked drawer held pens and pencils, notepads, stamps and envelopes, just basic office supplies. The only strong impressions she got were of efficiency and strength and those were the impressions she'd already had. There was nothing personal, not a single piece of paper that told her anything about him and she finally gave up.

When she heard the door being unlocked, Chloe's heart quickened and she got to her feet, twisting her hands together in mingled anticipation and dread. Jax came through the door, followed by two other men, all of them laden with bags and boxes. They trooped into the kitchen, setting everything down and then they stepped back, the two strangers eyeing Chloe.

"Chloe, this is Finn," Jax said gruffly, gesturing at the stocky man with red hair and beard, "and this is Slade. Both of them will be eating with us tonight."

The two men nodded at her while they made short work of putting away the supplies they had brought in. In just a few minutes, the kitchen was fully stocked with groceries, the refrigerator and freezer were full, and there was an extra case of beer in the pantry. Apparently, the two knew where Jax put everything, or maybe they always did everything for him. Jax pulled out four cold beers and passed them around. Chloe felt surreal as she accepted the beer from her captor and drank with two of the men who had been prepared to "take her out."

Jax looked her over and commented, "Everything fit okay?"

She nodded and said, "Perfectly."

He said, "Good. Come with us and we'll show you a bit more of our place. I imagine you could stand to stretch your legs."

Again, she felt surreal, but she went with them, all of them taking their beers. They went down a long hallway lined with closed doors and Jax pointed out Finn's and Slade's quarters. Apparently, all of the living quarters opened onto the same hallway and Chloe's face burned as she remembered the screaming she had done the night before. The hallway ended in a large room that was furnished with desks and a long conference table. There were white boards standing along the wall as well as a couple of large bulletin boards.

"This is our workspace," Jax said.

Chloe was thinking hard. "How many of you are there?"

"Six. Finn is second in command, but everyone has their specialty and in a way, everyone is independent. But I'm ultimately in charge and responsible for whatever happens with us." He looked stoic as he said it. "You'll meet the other guys in time. Once you're settled in."

Chloe gulped her beer, not wanting to think about actually settling in at this place. She wanted her own life back and she knew she had to find a way to escape. She also knew that right then what she needed most was patience and information. She had to keep control of herself, maybe even make him think that she was accepting the situation. He would have to trust her before she would be able to have a chance at getting away.

Jax led the group to a doorway and shoved it open, revealing a fully equipped gym. "This is where we stay in shape. You can exercise here if you wish. I'll bring you whenever I can."

Chloe felt a surge of frustrated rage at his comment. He would *bring* her here to exercise? Like yard time at a prison? It was intolerable and she struggled to contain her flash of anger. Jax led them to the back of the gym and pointed out a steam room, then back to the front where another door led to a large kitchen with a long table that had ten chairs at it.

"Sometimes we all take our meals together. When that happens, we take turns at kitchen duty. If I have you fix a meal for all of us, I'll assign someone to help you. If there are any items that you need for the kitchen, you make a list and I'll see that it's purchased."

Chloe was on a slow burn at the way he was assuming command of her. She knew she had to keep it under control, but her temper was simmering and she sincerely hoped that the tour was about over. Jax pointed back the way they had come and showed her to yet another room, this one a large laundry room equipped with three washing machines, three dryers, a long rod for hanging clothes up and a long table for folding clothes. There were half a dozen laundry baskets under the table and shelves that contained the necessary supplies.

"You'll be spending some time in here as well as in the

kitchen. I'm sure you don't need any instruction on how to operate the equipment here."

She was about to lose the tenuous grip she had on her anger and the fact that she could hear a faint hint of mockery in his voice nearly put her over the edge, but just then there was noise coming from the front of the building and the sound of a heavy door slamming. There were voices calling out and Jax and the other two men moved quickly toward the noise. Two men in full gear were supporting a third man, who looked barely conscious. Finn moved quickly to help them and Jax went ahead of them and opened a door that they had not gone through on Chloe's little tour. It looked like some sort of a medical facility, with two exam tables and the men hoisted the apparently injured man onto one of them.

"What happened?" Jax asked tersely.

"We were at the meeting site and there was a scuffle between some homeless guys. It must have been a setup, one of them made a run for us and got Joker with a knife before Shadow put him down."

"How bad?"

"Not sure. Somebody fired a couple of shots and we took off; we had to get out of there and get him back here."

Finn was pulling off the injured man's jacket and Chloe could see that he was wearing a flak vest. In a matter of seconds, his vest and shirt were off and she caught a glimpse of an ugly, jagged wound oozing blood. Finn and Slade worked on him while the other two men handed them what they asked for. They cleaned the wound and Jax looked closely at it while Joker gave a weak groan in reaction to their ministrations.

"He'll be all right. Get him stitched up and give him antibiotics; we don't want him getting infected. Joker, you're okay, man." Jax patted him on the shoulder.

Joker gave another little groan and said, "Easy for you to say."

Jax grinned and said, "You got that right. Better you than me. Give him a painkiller before you start stitching."

Joker said, "Hell, give me a fuckin' drink."

Finn chuckled and said, "Yeah, he's all right."

Chloe had been staring at them and she thought they were all crazy. "What happened? What were they doing?"

Jax looked at her and said, "I told you. This is what we do and it's risky every day. So, the last thing we needed was for somebody like you to show up and make the danger worse."

Chloe's mouth dropped open in shock. She hadn't done a damn thing wrong and he said *she* put them in danger? They were obviously in danger all on their own; she had nothing to do with it. She had to find a way out of this insanity. And she had a sinking feeling that Jax was completely serious when he said that he was keeping her here, that her life was here now. She couldn't possibly accept it. There had to be a way out.

Jax said, "Coop, take her to my quarters. We've got things to take care of."

"Okay, boss."

One of the men who had brought Joker in took her arm and started to lead her away. She jerked her arm away from him and snapped, "Keep your hands off me. I can follow without you touching me."

He grinned and shrugged. "Okay, lady, whatever you say." He set off and she followed him.

When they reached Jax's quarters, Coop unlocked the door and stepped back, motioning her inside. Chloe said desperately, "Please. Just let me go. I won't ever say a word to anyone. Just let me out of this place."

He shook his head and said, "Are you crazy? I'd be a dead man. Step inside."

With tears of frustration in her eyes, she strode inside and heard him lock the door behind her. Standing there and staring around her, the tears gathered and threatened to fall until she dashed them away and cursed out loud, vowing that she had shed her last tear. An hour passed by; an hour that she spent pacing and thinking, trying to come up with some kind of idea. And she finally had to face the fact that gathering as much information as possible and making them come to trust her was her best chance of getting out. It rubbed her the wrong way to have to be that patient, but she really had no choice. She took a few deep breaths and tried to clear her mind and calm herself.

When Jax let himself in a few minutes later, she was much more composed. He said, "Change of plans. We're going to eat together tonight and I'm going to need you to do the cooking. I'll be back in half an hour to take you to the kitchen."

"Why not just take me now? I can look the place over, familiarize myself with where things are before I have to start the actual cooking. Then I might have some questions for you."

He stared at her for a long minute. "I don't know…"

"Why not? It's not like I'm going to go anywhere. I'm in your control."

After another moment, he said, "Fine. Follow me."

Feeling like she had won a tiny victory, she followed him back to the kitchen. "How's your man?"

"He's fine. He won't be feeling great for a few days, but he'll be okay. He's all stitched up; not the prettiest job in the world, but effective."

"That's good." Chloe said it absently, as if without thinking, and she felt Jax staring at her, but she kept her attention on the kitchen, walking forward to start checking out the cupboards and drawers. "What am I cooking tonight?"

"The plan was for meatloaf and baked potatoes."

Chloe nodded. "I can do that. I make an excellent meatloaf."

"Remember that these are big appetites. You can do salad or vegetables and dessert of your choice. Oh, and there's fresh French bread as well."

Chloe looked a little impressed. "Wow, those *are* big appetites. What time is dinner?"

Jax glanced at the clock on the wall and said, "With everything that's happened, we'd better plan on seven o' clock. You can find whatever you need in here, just look until you find it. Any problem?"

She shook her head. "No, not at all. It'll be ready at seven."

He looked at her for another second and said, "Okay. See you later, then." He turned and walked out.

Chloe was pleased with how that had gone. She busied herself with finding and setting out everything she needed to prepare the meal, then set to work. After she had the meatloaf and potatoes ready for the oven, she checked the time and poured herself a glass of wine. He hadn't told her not to, so she assumed that it was acceptable for her to do it. She sipped it slowly and baked a batch of chocolate chip cookies for dessert, deciding that they went well with a meatloaf dinner. There was a recipe box that she went through and a couple of good cookbooks. It was a well-equipped kitchen and easy to work in.

At six-thirty, Coop came in and said, "Boss sent me to set the table and see if you needed help with anything." Looking around at the already set table, he said, "I guess you don't."

"It's all under control," Chloe said. "Dinner will be on the table at seven. Don't be late."

He was grinning as he walked away. The girl had some spunk. And the meatloaf smelled great. He wasn't about to tell her that he was the one who'd gotten out of cooking that evening. Chloe had dinner on the table at exactly seven and the men were prompt as well, taking their seats and making gruff comments about how good the food looked. It wasn't long before Chloe knew that Coop had been the one assigned to cook the meal, from the way the others poked fun at him about how much better off they were with Chloe's cooking. Jax's hard expression never changed and Chloe wondered with a sinking heart if it would ever be possible to actually please him. She pushed the despair away and concentrated on listening carefully to their conversation, trying to catch something useful.

But by the end of the meal, she hadn't heard anything that would help her. Still, she stored the conversation away to examine later. She'd been quiet throughout dinner and the men mostly talked around her.

Jax stood up abruptly and said, "Coop, you're on cleanup."

Coop started to protest but stopped quickly when Jax shot him a warning look.

Jax took Chloe by the arm and said, "Let's go."

She followed him without a word and he led her to his quarters, locking the door as always. "You did well. Your cooking is acceptable, so we can make use of you that way."

There was an immediate spark in her eyes and she snapped, "Gee, thanks for the compliment. It's always been my dream, to have somebody "make use of me"!"

Jax stared at her, standing there defiantly, her breasts heaving with her quick breaths and fire in her eyes, and his manhood stiffened in response. She was a feisty little shit and he ached to put his hands on her again. He saw her hardened nipples poking at her sweater and realized that she'd unconsciously run her tongue around her full, lush lips. He imagined those lips closing around his cock and he went even harder, the desire for her rolling over him in a wave. But he had work to do and pleasure was going to have to wait.

"I'm going out," he said. "I don't know when I'll be back." He strode to the bedroom and grabbed a jacket out of the closet and left without another word.

Chloe was left staring after him, unbelieving. That was it? She slowly realized that her panties were damp and her breasts were aching. What an asshole.

Chapter 3

It was late that night when Chloe heard the door open and close quietly. She'd been lying awake for hours, thinking and waiting, and she turned her head to look at the clock. Three am. Jax came into the bedroom and opened a drawer, then went to the bathroom. She heard the shower running and when he finally came to the bedroom, he gave a heavy sigh and lay down on the bed.

"Where did you go?" Chloe asked, immediately wondering why in the hell she had asked it.

"I had something to take care of."

"Ah. That explains it. Something else I don't need to know."

Jax said simply, "Nobody attacks one of ours and gets away with it. It had to be dealt with."

Maybe she shouldn't have asked, but she'd started down this road and, as usual, she said what she thought. "And that's what you did? Dealt with it? What does that mean?"

"It means that person won't attack any of us again. Ever."

A chill ran over Chloe. "What kind of person are you?"

Jax propped himself up on one elbow and said, "I'm the kind of person you don't want to fuck with, Chloe. The best thing you can do for yourself is learn quickly that you can and will obey me, whatever I say to you. Don't question it, don't object to it, just obey without hesitation. You'll be fine and you'll be protected if you just learn to do that."

She blurted, "You don't *own* me, Jax!"

"Maybe not yet. But I will. Make no mistake, this is a lesson that you *will* learn. Your life depends on it."

She had completely lost her patience. "Why don't you stop with all these cryptic little hints that my life is in danger, that I've done something so dangerous that I can never leave your protective circle. Shit, that somehow I've endangered all of you."

Quick as a snake striking, he gripped her chin and looked directly into her eyes in the dark. His voice was cold as steel. "They're not cryptic little hints. They're facts. I'm getting tired of telling you, over and over. Your life is in danger and you caused it by coming here."

"But you said I was set up."

"That makes no difference. What's done is done. I'm not going to tell you again. You are going to stop arguing with me and follow my instructions. And if you don't, I will punish you. You've had enough time to accept your situation."

She let out a breath and said, "You're a beast."

He smiled without humor. "Now you're getting it. I'm not a nice guy, I'm not your friend. But I'm responsible for you now and I take my responsibilities seriously. I'll punish you when you need it and I'll fuck you when I please. And you will learn to accept it; hell, you'll learn to love it, beg for it. You. Are. Mine."

He released her and she fell back against her pillow, breathing hard. Tears burned in her eyes but she refused to let them fall. He thought it was only a matter of time until she did everything he had just described. She would prove him wrong; she would never give in. She would never be his.

———

Chloe was up early in the morning. She'd thought about her situation until she'd fallen asleep in sheer exhaustion and she'd decided that it was necessary to do whatever she could to convince Jax that he could trust her. If that was even possible. He was the most guarded person she'd ever met and it wasn't going to be easy. She had one weapon only; she knew he wanted her and she knew how to make him want her more. So, she set out to make him want her all the time. She made a list of things she needed that she hadn't thought of before and gave it to him. There was makeup and fragrance on her list. She didn't know who the hell would shop for it, but that wasn't her problem. She wrote down her favorite shop and some instructions on what to ask for. Jax gave her an exasperated look when he read the list.

"Is this really necessary?" he asked.

She gave him an innocent look. "You said to write down anything that I needed. I need those things."

She moved around the kitchen, preparing breakfast, and conscious of how she moved. When she concentrated on flipping eggs without breaking the yolks, she touched the tip of her tongue to her upper lip; she closed the pantry door with a little sway and push of her hip. Her top two buttons were open, flashing a hint of cleavage when she turned. While she waited for the toast to pop up, she placed her hands on the small of her back and stretched, seemingly unconscious of the fact that her breasts jutted out enticingly when she made that particular move.

Jax watched her, enjoying the show, his cock twitching and heat rippling across his groin. It was obvious what she was doing and he decided to play along. He walked up behind her and put his hands on her upper arms, lightly stroking up and down. His hands moved down to her waist, his fingers splayed over her belly, igniting her nerve endings and making her swallow hard. Suddenly she felt like she wasn't controlling the game anymore; her belly rippled with heat and her skin was hyper-sensitive, as if he was strumming her body like a finely tuned instrument. Her taut nipples ached for his touch and her pussy felt swollen and wet. Jax lowered his head and nuzzled her neck, making gooseflesh rise on her skin. When the toast popped up, Chloe jumped and Jax chuckled.

He stepped back and said casually, "We'll have to continue this later."

Her face flushed, Chloe slapped butter onto the toast and set it on the table, then carried a platter of sausage and eggs to the table as well. Jax got milk and juice out of the refrigerator and topped off her coffee when he poured his own. They ate breakfast with little conversation and he watched her squirm a little on her chair, his eyes amused. The fact that he was aching to bury his rigid member in her tight, hot depths was beside the point. He managed to quell his response to her by the time he finished eating and he let her know that they would be on their own for dinner that evening.

"I'll be gone for the day. I'm leaving you Coop's phone number. He'll be here all day and if you want to go to the gym or the big kitchen, call him and he'll take you."

Chloe whirled around to face him. "I don't know why you can't at least let me have access to the rest of the building. It's not as if I have any way to get out. How would you like to be cooped up in this little space twenty-four hours a day?"

"You haven't earned the right to have the run of the

building yet. If you got half a chance, you'd make a run for it. I can't afford to let that happen."

"Ooh!" She struggled to control her temper. It wasn't getting her anywhere and if she couldn't start changing his attitude toward her, she was never going to get a chance to get away. With a deep breath, she gave him a nod. "All right. I really want... no, need, some more freedom. Whatever I have to do to earn the right, that's what I'll do. How do I do that?"

He stepped close to her and looked her in the eyes. "You accept your life as it is now. You accept me and you obey. It's not that hard. That yielding is part of you; just stop fighting it. I've seen it. You just have to let go." As he walked out, he had the thought that she was really in need of another lesson to show her what he meant. She'd done all the adjusting she was going to without him giving her another chance to submit. The next time she pushed the boundaries, he would give her that lesson.

Jax had a trying day. Two of his men were on surveillance for the third day, with nothing to show for it. The mission they had to undertake required more information before they could carry it out and the longer it took to gather the information, the more difficult it would be. It meant that as soon as they had what they needed, they would have to act without delay. They were all tense from the waiting and it couldn't be over soon enough to suit Jax. Their target was a real scumbag and there was no doubt that taking him out was going to be a benefit to anyone the asshole had ever been in contact with. But the waiting was really starting to wear on them all. When his radio crackled, Jax grabbed it and hoped for good news.

"Hey, boss, we're coming in." There was grim satisfaction in Finn's voice.

"Got everything we need?"

"Got it. We're a go tonight."

A grim smile crossed Jax's face. "We'll start getting everything ready."

The rest of the day was a burst of activity, the tension relieved by the fact that they were finally going to act. The six of them pored over the pictures and data the surveillance had finally provided, until they all knew their parts perfectly. The gear was already ready to go, but they meticulously went over every piece, checking, cleaning it yet again, and packing it all up. Finn ordered a bag full of sandwiches from a local place and Coop went to pick them up. By the time the sun started to set, they were ready to go. As they filed out, Jax had a fleeting thought for Chloe, but he shrugged and put her out of his mind. This was business and Chloe was unimportant at this moment in time.

Chloe paced the apartment, fuming. She had made chicken and rice, with a salad and crusty rolls, and it was well past dark now with no sign of Jax. It was bad enough that she was kept here in this apartment and ordered around like a slave, but now he didn't even bother to show up for the dinner he had ordered her to cook. It was intolerable! It was true that he had said he didn't know when he would be back, but this was ridiculous. Surely, if he expected her to make dinner for the two of them, he expected to actually be there to eat the dinner. She ignored the little kernel of worry that hovered around the back of her mind. How could she be worried about the brute who was holding her prisoner?

It was late that night and dinner had gone cold hours before, when she finally heard activity in the building. Apparently, they were all back. She could hear jubilant voices and the sounds of a celebration of sorts. And still, she sat there alone in the apartment. It was more than an hour later when the door finally opened and Jax walked in. His face was more relaxed than she'd ever seen it and he had a beer in his hand. He pulled off his boots and dropped his jacket on the couch. Her eyes widened as she saw that he was wearing a flak vest that soon followed his jacket to the couch. He tipped his beer back and emptied it in one gulp.

"Get me a beer," he said. "Get yourself one too," he added generously.

The look she shot him would have frozen a lesser man in his tracks. Without a word, she got two beers out of the refrigerator and handed him one. She opened hers and swigged down a third of it. "Your dinner is cold," she said.

He waved a casual hand and said, "That's all right. We ate before we left."

She couldn't believe her ears. Her temper, already at a simmer, began to bubble up to a dangerous boil. Her voice was level as she said, "The dinner that you ordered me to cook? For the meal that you said we'd be on our own for? You just ate something else instead?"

He gave her a quizzical look. "That's right. We had a mission and we needed to fuel up first."

Her tone dripping with sarcasm, she said, "Nice of you to let me know."

"I'll let you know what you need to know. Your presence here is insignificant when there's a mission."

She gasped at his words. "Then fucking let me go! If my presence here is insignificant, I'll be more than happy to get out of your way."

"You already know that's never going to happen and I'm getting tired of repeating it. I don't expect to discuss it again."

Outraged, she stomped her foot. "Well, I want to discuss it! You can't do this to me and I demand that you let me out of this hellhole!"

Now, there was a dangerous glint in his eyes. He set his

beer down and began to roll up his shirtsleeves. "You clearly haven't learned anything yet. I told you that I would punish you when you need it and you need it so badly."

Chloe's eyes were wide and she backed away from him hastily. He came calmly after her and she dashed around the table, frantic to get away. The chase ended abruptly when she tripped over his boots and he snatched her off the floor, his arm around her waist. He snagged one of the kitchen chairs with his foot and pulled it out, holding his shouting, flailing, kicking burden firmly. He sat down and hauled her across his lap and began spanking her, hard and fast. She wailed at the sting of his hard, calloused hand striking her squirming bottom with brutal force. He stared at her wriggling form, struggling to escape from his punishing hand and his member stiffened and the ache in his groin grew. He wanted bare skin under his hand and he rolled her to the side so he could undo her jeans. He wrestled them down over her hips and then yanked her panties down to expose her pink cheeks.

Jax laid a hand on her ass and squeezed one cheek, stroking with his fingers. Chloe sucked in a breath at the electric sensation that shot through her groin and she squirmed against his thighs and arched her back, lifting her buttocks in an unwilling plea for more. The heat was coiling in her belly, spreading and consuming her, and she felt moisture trickling from her sensitive pussy. When he smacked her bare bottom, she raised her butt to meet his hand and he rained hard spanks down on her beautiful ass, quickly turning the creamy skin red. Each smack raised the heat level that consumed her and she squirmed mindlessly, her whole body swept with the sensation of pain and pleasure.

Jax spanked her harder, the ache in his stiff cock nearly intolerable. He wanted to bury it inside her, he wanted to jam himself into her and empty himself in her. But he had to punish her first, although her reactions were telling him that she wasn't suffering at all. He knew her luscious, sweet pussy was swollen and dripping with her arousal and the knowledge intensified the ache and need that was consuming him. He spanked the tender spot at the top of her thighs and she finally cried out from the pain. She had kicked off her jeans and panties and when she squirmed, he could see her plump lips, glistening with her juices and he could smell the fragrance of her arousal.

Chloe had lost the ability to see the room around her; she was consumed with pain and need. Her pussy ached for his touch and she wriggled against his leg, desperate for relief. The pain of the spanking increased and mingled with the fierce pleasure that grew and grew. She wondered dimly if it was possible to come simply from the stimulation of the spanking. Unconsciously, she spread her legs wide and he suddenly slapped her swollen pussy with his fingers and she nearly screamed at the shock of it. He did it again before she clamped her legs together, and with a savage growl, he jerked her up and pulled her shirt off, popping buttons all over the floor. It took one more second to undo her bra and then she was naked on his lap. She could feel his cock bulging against the crotch of his jeans, and with shaky hands, she reached down and released him.

Jax let out a groan and took her by the shoulders, raising her up as he stood and pushing her back so there was a space between them. The need for her coursed through his body and his senses were heightened, the electricity crackling between them. With one hand, he unbuckled his belt and jerked it free from his pants. Her eyes widened with dread and excitement all mixed up.

"You have a lesson to learn," Jax said hoarsely. But he had to be rid of the confining jeans that constricted him.

Chloe's body crawled with gooseflesh, her thighs damp and her nipples erect as she watched him strip off his pants.

His member stood proudly and she reached for it, wanting her hands on him. But he turned her around and bent her over the arm of the couch, ignoring her protests. The fabric of the couch rubbed against her crotch and her taut nipples and she squirmed her reaction before the leather snapped across her reddened cheeks. The stripe of fire bit across her ass and she cried out at the pain, clenching her fists and kicking as the belt cracked across her bottom again and again. She was lost in a sea of pain and, impossibly, a growing swell of pleasure mingled with the pain. She couldn't tell which was more intense, it was all becoming one and there was nothing in her world but sensation.

Jax swung the belt again and watched her mindless struggles; he could see how aroused she was and after a last stroke of the belt, he dropped it and slid his fingers between her thighs. He explored her wet, swollen folds and pushed a finger into her tight, hot channel, adding another finger when she squirmed against his hand. He couldn't wait any longer; his cock was going to explode if he didn't take her. Spreading her legs with his hands, he rammed himself into her, burying the full length of his iron hard erection in her hot, tight depths. He pulled back and plowed into her again, jerking her fiery, red buttocks against his belly and grinding against her. He thrust into her as hard as he could, the flame in his cock growing ever hotter. Chloe cried out in a wordless, guttural groan and began to quiver as the orgasm gathered and swelled. He wanted to make her wait, but he was beyond waiting himself and he pumped on until she screamed her release, shuddering and quaking with the waves of pleasure and he went on until he knew he was going to come, then he jerked himself free and pressed against her tiny, dark hole.

Chloe cried out in panic and struggled, but he pressed harder, beginning to enter her most private opening. The pain grew even while the quivers of her orgasm still shook her and she was engulfed in it, screaming again when he pushed himself fully into her. He was still for a minute and she felt herself stretching around the fullness of his cock. When he began to move, a new sensation began to mingle with the pain and the pain gradually decreased. Unbelievably, her pleasure grew again and as he rocked deeper and harder, the exquisite pain became one with the building pleasure. She was climbing again, another climax gathering, and there was nothing but pure sensation, sensation she'd never imagined. The room spun around them and Chloe gasped in shock.

"Please! Please!" she gasped, begging him.

"Please what? Please stop?" Jax spit out the words as he thrust forward.

"No! No, don't stop! Don't stop, I need... I need more." She was mindless in her desire.

He knew he was about to explode inside her and he pumped hard as he felt her begin to shudder again with the climax that was sweeping over her. He reached between her legs and fingered her hard little bud and sent her to a screaming orgasm and then, with a roar of triumph, he emptied his seed into her, pulsing and throbbing until he was drained. Chloe was quivering, little aftershocks of pleasure shaking her as she felt him come. She was utterly drained and completely satiated, wet and sore, inside and out and yet completely satisfied. She was shocked by the shameful act they had shared and yet her pussy throbbed at the thought of doing it again.

Jax reluctantly pulled away from her and she made a tiny little sound of protest as he did. That little whimper told him everything. She was his; she might not know it yet, but she was and he was never letting her go. His cock was already stirring; the sight of her, stripped bare and marked by his hand and his belt, was nearly more than he could resist. But she'd had enough for one night. She struggled to stand and he reached out to steady her as she swayed on her trembling legs. Her face burned with shame but her eyes were dark and heavy with the aftermath of her passion and she couldn't hide the satisfaction she felt. And with a bright flash of recognition, she knew that it would happen again and there was no way she could resist him; her body would welcome his touch and she would do anything he wanted her to.

Chapter 4

Chloe was quiet the next day. Jax cooked breakfast and after they ate, he left for his workday but told her that he would be back later in the afternoon. He took his flak vest with him, along with a basket full of his laundry. Chloe took care of the mess in the kitchen from breakfast and their uneaten dinner from the night before. She wandered across the apartment to the bookshelves, looking over the assortment of titles. She felt achy and sore all over and when she moved, her bruised bottom reminded her of all that had happened. She wondered idly why she didn't hate him; even her outrage over being kept there seemed to have faded. She must have lost her mind; the thought of his touch made a ripple of heat crawl through her belly. Maybe she was just tired. It had been a very short night, after all.

When Jax came in that afternoon, he found her asleep on the couch, lying on her stomach with her head pillowed on her arms. He stood looking at her, at the tendrils of auburn hair escaping from the thick tail and pink flush of her cheeks and something stirred in him, something more than the twitch of his cock. He turned away abruptly and told himself that it was just the sense of responsibility he had for her. And yet, he had an uneasy suspicion that it was more than that. It was a ridiculous thought. He wasn't a man who could have relationships that normal men had. The life he lived wouldn't allow for it. He'd done things that he could never share with anyone else, especially someone he cared for. And he would do those kinds of things again. It was his job and there was no escaping it. He left the bag he carried on the table and let himself silently out of the apartment again.

Chloe slept for another half hour and then gradually came awake, stretching and wincing at the ache in her bottom. But she felt a little better after the nap and she wondered if she should find something to cook for dinner. Jax hadn't told her if he expected her to cook, but he'd fixed breakfast, so she decided it would be sensible for her to take care of dinner. She got up and started for the kitchen, stopping at the sight of the bag on the table. It hadn't been there before. Jax must have been there while she slept. Curious, she looked into the bag and had to smile when she found perfume and makeup inside, along with the other things she had put on her list. There was her favorite lipstick; it was all exactly what she had wanted. She decided that Jax was a very strange man.

By the time Jax came in again, Chloe had a pot of potato and bacon soup simmering. She made a salad to go with it and a pan of brownies for dessert. She was wearing a touch of mascara and eyeliner that accentuated her emerald eyes and lipstick that made her luscious lips even more luscious. He could picture her leaving that lipstick on his stiff cock and he forced the thought away with an effort.

"That smells good," he said gruffly.

She gave him a wide-eyed smile and said, "Oh, you mean the soup?"

"Yes. What else would I mean?"

"Um, maybe the brownies."

Jax said, "They smell good too."

"Are you finished for the day?"

"Yep. There was a lot of paperwork to clear up, but it's done." He watched her move about the kitchen and he thought how much he'd like to get her out of her clothes and then he gave himself a mental shake. "Do I have time for a shower before dinner?"

"Sure. It's ready whenever you are."

He stood under the hot water and pictured Chloe, naked and sprawled invitingly on the bed, and he groaned in frustration. He finished his shower with a blast of cold water and then toweled off briskly. He put thoughts of what he'd like to do with Chloe firmly out of his head and went to the kitchen, dressed in flannel pajama pants and a t-shirt.

Chloe looked at him and felt her nipples tighten. He was a mouthwatering sight, the tight t-shirt outlining the hard muscles of his belly and chest, his hair still damp from the shower. Desire shivered down her spine and she told herself silently to stop it. "Ready to eat?" she asked brightly.

He was bemused, wondering why she wasn't pissed and outraged. Then again, he had predicted that she would learn to accept him; maybe it was happening. He got a couple of beers out of the refrigerator and sat down at the table. Chloe ladled out bowls of the hot soup and brought them to the table, then gingerly seated herself.

"Thank you for getting me the things on my list," she said.

"I told you I'd see that you have what you need."

"Yes. You did tell me that." They ate in silence for a while.

"This is good soup," Jax said. "Potato soup was my favorite when I was a kid."

It was the first time he had said anything personal about himself and Chloe was just a little bit shocked. "Was your mother a good cook?"

Jax grunted. "No idea. My aunt could cook." He kicked

himself mentally for the slip. He didn't talk about his life, not ever.

"You lived with your aunt?"

"Forget I said anything."

Chloe's eyes snapped and she said shortly, "Fine. You were almost human there for a second."

Jax refused to take the bait and they ate in silence again. Chloe was fuming as she stabbed at her salad with a fork. She finally heaved a huge sigh and tried again. "Jax, I can't just sit here in this apartment day after day with nothing to do."

He studied her for a long minute. He had to admit that, in her place, he'd have gone stir crazy inside of ten minutes. But there was no way he could let her out of the building; she'd be dead by the end of the day. "What did you do before? I know you were a messenger, but was that all you did?"

"No, that was just to pay the bills. I'm a writer. Well, I'm working on becoming a writer. I've written a few short stories but they haven't been published. I want to write a novel, a thriller."

Jax thought it over. If it would keep her busy, maybe he should give a little. "I don't see why you couldn't write here."

Chloe felt a little thrill of excitement. "I'd need a computer, a laptop would be fine." Her mind was racing.

Jax said slowly, "I can get you a laptop. But you need to understand that you'll be working offline. You won't be allowed to be on the internet."

She was instantly disappointed, but she hid it well. "If I can just write, it would be great."

"All right. I'll take care of it tomorrow."

She sent him a beaming smile and he felt his gut clench. It was the first time he had ever seen her smile and it was as if he'd taken a hard punch. He kicked himself mentally, over and over. He couldn't afford to have these kinds of feelings. She was his responsibility and nothing more. He had no right to have more. He could use her to his heart's content, but he could *not* have feelings for her.

"Thank you. Really, thank you." Chloe forced herself to thank him, even though the words stuck in her throat. But this was something she might be able to use to get her freedom back, so she would play the part to the hilt. He had to trust her if she was ever going to escape.

"You're welcome," Jax said gruffly. He went to the stove and ladled more soup into his bowl. He hoped he wasn't making a mistake, but as long as she didn't get internet access, it should be fine. It wouldn't be a problem to deny her access to the internet.

It was the best Chloe had felt since she'd come to this place. She would have something to occupy her mind and she would watch and wait for her chance to get online. There had to be a way to do it. She knew perfectly well that Jax and his men used it. And the bizarre story that was happening to her would make a great book. She felt energized and hopeful for the first time since stumbling into the whole mess.

The next day, true to his word, Jax brought her a laptop. "It's set up and ready to go," he said. "You can write all you want to. We're going to be gone for the evening, so you don't have to worry about dinner for anyone but yourself. We're going to be getting pizza."

Chloe was smiling again as she ran her hands over the computer. "I can't wait. Pizza… that sounds good."

Jax's cock twitched as he watched her and he said gruffly, "I'll get you one before we leave. What do you want on it?"

The offer took her by surprise. "Really? My favorite is double pepperoni and mushrooms."

"Okay. I'll be back before we go." And he left the apartment.

Chloe sat down with the laptop and she was soon immersed in a new idea for a short story. She lost all track of time and when Jax came through the door with a pizza box, she realized that several hours had gone by. Her stomach growled as she caught the delicious aroma of pizza and she smiled at him again. "That smells wonderful!"

"It's all yours. Enjoy. We're headed out and it'll be late when we get back. Here's a cell phone. It will only dial me. If you have any kind of emergency, you can call me."

Her mouth dropped open as she took the phone from him and she thought that all phones could dial 911. But after he left, she discovered quickly that this phone wouldn't. She set it aside and helped herself to a big slice of cheesy, loaded pizza. It was absolutely delicious and she opened a beer and sat down to enjoy the unexpected treat. She switched on the television and watched while she ate, flipping through the channels and settling on local news. There were the usual shootings and auto accidents, robberies and other depressing news. Then they spent some extra time reporting the story of the sudden and tragic death of a prominent, wealthy businessman. He'd been found dead in his own hot tub, naked and with a drink sitting on the edge of the hot tub. There was no evidence of foul play, the news anchor said solemnly, but the cause of death was pending an autopsy.

The local news ended and the national news came on. The story she'd just heard was featured on the national program as well. But they delved into the dead man's story a little deeper. For years, it had been rumored that the man had a thing for young girls and had founded a smuggling operation that brought the girls to him to choose the ones he wanted and to sell the others to the highest bidder. He'd been investigated more than once, but somehow there was never the evidence needed to charge him.

"Good riddance," Chloe muttered. "Couldn't happen to a nicer guy. Whatever caused it, I hope it was painful." She turned off the news and found a lighthearted romantic comedy, then got herself another slice of pizza. It was late when Jax got in and he found her asleep on the couch in her pajamas, the TV still playing quietly.

He went back and showered, careful to be quiet about it and then he picked her up and carried her to bed. She stirred and mumbled something to him, but then fell promptly back to sleep when he pulled the covers over her. He turned off the TV and the lights, and then he stretched out on the bed beside her, breathing in her fragrance and thinking about the feel of her soft skin. It was a long time before he fell asleep.

More than a week went by quietly. Chloe was occupied with the story she was writing and it kept her mind off the predicament she was in, at least a little bit. Jax continued to be pleasant to her and they ate breakfast and dinner together most days. Chloe developed a routine of going to the gym each day after breakfast and Jax decided to accommodate her by making it his workout time too. The two of them went through their workouts, surreptitiously sneaking glances at each other and pretending to ignore each other. But the sexual tension was there; in fact, the other guys joked to each other about it.

Jax called a meeting one day and after it was over, the activity level in the building increased. Chloe figured they must be getting another mission, whatever that might be. The men spent hours in the office, poring over plans and maps. Finn and Coop were sent someplace and were gone for several days and, as usual, nobody said anything that Chloe could overhear about what they were up to. Jax was at a high level of tension and something seemed different in the atmosphere of the headquarters. She wanted to ask him what was going on, but she didn't know if she dared.

After a couple of days of this, Chloe was startled when Jax entered the apartment, flinging the door back with a loud bang. He paced the floor, running his hand through his hair in frustration.

"What's wrong?" Chloe asked hesitantly.

He turned a bitter look on her. "What's wrong is that everything is fucked up. Ever since that damn envelope you brought here, I don't know if we can trust anything. We're doing everything we can to check things out, but there's still doubt."

"I'm sorry—"

He waved a hand in dismissal. "This one's not on you. You were set up; you were used. That's why I have to protect you now. We're the ones he's after, you were just a convenient means to that end."

It was the best thing he'd ever said to her about how she had come to be there. "What does he want?"

"He wants us all compromised. He wants us destroyed, dead if possible."

A chill went through her. "The man who gave me that envelope wants that?"

"No, he wouldn't have given it to you himself. He had someone do it. What we need to do is get to him before he gets to us."

"Can you do that?"

Grimly, Jax said, "We're going to have to. It's either him or us and I'm not going down. I'm not going to watch my guys go down, either."

"What can I do to help?"

Her words took him by surprise and he looked at her for a long time. "Chloe, I'm sorry you got mixed up in this. It wasn't your fault and I know you must feel like you're being punished for it. I hope you can understand that that's not the case. This guy who set you up is ruthless and I *have* to protect you from him. The only way I can ever let you go is if we take him out and we know that it's over for good."

Her heart leaped wildly at his words and she was shocked when, mixed in with the hope, she felt a strange disappointment at the thought of leaving. Slowly, she said, "I think I believe you."

His gut was clenched as he thought of her leaving. He had claimed her for his, but he knew that if they neutralized the enemy, he would have to let her go. The idea of her being gone left him with a cold feeling, one he'd never felt before. He had a sudden vision of the rest of his life going by filled with emptiness, and he swore silently. This was the worst mess he'd ever been in. He turned and walked away, slamming his fist down on the table when he reached it. He was shocked when he felt her hands on his back, stroking lightly and then sliding around his waist. With a strangled groan, he turned and swept her against him, his arms like steel around her. He gripped her ponytail and pulled her head back, taking her lips in a hard, bruising kiss. His tongue probed her hot, sweet mouth, tangling with her tongue and sucking it into his mouth. It took her breath away and her knees went weak as the heat shot through her belly and her groin, sharp as an electric shock.

Jax's cock was rigid, straining against his jeans and aching to be set free. His whole body ached for her, so strong that it was pure agony. What the fuck was she doing to him? Then she sucked his bottom lip into her mouth, her tongue swirling over it until he thought he'd lose his sanity if he didn't take her. Her body was vibrating with pure animal attraction and when she ground her pelvis against the bulge at his crotch, he let out a savage growl. She was reaching for his belt buckle when his phone buzzed. Cursing, he took an unsteady step backward and reached for the phone.

"Boss, Finn and Coop are back."

"All right. I'll be there in a minute." He clicked off the phone and stood there, breathing hard. "I've got to go."

Chloe was trembling. "Okay."

He grabbed the back of her head with one hand and pulled her mouth to his in a long, probing kiss. "This is not over," he said hoarsely before he went.

Chapter 5

There was an undercurrent of excitement in the office as Finn and Coop reported what they had found to the rest of them. They had pictures and diagrams of the building they would have to breach. They knew where the security alarms were and where the guards were. They knew what the targets were guilty of and knew they were out of reach of legal prosecution and justice. They knew there were more victims to come if they didn't carry out their mission. They had every reason to proceed and only one possible reason not to. And yet, there was no way to be completely sure.

"What's your gut feeling?" Jax asked.

Finn said, "I think we're good to go. We dug deep; we watched everything. There was nothing to indicate that Snake's involved in any way."

"What about you?"

Coop nodded. "Yeah, boss, I think it's a go."

Jax drummed his fingers on the table. "Something still feels wrong."

His men watched him in silence. It wasn't like him to be indecisive. Finally, he said, "I'm going to make a call."

He went over to his desk and got a phone out of a drawer. He dialed a number and waited. When the call was answered, he said, "It's Jax. I need to speak to him."

A couple of minutes passed and then the men could hear him say, "Yes, sir." He turned away and spoke quietly into the phone, listening for longer than he spoke. Finally, he clicked the phone off and returned it to the drawer. He walked back over to his men and said, "Okay. It's a go. They've got eyes on Snake and they say there's no activity. They'll continue to watch throughout our mission and sound a warning if anything looks suspicious."

The men visibly relaxed and Coop said, "Good. That's good to know, that they've got eyes on him."

"Agreed. We'll gear up in the morning and head out later in the afternoon."

The atmosphere in the office was almost festive. He decided to order dinner for them all that evening and send Joker to pick it up. In the meantime, he went back to his quarters to talk to Chloe. When he walked in, she looked up immediately, her eyes wide.

"Is everything all right?"

Jax nodded. "Our mission is a go. We'll be leaving tomorrow afternoon and we should be back the next evening. We're all going to eat together tonight and I'd like you to join us."

"Am I cooking?"

"No. I'm ordering dinner. I just want you to join us."

It took her by surprise, but she nodded her assent. "All right. This mission, is it dangerous?"

He gave a short laugh. "They're all dangerous. That's why we're so careful. I don't want anyone getting hurt on my watch."

"Did you check everything out? As far as the man who sent me?"

"We've checked it out every way we possibly can." He knew he was telling her too much, but maybe it was the way to make her understand how much danger she was really in.

She asked anxiously, "But you still can't be sure?"

He shook his head slowly. "Not one hundred percent. But we're sure enough to go."

"Why? Why can't you just call it off?"

Jax gave her a bleak look. "This is our job. This is our lives. Every one of us knew when we signed up for this that there was no going back. Someday, when we're too old to do it anymore, they'll let us retire and then we'll have to disappear. We took this life on and we knew what we were getting."

Chloe shivered. "It sounds awful."

"Unfortunately, it's necessary."

When Chloe walked into the communal kitchen with Jax that evening, she was greeted by a bunch of rowdy men, fired up and ready for tomorrow to come. Finn put a bucket full of beers on the table and everyone helped themselves. Chloe sipped her beer and listened to them give each other shit. She even had to laugh at them a few times. Jax watched her and listened and played along with the men, knowing he was getting a glimpse of Chloe as she had been before she had entered their world. Joker walked in, loaded down with boxes and bags and bringing delicious, spicy scents with him. Jax had ordered a Mexican food feast and they had literally a little of everything for dinner.

They ate, drank, talked, laughed, joked, and let off a lot of steam. When they were finally wound down, they all cleaned up the mess and then straggled off to their quarters, calling out their goodnights. Jax and Chloe walked back to his quarters and Chloe stifled a yawn and said, "I'm going to go brush my teeth and change clothes."

When she was finished, Jax took his turn and Chloe sat cross legged on the bed, brushing her hair. Jax walked through the door clad only in his undershorts and she could immediately read the look on his face. She set down the brush and stood beside the bed, gazing at him. When he took a step toward her, she held out a hand to stop him. He stood watching as she slowly pulled the tank top she wore off over her head. The lamplight lit her wondrous breasts with a warm, golden glow and she slowly ran her tongue around her lips. She cupped her breasts in her hands, the rosy tips pointing toward him and his cock went rock hard at the sight. Slowly, she pushed her pajama pants down over her hips until just a hint of the down between her legs was showing. With one more little motion, she let them drop to the floor. Sweat beaded on Jax's face as he watched.

Chloe covered her breasts with her hands and turned sideways from him, peeking over her shoulder at him and playing the shy maiden. A low growl escaped him and he stripped off his underwear, his proud member standing at attention for her. She licked her lips again and took a few hesitant steps toward him. He was mesmerized; she was teasing him, playing with him and he was totally captivated. He wanted her touch, wanted to feel her against him, but the game had captured him and he let it play on. Chloe picked up her hairbrush and dropped it on the floor, innocently widening her eyes at him before she bent prettily to pick it up, letting him have a look at her gorgeous ass and the down between her thighs. When she stood up, she looked at him with those wide, innocent eyes and looked pointedly at the hairbrush in her hand and then down at the fine fur at her crotch. With a saucy smile, she lightly brushed that fur with the hairbrush and Jax groaned at the sight.

She laid the hairbrush down and swayed toward him, not too close, and then around behind him. She stepped closer, until she could brush her taut nipples against his back with the lightest of touches. She pushed her pelvis forward until the soft fur brushed his ass. She reached around him and laid her fingers lightly at the tops of his thighs, stroking up his belly on either side of his rigid cock without touching it. Jax was actually trembling and Chloe felt full of power as she continued to tease him. Unable to bear it any longer, he spun around and reached for her but she pressed her hand against his chest to stop him. Standing on her tiptoes, she brushed his lips with hers, licking them lightly. She looked down to see one clear drop on the head of his penis and she bent and licked it off, making a shudder run down his spine.

Chloe moved around him, touching him, then backing away, and the burning ache inside him built and built. Finally, she stroked his stiff manhood with her fingertips, rubbing her thumb lightly over the velvety soft head and leaning forward at the same time to kiss his hard, flat belly. He could hardly contain himself as her fingers drew imagined designs on the length of his cock, and when she cupped his heavy balls in one hand, she drew a hoarse groan from him. She was bewitching, irresistible, and his cock twitched with the need to be buried in her. Still, she drew it out. When she sank to her knees, he shuddered in anticipation, and when her tongue traced a delicate line from his balls up the entire length of him, he shuddered again. Her hand massaged the orbs it held, her tongue swirled around the tip of his cock, and then she licked it like an ice cream cone.

Jax actually felt his knees getting weak and all he was conscious of was the feel of her hands and her tongue on him. When she finally took him into her mouth and sucked at him, he groaned and thrust deeply into her hot mouth and to the back of her throat. Her hands were busy at the length that she couldn't take into her mouth and she sucked strongly even while her tongue swirled in circles around him. The pressure within him was growing stronger and he knew he was about to come. But she pulled away from him and trailed kisses up his torso, nibbling at his ribcage and cupping his buttocks with her hands to pull him against her so that his cock nestled between her breasts. He filled his hands with her hair and she nipped lightly at his ribs until he couldn't take it anymore. She finally let him pull her to her feet and against him to plunder her skillful mouth with his.

Now it was Jax's turn to feast on her, devouring her tender breasts and raining kisses down her belly to the sensitive spot at the top of her thigh. She fisted her hands in his hair as he nibbled that spot and spread her legs to lightly stroke her swollen, wet center. He gently explored the swollen folds, drenched with her juices, and put a fingertip on the hard little bud that hid there. She arched her back with a moan and he pushed two fingers into her hot, tight channel while she squirmed against his hand. The electric bolts of pleasure shot through her, and when he nuzzled the inside of her thigh, she cried out, begging for more. He lifted her, cupping her ass with his hands and she let her legs fall open as his tongue explored her sweet pussy, laving her swollen lips and thrusting into her with sharp little jabs. Her heels drummed against the bed when he sucked her clit into his mouth and swirled his tongue around it. She was soaring on waves of heat, the desire sucking her into a whirlwind of sensation, more and more intense as his mouth devoured her.

Jax flipped her over on her belly and pulled her up onto her knees, thrusting his fingers into her dripping pussy and pumping deep inside her. He was near the end of his ability to keep from burying himself in her and when she began to beg him, nearly incoherent, he'd had enough. He knelt behind her and thrust himself into her with a shout, burying himself to the hilt in her sweetness and grinding against her. His heavy balls slapped against her clit and she moaned at the intensity of the feeling, growing and growing. His thrusts became harder and faster as she rocked back against him, wanting him to go even deeper. She was dizzy with sensation, carried away on waves of raw desire. When he thrust a finger into her tight opening, fucking her ass with his finger, she exploded with a thunderous, gut-wrenching orgasm. Shudders of ultimate pleasure shook her and her muscles contracted around him, milking him to his own climax so he pumped his seed into her with deep, throbbing thrusts until he was utterly emptied. He turned to his side and collapsed on the bed, pulling her tightly against him, both of them breathing in deep, hard pants.

Chloe slowly came back to reality, quivering with the power of what they had shared. She thought dimly that it was impossible to live through anything that intense, and yet she had. He was her captor. He even claimed that he was her owner. Everything told her that she should hate him and fear him. And yet, she lusted after him with every part of her being. She wanted to do what they had just done night after night. She couldn't imagine ever growing tired of it. His touch set her on fire; he brought her to places she had never dreamed of. Unconsciously, she snuggled closer to him and he felt her do it. He automatically gathered her closer; the place where he lay at that moment was the best place he had ever been.

In time, they went to the shower together. They didn't speak. They just washed each other, gently, with intimate touches and kisses, until Jax turned her around and fingered her beautiful ass, sliding one finger into her, stretching her and playing with her until he could insert another finger and then another. Until, when he pushed his cock into her, she welcomed him and she reveled in the way he filled her. When he rocked back and forth in an increasing rhythm, she met each thrust and when she shot into another powerful orgasm, she screamed her pleasure and only a moment later, he emptied himself into her again.

When they finally fell asleep, they were twined together in the bed, both of them drained and satisfied.

———

The morning brought tension as the men prepared for another mission and Chloe knew there were real dangers possible. She was jittery and Jax let her come with him to the equipment room while they packed up their gear. It was shocking to her, the amount of specialized gear that they carried and it was sobering to watch them do it. She didn't know exactly what their missions consisted of, but she had enough information to give her a good idea of what they probably were. She didn't know what to think of it all. She just knew that it was dangerous, and at any time they might not all come back.

Chloe made a lunch of soup and sandwiches for all of them and sat with them, nibbling at her food. They ate in near silence, which was really unusual for them, and when they were done with lunch, they started loading up their gear. When they were nearly finished, Jax walked her back to his apartment and handed her the phone he had given to her when he went on the last mission.

"I added another phone number to the phone. The first number is mine; you can call that if anything is wrong. The second one is only to be called if it's more than twenty-four hours past when we were supposed to be back and we haven't made it or contacted you. If that happens, you call that number and help will come. It's the best help I've been able to arrange for you and I don't know if it will be good enough, so we'll hope that it never happens. We should be back tomorrow evening, not too late."

Chloe was wide-eyed as she stared at him. All of it had suddenly become entirely too real. She took a deep breath and said, "Be careful."

Jax gave her a wintry smile. "Always." He started to turn away, then grabbed her and pulled her to him for a hard kiss. "I'll be back."

And he was gone.

Chapter 6

The hours crawled by. Chloe moved from one spot to another in the small apartment. She tried to write, she tried to read, she kept the TV on, tuned to the news and the volume kept low. She stared at the walls, the fact that there were no windows driving her crazy. She hadn't had a glimpse of the world outside this building since the fateful night she'd arrived at the door. She vowed that when Jax got back, something was going to have to change. Nobody could live this way. She looked over his books again, trying to find a clue into what exactly was going on here. There was a book called Way of the Mercenary that caught her attention and she took it down from the shelf. She leafed through it and realized that there were notes penciled onto some of the pages. Her interest piqued, she took the book with her to the couch and examined it more closely. What she found was chilling—savage men who committed acts of violence for money. Some of the notes that had been jotted down were chilling as well.

There were pages that struck her as eerily similar to what Jax's group of men were like. She knew that they were engaged in dangerous missions, but were they really this kind of a band? Soldiers of fortune? It was surreal, something from a dark and savage world that she didn't quite believe really existed. No, it was impossible. It was the stuff of the kind of book she'd like to write, but that was fiction. And yet some of the things she had seen… what kind of a place was this? What kind of men were they? And did she really want to know?

Chloe slapped the book closed and returned it to the shelf. She had to do something. She couldn't believe she was going to be confined to this space without human contact for more than twenty-four hours. It was maddening. She thought about her life before it had been snatched from her. She had no family. Her job was whatever she could get from day to day. She picked up envelopes and packages from several different places and delivered them. She brought back the receipts and picked up her pay. There wasn't an office where her presence was expected every day. So, nobody was missing her, nobody was sounding an alarm that Chloe Bennett had disappeared. It occurred to her that the person who had sent her here was perfectly aware of those facts. It was why she could be sacrificed to get to Jax and his band of whatever they were. She hung her head in despair.

The news caught her attention. There was a huge traffic snarl in Manhattan and a scuffle had broken out among angry drivers who had been brought to a standstill. Police were gathering there, trying to calm things down and the confusion continued to mount. It was just another day in a large, busy city. Chloe sat down with her laptop and began to write random thoughts. After a few minutes, she realized that her tension level had dropped a few notches and she kept writing. She decided to start a journal and realized that it was the best idea she'd had since Jax had given her the laptop. She went back to the night she'd brought the envelope to the door and recorded a history of everything that had happened. It kept her busy for several hours and when she finally stopped, she realized she needed a break.

Chloe went to the kitchen and opened the refrigerator, where she found leftover soup. She warmed up a bowlful and sat down at the table, turning the volume up on the TV a little to keep her company. She was nearly finished with her soup when the phone Jax had given her vibrated. It startled her so much that she dropped her spoon, staring at the phone.

"H-hello?"

"Are you all right?"

She felt a rush of relief when she heard Jax's familiar, deep voice. "Yes, I'm fine. What's wrong?"

"Nothing. We're in place. Now we have a long wait and I thought I ought to check on you."

It was the last thing she had expected to hear from him. "It's just very quiet here." She thought she heard him sigh.

"Quiet is good. I think I'll be glad to get back to it."

"Is everything the way it's supposed to be? No sign of... you know."

"No sign of a problem so far. I'm optimistic."

"Good." It was Chloe's turn to sigh. "I guess it's dumb to tell you to be careful."

"Nah, I'll take it." Her words gave him a curiously warm feeling. "Okay, I've gotta go."

She sat looking at the phone after he hung up and found herself whispering a little prayer for their safety. She looked at the time and realized that it was dusk and the sun would be going down soon. She had no idea when their operation would commence, but she knew it would be in the dark. She curled up on the couch with a cup of hot tea to warm the chill she couldn't shake off and flipped through the channels for a while. She ended up turning back to the news, even though she didn't expect to learn anything from it. The later it got, the more she felt the eerie quiet of the building. A deep sense of loneliness overwhelmed her and she knew that something had to change before the next mission.

Chloe went back to her laptop and wrote her feelings; she wrote about the loneliness and dread, the feeling of being left completely alone in the world. It was a haunted feeling and one she wouldn't wish for anyone to experience. She was tempted to use the phone, just to hear his voice but she knew that was a terrible idea and one that might actually put him in danger. She dismissed the idea as soon as she had it. She changed into pajamas and wandered around the apartment, too restless to remain still. It was late when she finally began to yawn and admitted to herself that it was time to sleep. She walked into the bedroom and stood staring at the empty bed; she just couldn't bring herself to crawl into it alone. So, she took her pillow to the couch and curled up under a blanket, the TV still playing softly in the darkened apartment.

Things started out well enough for Jax and his men. The house they were invading was a well-kept secret, at least it had been up until now. There were guards, but not an over-whelming number of them. Coop took out the guard posted near the alarm system with one quick, smooth thrust of his knife. The man slumped silently to the floor and it took only a minute to disable the alarms. He whispered the okay to Jax and Jax gave them the signal to go. In less than thirty seconds, they were all inside and two more guards were bleeding out on the floor. Jax, Coop, and Joker approached from the front and the rest of them went in through the rear. They counted the guards as they went, making sure they were all down.

There were three men in the room they were converging on and everything had gone smoothly. Finn and Slade crept closer, one on each side of the door, guns raised. Jax was just behind Finn and Coop was behind Slade. Shadow had a device he was using to listen to the conversation in the room and as soon as he heard all three voices, he gave a nod and the men surged silently forward. Silencers muffled the gunshots and a moment later, all three targets were dead on the floor. Shadow quickly took a picture of each man's face and they melted down the hallway and toward the back entrance to the house.

"Fuck, we're getting company," Shadow said grimly.

All six of them faded quickly into the dark outside the back of the house, but now they were cut off from their escape. Two vehicles pulled up and they heard doors slamming. A moment later there was a shout from inside the house and men with flashlights and guns spilled into the yard. Jax had led his men to the shelter of the trees at the edge of the yard and he motioned to them to spread out. A quick assessment told him that they had no choice but to take the newcomers out. Slade fired and one man went down, and before the others could take aim at the spot the shot had come from, Coop fired from thirty yards the other direction. Finn was next, from an entirely different spot. Shots rang out from their adversaries and they were on the move, circling around in hopes of flanking them and guided by the flashlights that were still on.

There was a shout. "Shut those fucking flashlights off!"

There was a flurry of gunshots and Finn went down. But then it was over. One man was groaning from where he lay on the ground; the rest were dead. Slade used his knife to finish the wounded man and the rest of them went about making sure the others were all dead.

"Boss!" Coop called softly, "Finn's down."

"Fuck!" Jax hurried over to him. "How bad?"

"He's alive."

"Let's get the hell out of here."

Slade and Coop lifted Finn and they all made a run for the vehicle that was hidden behind an outbuilding behind the house. They raced away from the scene of the carnage, head-lights off until they put some distance between them and the fucked-up mess they had left behind. Slade was checking out Finn, who came to with a groan while Slade eased off his flak vest.

"It's his shoulder, boss," Slade said. "He'll be fine, it was through and through. I've got to stop the bleeding." He worked efficiently, using the same powder that the military employed and applying Combat Gauze dressings while Finn cursed at him.

"Your fucking bedside manner sucks, man."

Slade grinned. "Yeah, he's fine."

Jax gave him a thumbs up and then got on the phone. "I need to speak to him. Now." He waited impatiently for the call to be answered. "No, I don't want to hold, I want him on the phone right now." He listened for a few seconds and then snapped, "I want to know what the fuck happened here! We got the mission finished and then hostiles showed up. Yeah, we've got a man with a GSW and a pile of dead guys lying outside around the house. That's right, your cleanup just turned into a much bigger job."

Finn said faintly, "Go, boss."

"I don't give a shit. You get that mess cleaned up and you make sure he knows I want some answers." Jax cut the call off and swore bitterly. "Fucking prick. Is everybody else okay? No injuries of any kind?" The others assured him that they were fine. "Shadow, did you get pictures of the visitors?"

"Got them all, boss."

"Good. Something really stinks here and we're going to find out what. We're also going to get away for a while. It's time for a break."

A little cheer went up and then Finn said, "We'll need to

take a nurse along with us, boss. I've got a lot of recovering to do."

They laughed at him and the atmosphere lightened a little. Slade opened a cooler and got out ice cold beers for all of them. They had several hours of driving time back to headquarters and they needed to stop for food before too long. It was soon daylight and Coop found them a little town with a local cafe and he pulled into a parking spot. They had all stripped off their protective gear and stowed their weapons while they drove and they put on regular jackets to cover their handguns. Finn's left arm was in a sling and he was a little shaky as they trooped into the restaurant, but he was okay and ready for a meal.

The waitress's eyes widened at the sight of the tough looking group but she shoved a couple of tables together for them and brought coffee right away. They celebrated when they found steak and eggs on the menu, and twenty minutes later they were digging into them along with piles of home fries and a basket full of freshly baked biscuits. There was a big bowl of gravy and a couple kinds of homemade jam as well as a pot of honey. They left the best tip the waitress had ever seen and she sent them off with coffee for their trip. They all felt better when they got back on the road. Finn was asleep within five minutes, and a few hours later they pulled off for gas and a bathroom break, then Joker took over the driving.

Shadow was busy with a laptop. He'd loaded the pictures he'd taken onto the computer and was studying each face carefully. Jax huddled over the screen with him and they discussed the mess in low tones so they wouldn't wake Finn.

"You're right, boss, something really stinks here. Everybody who was in the house was supposed to be there. The IDs we made during planning were exactly right. But the guys who showed up after, they're like ghosts. I know I'm just beginning the search, but I'm not finding anything at all."

Jax grunted. "That's a problem."

"Yeah. Maybe a big one."

"Any news breaking yet?"

"No. I'd say cleanup has been completed."

Jax said grimly, "It better be. We're leaving town asap. We're way overdue for some down time and we've got to do a real evaluation of what happened before we even consider going back for more. We can do that from a beach."

"What if our evaluation turns up big problems?"

"Then big changes will have to be made. They might have us for life, but we've got leverage against them too. They're not going to allow a mess like this to happen again. We're not taking missions unless they can do better." Jax was dead serious.

"That's strong talk, boss."

"I mean every word."

Shadow said, "I know you do. But if something's rotten at their end, I'd hate to see what they'd do to cover it up."

"You and me both," Jax said morosely.

"You think we need to move our base?"

"Yeah. No question. That's happening before we take on another mission."

"Good. I think we've been there long enough. Maybe too long. If Snake could figure out enough to be able to send us that message, then we were there too long. We need to disappear." Shadow had been wanting to say it ever since Chloe had been caught at their door.

"Agreed. And we need a plan to take the head off the Snake."

"It won't be easy."

"No, it's probably going to be the hardest and riskiest thing we've ever done. But it's necessary. We've got to get them before they get us," Jax said.

"Where are you thinking about moving us?"

"Someplace remote. A place where we can set up a perimeter and nobody can just walk up to the door. I never liked being right out in the open like we are. We need a fortress."

Shadow contemplated whether he dared ask his next question. Taking a chance, he asked, "What about the girl?"

Jax said shortly, "She goes with us. She's not safe any other way and she was set up. She's my problem."

"Understood." Shadow shut down his laptop. "I think I could use an hour of sleep."

It was near dusk when they got back. Chloe had paced the apartment for most of the day, and when she heard them coming in, she was left weak in the knees with the rush of relief that swept over her. She sank down onto a chair and waited. It was only a couple of minutes before she heard the lock turn and Jax walked in. Without thinking, she rushed to him and threw her arms around him. He hesitated for a split second and then his arms were around her, hard as steel, and he was plundering her mouth with his. When they broke apart, Chloe stared at him, her cheeks flushed with embarrassment at the way she had flung herself at him.

"Is everything all right?" she asked breathlessly.

"Finn took a bullet through the shoulder but he's okay. There were... complications. We all made it out okay."

"Oh, my God," Chloe was horrified. "Is he in the hospital?"

"No, he's with us. Slade patched him up. We don't go to the hospital; there would be way too many questions."

"You said there were complications. What does that mean?"

Jax said, "Nothing I can tell you about. But you might like to hear that we're going to be getting out of here for a while."

"Getting out of here. What does *that* mean?"

"That means that we're way overdue for some time away,

time to decompress, and we're taking it. So, I hope you like the beach."

Chloe was speechless. It sounded like he was talking about a vacation. How the hell did you take a prisoner on vacation? Then she thought about her reaction when he had come through the door and she had to wonder just how much of a prisoner she really was. What a screwed-up mess. But, honestly, any change from spending day and night in this apartment was going to be welcome.

"I love the beach," she said.

"Good. Come on, we've got things to do; you can come with me."

She followed him out of the apartment and down the hallway to the bustle of activity that was going on, guys hauling in equipment and stowing things away. Finn was ensconced in a chair, his arm in a sling and one foot propped up on a stool, directing the activity. She caught sight of some wicked looking guns before they were locked away in their cabinets and piles of flak vests and other protective gear were hung up on racks. It was all frightening and fascinating at the same time, and once again, Chloe had a surreal feeling, as if she had stumbled into a movie set from some crazy action movie.

"I'd better order some food," Jax murmured.

"Oh! I forgot," Chloe said, "I didn't know what else to do with myself today, so I cooked. There are two lasagnas in your oven and a big bowl of salad in the fridge. I figured if you all didn't come back hungry, I could always freeze the lasagna."

Jax was staring at her. "That sounds perfect. I appreciate it."

Chloe was flustered. "It'll be ready anytime now."

"Fantastic. Coop and Joker can go get it and bring it to the big kitchen." Jax sent the two men to get the food and soon they were all gathered around the long table.

By the time they were all finished eating, the men were ready to hit their showers and then their beds. Slade said, "Come on, Finn, I'll change that dressing for you and make sure everything looks good. Night, assholes. Oh, not you, Chloe. Thank you for the dinner."

And night settled in.

Chapter 7

Chloe was in the big kitchen making one of her favorite dishes, chicken and dumplings. There were two cherry pies in the oven, just beginning to smell good. The guys were busy packing up equipment. Everything had to be cleaned, catalogued, and packed for moving. Once it was all ready to go, it would be loaded into an armored box truck and driven to a location known only to Jax, at least at this point, where it would be locked into a bunker to wait for them to pick it up. And as soon as that was all done, they were going someplace to decompress. Chloe had no idea where they were going, but wherever it was, she was looking forward to it. Just to be outside with sunshine on her face and warm sand between her toes, she gave a little shiver of delight at the thought.

Jax was on the phone at his desk and every now and then, Chloe could hear him raising hell with whoever he was talking to. He was seriously pissed and it seemed that his quest for answers wasn't going very well. The news had broken early that morning about the murders at the house Jax and his crew had stormed. It was limited, however, to the dead men who had been found in the house; there was no mention at all of anything found outside the house, where their gun battle had taken place. The news anchor finished by saying that the main victim, Carlos Rivera, had long been rumored to be linked with organized crime. The investigation was ongoing. Chloe had seen the news report and she wondered just how much wasn't being said.

Jax dropped the phone with a frustrated curse and shoved his chair back. Direct questions weren't getting him anywhere. He was obviously going to have to find out what he needed to know in another way. In the meantime, they needed to get on their way as soon as possible. He walked over to Finn, who was seated in a comfortable chair with his feet propped up, directing the other men.

"Look at him, boss, just sitting there supervising. Hell, he was shot in the shoulder, not in the heart," Coop called.

"Yeah," Joker chimed in. "I didn't know our benefits included light duty." That was met with hoots of laughter from the other men.

"Shit, Joker, it's a good thing they don't," razzed Slade. "You get hurt every third time you go out. You'd be on light duty for the rest of your life."

Even Jax had to laugh at that one. Joker did have a knack for getting hurt, although it was usually superficial. He pitched in with the packing and by the time they sat down to dinner that evening, they had well over half of it done. The way it was looking, they should be able to leave the next afternoon, late. Chloe had packed her things that morning, keeping out whatever she needed for the next day and all the men would pack their personal gear first thing the next morning. They demolished the pot of dumplings and both pies and complimented Chloe on the meal. She was feeling oddly comfortable with the group and they had relaxed a little when they were around her.

When they went to bed that night, Jax pulled Chloe over and held her against him for a few minutes. Finally, with a heavy sigh, he kissed her on top of the head and said, "Better get some sleep. It's going to be a big day tomorrow."

"Good night," Chloe murmured, already drowsy.

Sometime during the night, she woke to find herself alone in the bed. Disoriented, she looked around until she saw Jax sitting in the chair at the desk, his chin propped on his hand, just staring into space. "Jax?" she called softly.

He turned and looked at her, then rose and came back to the bed. "Go back to sleep."

"What were you doing?"

He sighed and said, "Just thinking." He pulled her close and she cuddled against him with her head on his shoulder. He stroked her hair absently and when she drifted into sleep, he had finally fallen asleep too.

The activity level was even higher than it had been the day before. The men worked efficiently, their joking at a minimum as they set out to finish the job. By midafternoon, they were ready to load the truck. Chloe made use of the last of the sandwich supplies that were in the kitchen and they had a quick lunch before Joker and Coop went to get the truck. In a little more than an hour, they were on the road. Chloe rode with Jax, Finn, and Shadow in the big, dark SUV and the other three followed in the truck. Chloe drank in the sight of the outside world as they left the city and set out across the countryside, keeping to secondary roads. She vowed that if she ever had a normal life again, she would never take it for granted.

Shadow, sitting beside Chloe, handed her a shopping bag and said, "I have some things for you."

Curious, she looked into the bag and found a good quality ladies' purse.

"The saleslady assured me that you'd like it."

Chloe pulled it out and stroked the butter-soft leather. "I do. It's beautiful, but I don't understand."

"There's a wallet in there too," Shadow said. "I don't know what else you put in a purse, you can handle that, but I have what you need to put in the wallet."

He handed her an envelope and she opened it to find a full set of ID with her picture and a false name, right down to a birth certificate and passport. There was a high school diploma and a driver's license, social security card and some other papers.

"Brynn Kelly," Chloe said slowly. "This is supposed to be me?"

"We need to be prepared if anything comes up where you would need an ID. There's a history of Brynn Kelly in there. Read it and memorize it, so if you have to answer any questions, it comes naturally."

Chloe felt cold and she gave a little shiver as she stared at the new identity. She felt like it was the end of her life as she knew it. Her face was haunted as she turned her gaze on Shadow. "This is... I don't like it."

Shadow chose his words carefully. "Chloe, when you were sent to us, it was unfair to you and it put you in grave danger. There was no way to undo it. But we don't want to see you pay any more of a price for it than you have to. We know how to protect you. Let us do it."

She blinked back tears and then her face hardened. "All right, for now, I have no choice."

Jax was driving and he didn't speak, but he heard every word. He hoped that the moves they were making would improve things for them all, Chloe included.

Without another word, Chloe began putting things away in her wallet, then put the wallet in the lovely purse. She would add other things later, but she did have her lipstick in her jacket pocket and she put it in a little pocket inside the bag. When she was finished, she nodded at Shadow.

"Do I need to read it now?"

"No, enjoy the scenery. But at least take time to skim over it before we get on the plane. You've got time."

So, she sat back and watched out the windows until the sun went down. They stopped not long after for gas and a break, and they grabbed burgers at a fast-food place. Then they were on the road again. Shadow gave Chloe a small flashlight and she took out the history of Brynn Kelly and read it, growing fascinated at the weird idea of becoming someone else. She wondered how many people in the world wished they could do exactly that and she had the thought that at least she liked the name Brynn Kelly. She was nodding off when they came to a stop again, several hours later. She straightened up groggily and looked around. They were stopped on a narrow drive through a thick growth of trees. There was a stone wall ahead of them and the drive widened as it neared the wall, so Jax pulled the SUV over to one side and the truck rolled up beside them.

The men in the truck climbed out and so did Jax and Shadow. They all stood talking between the vehicles and then Jax reached in for a device that Finn handed to him. He punched some numbers into the device and then, in the wall ahead of them, two massive stone doors slid silently open. Inside the doorway, the floor sloped down and Joker hopped up into the truck and drove it through the opening and down the slope. Jax entered some more numbers and some lights came on inside the opening.

"You want to get out?" Finn asked.

"Can I?"

"Sure. I need to stretch my legs too."

Chloe got out quickly and walked closer. Joker had driven into a building, one with thick stone walls and a floor that sloped down to nearly a basement level. The lights were mounted along the walls, up high and only dimly illuminated the space.

"Put the go-bag in the SUV," Jax said.

Coop hauled a dark duffel bag out of the back of the truck and then closed the door and locked the truck up securely. He put the bag in the back of the SUV along with their luggage and they all got into the vehicle. Jax worked his magic with the remote-control panel again and the doors slid closed, leaving what looked like a plain stone wall. As they drove away, Chloe looked back and it was as if the trees swallowed up the whole place. Nobody, going by, would ever dream that the building was back there.

"What was that place?" Chloe asked softly.

Shadow said, "It's a bunker. Nobody knows about it but us."

"Almost nobody," Coop corrected with a grunt.

They were all silent and Jax drove on. Overcome with exhaustion, Chloe fell asleep and when she opened her eyes again, the first light of dawn was touching the sky. Jax had pulled up beside a long building and as he shut the engine off, the men were piling out of the vehicle. Jax took her arm and helped her out, then pulled her to the side.

"I want you to stay right beside me and keep quiet. I'll do the talking. If we need anything from you, I'll tell you. This should only take a few minutes and then we'll be in the air."

"But—"

"Not now, Chloe."

His face was so serious that she didn't say another word. She stayed close to his side as they all entered the building and Jax walked over to a long counter. The grizzled man behind it gave him a hard look before he broke into a grin.

"Goddam, Jax, it's been a long time. How you been?"

They shook hands and Jax said, "Can't complain. You look as fit as ever; how you been?"

The man gave a short hoot of laughter and said, "I guess I can't complain, either."

"Are we all set?"

"I got you covered. I go two, three weeks at a time without anybody showing up out here, so you're good to go." He pulled out some paperwork and stamped it, handing a copy to Jax. He spat a stream of tobacco juice into a can on the floor and said, "Who's the little lady?"

"Mine," said Jax. "That's all you need to know."

"Didn't your mama ever teach you to share?"

"Nope. It's not in my DNA," Jax said with a grin.

"Well, grab your bags and follow me."

There was a flurry of activity as the men unloaded the SUV and Finn made sure there was nothing left inside it, then they all trooped after the old man, through the building and out a side door to the open pavement, where a sleek plane was sitting. The men made short work of loading their things into the cargo hold and two more younger men were introduced as the pilot and co-pilot. They all climbed the stairs into the plane and Jax handed the keys to the SUV to the old man, who took them with a grin. Then, with a final handshake, Jax turned and boarded the plane. The plane seated ten passengers, so they were seated comfortably, and a few minutes later, they were in the air.

Chloe gripped the armrest and gazed out the window and down at the landscape below them. Jax was sitting across the aisle, looking out the window on the other side of the plane. The drone of the engines was soothing to her and she felt an enormous relief at the fact that they were putting distance between them and the threats that had seemed to be all around them back at the headquarters building. When the plane finally landed, it was on an island. As they descended,

Chloe could see sandy beaches, palm trees, blue, blue water, and a small airstrip with a small building beside it. The men were in good spirits as they departed the plane and unloaded their bags. There were two beat up old SUVs waiting for them and after Jax handed an envelope to the pilot, he spoke to a man who was slouched in a lawn chair outside the little building. Then, with a nod, he turned and signaled to his crew and they piled themselves and all their bags into the two vehicles.

Jax drove one of them and Coop the other, with Jax in the lead and Chloe beside him. They drove a couple of miles through a wooded area that made Chloe think of the jungle, over a rutted road that was little more than a trail. When they drove out of the woods, they were at a wide beach dotted with small cabins. There were several firepits and a volleyball net, surfboards and boogie boards propped against the cabins, and a couple of kayaks off to the side. There was plenty of firewood stacked up and ready to burn and each cabin was equipped with a fully stocked refrigerator and a two-burner stove. Jax led Chloe to one of the larger cabins and ushered her in. He took her by surprise when he grabbed her and planted a kiss on her mouth.

"This is home for the next few weeks," he said. "What do you think?"

"I think it's amazing," she said. "And I think I don't have a damn thing with me that's suitable for the beach."

"I took care of that for now." He led her through a short hallway, past a tiny bathroom and into a bedroom. There were wispy white curtains at the window, drifting in the breeze and there was a large shopping bag on the bed. "There you go, see if that'll do. Tomorrow, I'll take you to the other side of the island and you can buy what you want. Oh, and add this to your wallet." He handed her a wad of cash.

Chloe was speechless. She dumped the bag out on the bed and found perfect things for the beach—gauzy shirts and skirts, sandals, a swimsuit, a king-sized beach towel, sunglasses, a big straw hat. And every piece was in the perfect size.

"How do you do this?" she asked, shaking her head.

"Is it all right?"

"It's perfect. I need to change clothes."

When she emerged from the bedroom, Jax took one look and gave a long whistle. Impulsively, she made a little spin and made him laugh. He pulled her against him and gave her a gentler kiss.

"Are you as hungry as I am?" he asked when the kiss ended.

Chloe laughed and said, "I'm starving!"

"Let's raid the refrigerator."

They found fresh seafood salads, ice-cold beer and, on the counter, a bag of crusty rolls. They carried it all out onto the little porch along the front of the cabin, which held two chairs and a small table, and ate while they watched the waves glinting in the sun and the antics of Jax's guys set free. It was the best Chloe had felt since the night she had walked up to Jax's door. She felt free and, for once, she wasn't scared. Maybe it wouldn't last long, but she was going to enjoy every minute of it while it did. It made her wonder what it would be like if Jax wasn't the man he was, if he just had an ordinary job without danger and death. But he didn't and, according to him, he never would. She decided it was time to shut off her head and just enjoy things while she could.

After they ate, Jax told her that he needed to talk to his men for a little bit and Chloe went to the water's edge and slipped off her sandals, wading in the warm, shallow water. It was the most beautiful beach she'd ever seen and she drank it in, the sights, the smells, the delicious warmth of the sun. It was perfect; not too hot, but the water was warm and she thought for a second that she could live there forever.

Jax was finished before long and he sat in the sand and watched her, thinking that if they could just stay there forever, all his problems would be solved. He was an idiot. When Chloe saw him, she ran across the sand toward him and then plopped down beside him.

"It's so gorgeous here! Have you been here before?"

Jax said, "Yeah, we have. We have a few places and we alternate where we go. Even when we take a break, it pays to be careful. This is a favorite with all of them, though."

Chloe said with feeling, "I can see why. It's like paradise."

Jax thought *yeah, we go back and forth, from paradise to hell. It's really getting old.* But he kept silent, unwilling to ruin the moment.

Chapter 8

The days drifted by, blissfully peaceful. Chloe would sit on the porch with her laptop, continuing to write; a story was beginning to form and she was letting it make its way at its own pace. She walked on the beach, swam in the warm, salty water, and Jax took her to the other side of the island to shop in the funky little stores and the village marketplace. They cooked over the open fire and drank ice cold beer that they pulled, dripping, from coolers full of ice. She sat, laughing, as the guys tried to teach themselves to surf and made outrageous bets with each other over who could stay up the longest. One day they rented a charter and went out fishing and the swordfish that Coop caught fed them all for two days. Joker fried potatoes and onions in a cast iron pan over the fire while they roasted the fish with butter and herbs, garnished with fresh lemon.

Jax and Chloe made love at night in their cabin, bathed in balmy breezes from the open window. She wasn't sure what had happened, but it was as if when they'd gotten to the island, they had met all over again without any of the circumstances that had really happened when they met. Jax was the most relaxed she'd ever seen him and Chloe simply refused to think about the reality of their strange relationship. She let her feelings lead her and just enjoyed it. Deep down, she knew that eventually it would come to an end, but she would face that when it happened.

Jax knew he should resist what was happening between them. He didn't have the right to this kind of relationship, however long it lasted, and he knew that eventually he was going to hurt this woman who had found a way into his heart. He was going to hate himself when that time came, but he wouldn't have a choice; he would do whatever it took to keep her safe. He was cruising toward disaster and he made the choice to take what he could while he could. It made him despise himself even more, but he seemed to be powerless to resist her.

Jax and Shadow spent time each day searching for information that would tell them the truth about the forces that controlled them but they were making little progress. They had been unable to identify any of the men who had attacked them that night; it was as if they had never existed.

"Shit, Shadow, they were hidden better than we are. Who the fuck *were* they?"

"I don't know, boss, but maybe we should look at it differently. Instead of trying to figure out who they were, maybe we can figure out who sent them."

Jax thought it over. "Well, we have our suspicions. We just have to confirm or refute whether either party was responsible. Where do we start?"

"Find out exactly what both those parties were doing during the time in question. We've got to track everything they did and everyone they communicated with."

Jax sat back and said, "Well, that sure won't be easy, but at least it's possible. Let's do it."

"I'm on it."

"But you're still on break, so a couple of hours a day is it. I'll work with you."

Shadow gave him a grin. "I won't argue with that."

"I want us all to be fresh when we leave here."

"Have you made a decision on where we're going to go?"

Jax said, "I've narrowed it down to two possibilities. I'm going over all the pros and cons and once I think I have all the info, we'll have a meeting and discuss it."

"Sounds good. Now, I'm going to take one of those kayaks out for a while. Want to join me?"

"No, I think I've got something else in mind."

Shadow snickered at him. "Yeah, I bet you do."

Jax flipped him off and said, "Don't be an asshole."

"Hey, I like the lady. I don't blame you."

"I like her too. I'm going to end up fucking her over and I don't like that."

Shadow tilted his head and said, "Then find a way not to do it." He got up and walked away.

"Son of a bitch," Jax muttered. "Just find a way." He went to find Chloe.

Chloe had just finished writing for the morning and she was shutting down her laptop when he walked up. "All finished?" she asked.

"Yeah, we're done. You too?"

"I am all done for today."

"Want to go to town and have tacos?"

"Ooh, that sounds great. I need some lotion too."

Jax grabbed her and squeezed her butt. "I'll give you some lotion, baby."

Chloe actually giggled and it made him grin. "Let me go put my hair up." She was back in a flash and Jax felt his gut clench as he looked at her. She had developed a light, golden tan and she was wearing a gauzy, wraparound skirt that fluttered around her calves and a filmy white shirt over a form fitting white tank top and bright turquoise sandals. She looked good enough to eat and Jax had another piercing moment when he desperately wanted to stay there forever.

He took her hand and they got into one of the vehicles and started off for the other side of the island. He cranked up the radio and Chloe sang along, laughing and ad-libbing when she didn't know the words to the island music. They spent the afternoon eating whatever struck their fancy, window shopping, and Chloe got her lotion. Jax was careful to call her Brynn whenever they went into town and she was beginning to get used to it. They stopped at a pushcart that was operated by a local they had made friends with and he greeted them with a huge grin.

"Brynn and Jax, my friends! It's good to see you!"

Jax winked at him. "It's good to see you, Andre. We need something cold."

Andre winked back and said, "I have just the thing for you." He pulled two beers out of the ice and handed them to Jax and Chloe.

"Perfect," Jax said, handing him a twenty-dollar bill and refusing the change. "What's happening today? Anything exciting?"

"Ah, the widow down the street is trying to get me to come to her home for dinner, but I know what she's up to. She wants a taste of Andre's sausage and she just isn't my type."

Chloe nearly spit her beer out laughing.

Jax considered the dilemma carefully. "But maybe her bun *is* Andre's type, eh? Maybe you should give it a try."

Andre leaned forward, looking earnestly at Jax. "But she got *six* babies! I don't know, I think maybe it's better to stay away."

"Ah, now, that changes things. Yes, I agree, it would be safer to stay away. Thanks for the beer, my friend, we'll see you soon."

They wandered on down the street, Chloe still giggling, and when she could stop, she said, "Poor Andre! I think *all* the ladies are after him."

Jax said solemnly, "They've all heard about Andre's sausage."

Chloe was lost in peals of laughter again. Watching her, Jax knew he was going to store this day away in his memory for the rest of his life. Three weeks had already slipped by and he had a growing feeling that bad things were going to catch up with them soon. That night he held her long after their lovemaking was over, holding her close and watching her sleep. He silently cursed the man who had sent her to him and the danger it had put her in. He already knew, maybe he had known from the start, that he couldn't bear it if something happened to her. He had to make sure that could never happen. Then, once it was done, he could let her go, let her get away from his doomed life. Shadow was wrong; there wasn't a way to keep from hurting her. He had to set her free from his poisonous life, for her own sake. It was hours before he drifted into a fitful sleep.

Two days later, Jax was ready to meet with his men about where they would move their base to. They sat on the beach under the palm trees, cooler beside them, beers in their hands and set off into a serious discussion. Jax described the two locations to them; both were in remote places, away from cities and even large towns. Both were in protected places that they could defend easily with a little preparation. One was a large, sprawling house with a good-sized building behind it that had once been a workshop; so, it had a concrete floor and was fully wired and insulated. The other was an industrial building. It would take a lot more to set up for them, but it had thick, concrete construction and would be harder to breach. Jax had noted a lot of pros and cons for each of them and they discussed it carefully, studying the pictures and blueprints. One big con for the industrial building was how long it would take to convert it for their use. At the end of the day, they concluded that it was just not feasible to take on such a big renovation. With a vote, they all agreed on the house for their next base and the decision was made. Now Jax had to inform the boss he answered to.

The conversation didn't go well. It came as a surprise to the man they called Gunner and he was not happy about being surprised. But Jax stood firm, pointing out that he still hadn't been given any answers about their last mission and security had to be increased. The location would remain undisclosed until Jax felt it was safe to disclose it and Gunner really blew his top over that.

"You work for me, you son of a bitch!" Gunner railed at him.

"No, you know that's not true," Jax said calmly. "We work for our country and so do you. So, while we're setting ourselves up with better security, you might want to clean your own house. And we're going to need funds wired to our account."

"You'd better not waste any time getting set up. You're going to need to be back in operation if you want to play this game."

Jax said, "This is not a game, not for us. Every time we take a mission, it's our lives on the line. So don't threaten me."

"You get paid well for putting your lives on the line."

"Yeah, we do, and part of the deal is that we can depend on your end. So, you make fucking sure that your house is clean. There's not going to be another fiasco like we had last time."

Gunner said, "Are you threatening me?"

"Nope. I'm telling you how it has to be."

There was a moment of silence and then Gunner said, "The money will be wired within the hour. Verify it and then get busy."

That was it. Their break was over. Jax called his men together and let them know. Then he said, "Coop, you and Joker go to town and get the biggest steaks you can find and lobsters, too. Tonight, we feast."

"You got it, boss," said Coop.

Jax went to talk to Chloe. "Our break is over, babe. I just spoke to Gunner and we've got to set up our new base as quickly as we can. They want us back on the job."

Chloe sucked in a deep breath. "It went so fast," she said faintly. "Now what?"

"Tonight, we feast and drink and enjoy ourselves. Tomorrow, I call for our flight out and we get packed up. But we don't worry about it tonight. That's a rule."

She smiled at him, but her eyes were somber. "Okay. Tonight, is for fun."

And they enjoyed themselves. Coop made buckets of margaritas and Finn and Slade set steaks to sizzle over the fire, with lobsters cooking over another fire, drenched in butter. It was the best meal Chloe had ever tasted and they gorged themselves and drank too much. They danced under the moonlight and the flickering firelight, and late in the evening everyone except Chloe and Jax stripped down and ran into the water, jumping and splashing like children. And, later, Chloe and Jax sated themselves yet again, feasting on each other's bodies, giving and taking until they collapsed in loose, exhausted satisfaction. They fell asleep with the moonlight playing over their skin and slept the deep, dreamless sleep of oblivion.

The next day, the whole bunch of them were quiet and subdued, packing efficiently and preparing to leave paradise. Jax had made his calls early and they had only a couple of hours before their plane would arrive. Chloe stood in the cabin and looked around at the little place they had enjoyed so much. When Jax came up behind her and put his hands on her shoulders, she leaned back against him and sighed.

"Thank you for bringing me here. I never imagined a place like this. I might have gone my whole life without experiencing anything so beautiful."

Jax felt like a dog. He wanted to tell her that he would bring her back again, but he didn't dare say that. He knew one thing for sure; she didn't deserve what had happened to her. For the millionth time, he cursed the Snake who was their enemy. His primary goal, once they got set up in their new base, would be to put him down forever. And then he would have to set her free. He shook off the thoughts and kissed her neck.

"Andre sent us a gift," he said.

Without turning around, she said, "It's not a sausage, is it?"

It startled a chuckle out of him. "No, it's a six pack of island brew."

"Ooh, that's a good gift. What a nice guy."

"He is. And we need to go now."

Chloe felt tears burn her eyes, so she shook them off and squared her shoulders. "Okay, let's go."

They were even quiet on the flight back, talking softly now and then or napping. When they landed, Jax settled up with the pilot and the grizzled old man who ran the airstrip. Coop checked out the SUV, which was still parked where they had left it, sweeping it with an electronic device for anything suspicious. They loaded their things into the back and hit the road.

They drove for hours, stopping only for gas and food, well into the night and pulled into the hidden bunker where they had stashed the truck, carefully checking everything out before they got out of the SUV. But things were quiet and exactly the way they had left them. They took a few minutes to stretch their legs and then they were on the road again, Coop driving the truck and following Jax in the SUV.

The next time they stopped, it was getting light outside and they needed breakfast. Again, they were staying on secondary roads and away from big towns and cities. They fueled up the SUV and the attendant told them where to find a good cafe. Forty minutes later, they had refueled themselves and Jax turned the driving over to Shadow for a while. He made a call and left a short message for Gunner and then he stretched out his legs and went instantly to sleep. Chloe had slept quite a bit overnight, so she quietly watched the road. They drove all the way through the day, stopping only when they had to and Chloe watched the terrain with fascination. Toward evening, they had driven into a more mountainous area and Chloe thought the elevation had been slowly rising. As the sun set, the road got lonelier and the surroundings more rugged.

Jax was driving late that night when he slowed down and proceeded at little more than a crawl over what felt like a rough, rutted drive. They seemed to be on it for a long time and then he drove onto more level ground and pulled to a stop.

"Hey, kids, we're home," he called.

There was one light high on a pole in the gravel barnyard they were parked in and otherwise, it was pitch black outside. They all climbed stiffly out of the vehicles and stretched out the kinks as well as they could.

"I'm not sure what we're going to find in here," Jax said. "The woman I dealt with said that most of the furnishings were left by the previous owners, and the electricity and heat were left on so hopefully we won't be completely roughing it tonight. Let's go check it out."

They all followed him as he unlocked the front door and opened it wide. He hit the light switch beside the door and, sure enough, the lights came on. The interior of the house was rustic, with lots of wood and there was definitely furniture left behind. There were deep leather sofas and chairs, heavy wooden tables and bright, western themed rugs and throws. There was a huge stone fireplace in the big main room they had walked into and, way at the back of the room, hallways branched off in both directions before they walked on into a large, beautiful kitchen that was equipped with another fireplace. Chloe's eyes were wide as she took it all in. They turned left down one hallway which had a door into a formal dining room, followed by a door into a large den. Across the hall was a full bathroom with large closets on each side of it and down where the hall ended, there was a sweeping staircase heading up. Down the hallway to the right, they found an office and a large library with a matching staircase at the end.

"Not bad," Jax said. "There are supposed to be six bedrooms upstairs, each with its own bath."

Chloe was absolutely shocked at the size and beauty of the house. She walked up the stairs with the others where, sure enough, there was a large sitting area at the top of the steps on each end and six bedrooms opening off the two long hallways. Jax peeked into each bedroom and easily located the master.

"Okay, I'm here. You guys pick a room and bring in the bags. Also, there's a box of food to bring in. At least we can have peanut butter sandwiches and fruit before we get stocked up tomorrow. And, Coop, you come with me and we'll get the truck pulled into the building out back."

Chloe went outside with the others; she was capable of getting her own bags and after she stowed them in the master bedroom and Slade brought in Jax's bags, she returned to the kitchen downstairs to check out the box of food and the cupboards and pantry. There was nothing edible, but apparently the previous owners had either been in a hurry to leave or they wanted all new things after they moved out. The kitchen was fully stocked with pots, pans, utensils, dishes, everything one could need to prepare food. The pantry was a walk-in and contained a large upright freezer that was turned on and working, but completely empty. Same with the refrigerator. It was as if new owners had been expected to walk in at any moment. The linen closets were stocked and it appeared that all the beds were freshly made.

Jax came back in with Coop trailing behind him and said, "I don't know about any of you guys, but peanut butter and jelly sounds damn good to me right now."

Within minutes, they were all wolfing down sandwiches and fruit, washed down with bottles of water they had carried along with them. They cleaned up the mess quickly and were finished for the night.

"I suggest we all get to sleep," said Jax. "We've got a helluva lot of work to do after tonight."

Chapter 9

The next morning, the disciplined men were all up early and ready to go. Chloe woke up at the first hint of sunlight peeking through the windows but Jax was already gone. She pulled on jeans and a sweatshirt, brushed her teeth and hurried down the stairs where she could hear voices in the kitchen. The table was littered with the remains of peanut butter sandwiches and there were still bananas and oranges. Chloe helped herself to a banana and listened as Jax assigned his men to various tasks. When he saw her, Jax beckoned to her and they stepped to the side to talk.

"Things are different here," Jax said. "We don't have fully equipped quarters of our own, so taking meals together will be the easiest thing to do. I'd like to be able to count on you to do most of the cooking since we'll be really busy getting things set up."

Chloe thought about the fact that he was actually asking for her agreement to his request and she was pleasantly surprised. "Yes, of course. I don't mind cooking."

"You won't have to deal with cleanup, the guys will take

turns with that. And if you need a break, someone can step in and fix a meal. So, Finn is going to town for supplies."

Chloe saved him from asking her. "I'd like to go with him if that's okay. It'll make it easier for me to plan meals."

"Good. You don't have to buy a ton of meat. I'm going to fill that freezer with a freshly butchered beef cow and a hog, so fish and chicken will be mostly what you need to get. But the pantry is completely empty, so you'll need all the basics."

She gave him a little grin. "Any special requests?"

"I'd go for that lasagna of yours anytime. Coop! Is that truck unloaded?" Distracted, Jax moved away and Chloe looked around for Finn.

She found him in the office, making a long list. "I'm going to go with you," she said. "I'm going to be doing most of the cooking, at least for now, so Jax wanted me to go along."

Finn gave a sigh of relief. "Oh, good. I'm not sure I'm a good one to be stocking the kitchen. The only thing I'm absolutely sure we need is a coffeemaker and plenty of coffee. And beer."

Chloe laughed. "I think we can manage more than that."

"Do you want to make a list?"

Chloe said, "Yeah, that would be sensible. Give me an hour, is that okay?"

"Absolutely. I've got other things I can do until then."

She sat down and made an organized list of necessities and then a week's worth of menus. Then she went back to the kitchen to see what else she needed as far as small appliances. When she had made her list as complete as she could, she found Finn and told him she was ready to go. They bounced along the rutted driveway, an overgrowth of trees on each side of them until they finally reached the road.

"Where are we, Finn?"

"Montana," Finn replied absently. Then he kicked himself

mentally. He didn't know how much Jax wanted her to know and he hadn't given him any instructions.

"Oh, that's right," Chloe said. "I remember seeing the Welcome to Montana sign last night." Finn heaved a small sigh of relief and Chloe hid a smile. "How long have all you guys been together?"

"Seems like forever," Finn joked, evading the question.

Chloe silently awarded him a point. "The beach was great, wasn't it?" she asked wistfully.

"It always is. I always thought I'd like to retire there someday."

"Have you been there a lot?"

Finn didn't see any harm in answering that. "Several times. It's my favorite place in the world."

"I can understand that," she said with feeling. "It's the most beautiful place I've ever seen."

Finn was curious. "How old are you, Chloe?"

"Twenty-four," she answered.

"Just a youngster." He grinned, but inwardly he was sickened. Her life had essentially ended at age twenty-four, when she stumbled into their world. She belonged to Jax, but Jax wasn't the only one who would step up to protect her.

"How old are you, old man?" she asked teasingly.

Finn groaned and said, "I'll be forty soon."

"Shockingly old," she said and laughed.

Finn laughed too. "Feels even older when you get shot."

"Are you all healed now?"

"Close enough. It's a little sore yet but it's in good shape."

Chloe shivered a little. "I can't imagine getting shot."

Finn said, "That's a good thing. I wouldn't recommend it."

"How far is it to the town we're going to?"

"It's about forty minutes from base. That's a good distance. We can stay under the radar a helluva lot easier than when we were in the city."

"Maybe I can go outside," Chloe said absently.

"I'd say that's a given. Look at you now; you're going to town."

She gave him a radiant smile. "That's true. It's a treat." After she said it, Chloe wondered at herself. Where had her outrage gone? Thinking it over, she realized that she had come to accept the fact that the danger she was in was real.

Finn turned off the little road they were on and they began to see a house now and then, although most of the land looked like pasture. When they began to pass some little groups of houses scattered here and there, Chloe realized they were getting close to the town. As they drove past the sign that said Welcome to Madison, it was clear that it was a very small town. Finn drove slowly down the main street, checking it out. There were several restaurants and a bar, including a home-town cafe, a Mexican restaurant, and a pizza place. There was a small strip mall with a department store and Finn pulled into a parking spot in front of it.

They found a decent coffee maker, a toaster and electric mixer, and picked up a few other household items. The cashier, a friendly, fifty-something woman, tried to chat them up, obviously curious, but they managed to talk to her without offering any information. She told them where the grocery store was as well as a building supply store a few miles out of town and a farm store on the other end of town. Finn sent a text message to Jax and gave him the address of the building supply store before they went on to the grocery store. When they came out, the bagboy loaded their three full carts full of groceries into the back of the SUV and Finn tipped him, enough to make the boy stutter his thanks, and they started back.

With some help from Finn and Shadow, Chloe got the kitchen in order and everything put away. She had bought tubs of chicken salad and other salads for lunch, along with chips and a bag full of cookies from the store bakery. The lunch break was a quick one, since there was so much work to do and Jax and Coop were headed to the building supply store afterwards. The entire place bustled with activity all day and Chloe was busy in the kitchen putting together two big pans of lasagna for dinner. The work center was going to be set up in the building outside, although they would use the office in the house for meetings and some of the planning. Shadow had Slade helping him wire all kinds of electronics around the place and putting in multiple security alarms and surveillance cameras.

It was several hours before Jax got back, with the truck fully loaded. All the men worked to unload it and placed everything where Jax wanted it, well organized and separated into stacks of items that would be used together. There were two generators, lumber, hardware, tools, electrical supplies, and they had also left an order at the store that they would pick up in a couple of days. Jax had given them a fake name and address, the opposite direction from the store from where they actually were and explained that since they owned their own truck and the crew was being paid for loading and unloading, there was no sense having the store deliver to them. It was less work for the store, so they were pleased with the arrangement.

When Chloe put dinner on the table that evening, it was for six exhausted men. After they ate, she took pity on them and excused them from cleanup duty for the night. Grateful, they went off to hit the shower and their beds and Jax helped Chloe clear the kitchen. The dishwasher was an industrial model and she was grateful for it, especially that night. When all she had left to do was wash off the table and countertops, she shooed him off to his own shower.

He bent to kiss her and said, "I know one thing for certain.

I'm glad this house has two water heaters to serve all those bathrooms."

Chloe laughed and said, "I'll set the dishwasher to start during the night."

Jax looked impressed. "You can do that?"

"Yep. This is a nice one."

"Okay. I'm going to check all the locks. I'll see you in bed."

But when Chloe finished what she had to do and walked upstairs with her half glass of wine, she found him stretched out in the bed, sound asleep, his hair still damp against the pillow. The ceiling light was blazing away and she turned on a small lamp and turned off the light. There was just a warm glow in the bedroom then and she sat in a chair and sipped her wine, watching him sleep. There was a warm, liquid pull low in her belly as she gazed at him. The weeks on the island had changed something and she was afraid that it was not going to turn out to be a good thing. How could this situation end in any way but badly? She drained her wine and went to take her own shower.

The work went on from dawn to dusk each day and when Chloe watched them, she was struck by the fact that the men were like a well-oiled machine, working so well together that they almost looked like they shared the same brain. Since they had decided to put the workspace in the outbuilding, there wasn't a lot to do in the house, other than all the electronics that Shadow was in charge of. There were several spots within the house where Chloe could contact whoever was in the barn, as they called it, and it made her feel that much safer to be able to call for help if she was alone in the house. Shadow spent time on the computer every day, searching for any evidence that their whereabouts were known to anyone. Their history before this, little as it was, had been erased from view and their first priority, once they were finished setting up, would be developing a plan to take out the Snake.

On their seventh day there, Jax gave Chloe an evening off her cooking duties and ordered pizzas from the nearest pizza place. It was an even smaller town than the one they went to for supplies, but it was considerably closer. It was a large order and he paid for it over the burner phone he was using with a credit card in a false name. He sent Coop to pick it up and to get a couple extra cases of beer. When he came through the door, loaded down with boxes and bags, the guys actually sent up a cheer. Joker hustled out to bring in the beer and Slade opened a cooler and loaded it with beer and ice. The atmosphere was as close to party-like as it had been since they'd been on the island and a lot of laughter went on as they feasted on pizza, wings, garlic bread, and even a little salad.

"Let's have a toast," Finn said. He waited until bottles were raised and said, "Chloe, I just want to say that you've been doing a damn good job of keeping us all fed. Let's hear it for Chloe!"

They were rowdy as they drank to Chloe and she laughed at them. "Thank you, guys. As long as you all keep on doing cleanup, I'll keep on cooking."

Joker asked plaintively, "But, Chloe, can I make a request? Please?"

"Okay, let's hear it."

"Could you make that meatloaf again that you made the first time you cooked for us? Damn, that was the best meatloaf I ever ate. My mom couldn't make that for shit."

The guys broke up, laughing at him. And Slade said, "Well, while we're talking requests, how about more cherry pie?"

Chloe was giggling at them and Shadow gave Jax a

pointed look as she said, "Okay, you guys are on. Next week I'll pick a night and make meatloaf and cherry pie."

"Yes!" Joker gave a triumphant fist pump.

"Geez, Joker, you're such a dumbass!" Coop was laughing hard.

"Hey, I resent that," Joker complained. Within a minute, they were arm wrestling and the other guys were cheering and placing bets.

A little while later, with the arm-wrestling tournament going full steam, Chloe noticed that Jax and Shadow had gone down to the other end of the table and were sitting there, talking quietly. She watched them, noting the serious looks on their faces and the way that Shadow was jabbing at the table with his forefinger. Something was going on. It hit her hard that the four weeks that had just passed couldn't be further from life as it was normally with these guys. A chill ran down her spine and she took a swig of her beer and tried to turn her attention back to the fun.

Jax finally nodded at Shadow and banged a fork on his beer bottle to get everyone's attention. "Hey, guys, we've got something to talk about."

They quickly calmed down and faced him, quiet.

"Shadow's been combing the internet, looking for signs of the Snake making a move. He might have found one."

There was a little murmur from the others.

"A couple of days ago, our last base building was breached. Of course, we were gone and we left no traces of ourselves there. But one of the Snake's lieutenants was spotted by a traffic cam outside our building. Now, I can't think of any reason for that, unless they had an idea that we'd been there. He's getting info from somewhere and it's sure not from any of us. Taking out Snake is a top priority for us, but if we don't figure out where he's getting info from, we've got a problem. Any ideas?"

Slade asked, "Has Gunner told you anything at all about what happened on the last mission?"

"No," Jax said moodily. "And I know damn well that he knows something. We're trying to trace everyplace that he and his group have gone since then and who they've been in contact with. As you know, it's damn hard to trace anything they do."

Finn said thoughtfully, "Does Gunner know about Chloe?"

Jax's face went stony. "No, and it's going to stay that way."

Finn was thinking out loud. "So, Snake had someone send Chloe with his message, knowing that she'd probably never make it out of our base. And you called Gunner and raised hell about Snake being able to send a message to us."

"Yeah, but I never mentioned how the message got to us. As far as Gunner knows, the message was slipped to one of you on the street."

"But Snake knows better than that. He sent Chloe to our address."

Jax thought for a minute. "And then our mission went sour. We don't know the first thing about the guys who showed up. What did our targets have to do with Snake?"

Shadow looked up, giving him a grim look. "I don't know yet, but I'd bet a year's pay there's a connection."

The other guys stared at each other, looking seriously disturbed. "So that means the leak is most likely coming from…" Finn couldn't finish the sentence.

Shadow said, "Yeah. Too many things just don't add up right."

Coop said, "Fuck. We are fucked."

Jax said, "Not yet. But we're going to have to be faster and smarter."

Finn said, "But we don't know anything for sure."

"No. We have to keep digging and we have to suspect

everyone. We don't have any trust for anyone except each other. Clear?"

"Clear, boss." They said it nearly in unison.

Shadow was thinking hard. "Boss, what if we give them all a push?"

"What do you mean?"

"Both of them clearly know about our last base. What if we turn them against each other?"

Jax's brain was working hard too. "How so?"

Finn was following Shadow's train of thought. "If the base building blows all to hell, who did it? Neither of them know that we know the building was breached."

Jax sat back and thought it over. A slow smile was beginning to stretch across his face. "We have to be invisible."

Coop gave him a grin. "We can do that."

Jax said, "Joker, you feel like playing?"

Joker looked eager. "You bet your ass, boss. I haven't gotten to play in a long time."

"All right, tomorrow we've got planning to do." Jax felt a savage pleasure at finally having a path to follow.

They were all grimly pleased and anxious to get started.

"Beers are on me, guys!" Jax said, pulling the cooler open.

Chloe had sat there listening, trying to go unnoticed, but she hadn't heard much and had no idea what was going on. At least, not much of an idea. But she suspected that they were planning to blow up the building they had lived in not long ago.

Chapter 10

There was a planning session going on in the office. Chloe had offered to bring in food and drinks, but she'd been turned away with a terse word of thanks. The meeting had been going on for a long time and she finally went to the kitchen, frustrated, and made chicken noodle soup. She was wandering around, trying to decide on something to bake, when Shadow came out and came into the kitchen.

"Hey, Chloe, is everything okay here?"

"Yeah, everything's fine. How about in there?"

"It's a little tense, but we're hashing things out. Damn, something smells really good in here."

"I made chicken noodle soup."

"You're an angel. Can you make some sandwiches to go with it?"

"Sure. How about grilled ham and cheese?"

Shadow kissed her on the forehead and said, "Perfect. How long?'

Chloe glanced at the clock and said, "Give me twenty minutes."

"You got it. I'll chase them all in here if it has to be at gunpoint."

She had to grin as she watched him hurry back to the office. When they all filed into the kitchen, she hid a smile at the scowl on Jax's face. He apparently hadn't gotten his way. They all ate quickly and then thanked Chloe and hustled back to the office. Shadow gave her a wave and a grin as he took up the rear. They were in there another two hours before they finally finished and came out.

The next two days, most of the guys spent all day in the barn. A couple of trips to town were made and Joker seemed to be the one with authority for the time being. On the third day, the crew made preparations for a road trip.

Jax sat down with Chloe, a serious look on his face. "Joker, Coop, Slade, and I have to make a trip. Finn and Shadow are going to stay here. We'll be gone for a few days. You need to do whatever they ask you to. They're responsible for your safety while I'm gone, so keep that in mind."

Chloe was staring at him. "What are you trying to say, Jax?"

"I'm saying, don't try anything while I'm gone."

"Like what? What the hell would I try?"

"Chloe, I understand that you want nothing more than to get away, get your freedom back, but I need to know that you're going to behave while I'm gone. I need to be able to concentrate on what I have to do."

She shook her head incredulously. "Don't you worry about it, Jax. I'll be a good little girl while you're gone. I wouldn't do anything to cause Finn and Shadow problems."

He realized uneasily that she hadn't made any such promise about causing *him* problems. "Okay, good. I just can't afford to be worrying."

She gave him a narrow look. "Oh, you're concerned about

having to *worry* about me? Well, don't. I'll be just fine here with Finn and Shadow."

It was the answer he had wanted, but somehow it didn't make him feel better. He opened his mouth to ask another question, but he decided it wasn't going to help. He went off to make his preparations and Chloe stuck her tongue out at him as he went.

By late afternoon, they were ready to leave. Chloe had made a cooler full of sandwiches at Coop's request and bagged up a batch of homemade cookies as well. Jax fidgeted around as Coop and Joker put them in the SUV and Chloe ignored him. When everything was ready, Coop, Joker, and Slade stood, looking expectantly at their boss until he waved an arm at them and sent them outside. He grabbed Chloe by the hand and led her upstairs to their room.

"Goddammit," he said, "I just wanted to make sure everything would be all right while I'm gone."

Chloe said sweetly, "Everything will be fine, *boss.*"

He swore under his breath and grabbed her by the back of her head, pulling her against him for a deep, bruising kiss. He kissed her until her knees went weak and when he finally pulled away, her head dropped back and her eyes remained closed. He brushed her mouth again with his and said, "Behave yourself."

Breathlessly, she said, "I will. Be careful."

He started out of the room and stopped when she called his name.

"Really, Jax. Be careful."

He gave her a grin. "I will."

She watched them from the bedroom window, loading the last few things in the SUV and joking with each other before they got in themselves. Jax had a few last words for Finn and then he opened the driver's door. He started to get in, but then he stopped and turned, looking directly up at the bedroom window where she stood. He gazed at her and when she raised her hand to him, he returned the gesture and gave her a nod before he climbed into the vehicle. She stood there watching him drive away until they were out of sight, swallowed up by the trees along the driveway.

Chloe went back downstairs and Finn came through the back door. "We're going to do some work in the barn. Do you need anything?" he asked.

"No, I'm going to do a little laundry and then I'll start dinner."

"What time do you want us in here for dinner?"

She smiled and said, "Seven is good for me."

"Okay. Just give us a shout over the magic electronics if you need anything."

Chloe laughed at his description of Shadow's network of devices and gave him a little wave as he walked out. She went back upstairs and started a load of laundry, then went back down and wandered into the office. There were some papers scattered over the table and she looked at them idly as she drifted around the long table. There were discarded notes they had scribbled during their meeting and Chloe didn't see anything that caught her attention. Besides, Jax wouldn't have left anything of significance there, right? She realized that Finn could be watching her right then and she casually gathered the papers up and stacked them in one neat pile at the end of the table where Jax always sat, gathering up pens and pencils and laying them on top of the papers. She pushed the chairs neatly up to the table and turned the light off as she left the room. It wouldn't do to have Finn getting suspicious of her. She told herself that she needed to be careful about what she did; Jax had probably instructed the two men to keep an eye on her.

Chloe went to the kitchen and started the casserole she had planned for dinner while her peach cobbler baked. She realized that the place seemed way too quiet with four of the men gone. She wondered exactly what they were doing on this trip. She'd heard enough bits and pieces that she was pretty sure they had gone back to the old base building. She had no idea why or what they were going to do there, but she thought it had something to do with the man who had set her up, the one they called Snake. She shivered a little at the thought of him. By the time Finn and Shadow came in for dinner, she'd had enough of her own thoughts.

While they ate, Chloe made an attempt to get some questions answered. "Are they on a mission?" she asked.

Shadow said, "No, they're tying up some loose ends."

She waited for more, but that was all he offered. "How is the barn coming along? You must be almost finished with it, aren't you?"

Finn said, "We're getting there."

She tried a different tack. "How many missions do you guys have in a year? Is it one right after the other?"

Finn said, "It just depends on what comes up. Sometimes there's a long, dull stretch between missions."

Shadow said, "Yeah, that's when we enjoy each other's company the most. When we're tearing our hair out from boredom." The two men laughed.

Chloe said, "I'd think you'd be glad when there's no mission."

Finn looked blank. "Why's that?"

"Well, because it's so dangerous."

Shadow drawled, "Danger is my game, missy."

Finn snorted out a laugh. "You asshole."

Chloe had to laugh too, but she still couldn't understand how they could look forward to a mission where they would be risking their lives. "You guys are weird."

Shadow looked offended. "Weird? I can see dark, dangerous, mysterious, hot, sexy, but weird? I just don't see it."

Finn was smirking at him. "Shadow sees himself as the modern-day double o seven. Joker says he's more like Deputy Dawg."

Shadow looked even more offended. "Now that's just hurtful. I'm the backbone of this operation; everybody knows that."

Now Chloe was giggling. "I bet that would take Jax by surprise."

Shadow waved a dismissive hand. "He knows it. Hell, if it weren't for me, he'd just be a-a badass boss without me."

Finn was laughing. "You really are a jackass, aren't you?"

Chloe leaned forward and said, "He's trying to flush the Snake out, isn't he?"

Finn abruptly stopped laughing, looking guardedly at her. Gently, he said, "Now, you know we can't tell you that, don't you?"

Chloe said simply, "You don't have to."

"Shit," Shadow muttered.

"I've thought about all of this a lot," Chloe said. "I don't know why I got picked to be thrown into this whole mess, but I didn't choose it. And yet, I'm starting to feel responsible for what's happening, for putting everyone in danger like Jax has said all along. And, again, I don't know what I can possibly do about it. But now there are four of you doing something risky because of me. I don't like this; I don't like it one bit."

Finn and Shadow looked at each other and finally Finn said, "Chloe, you don't need to feel responsible for any of it. The Snake has been out to get us, especially Jax, for a long time, long before he decided to toss you into the mix. This is all on Snake, not on you. We've needed to take him down for a long time, but he's a tough enemy. He dumped you into the middle of it, fully expecting that you wouldn't live out the night, that night you delivered that envelope. And that pissed all of us off. We come up against a lot of really evil people,

people who have no regard for human life, but he's the worst of them. If he had the chance, he'd do it all over again to some other unsuspecting woman. He's not even worthy of being called a human being. He's a monster and we're going to put an end to him. Is it for your sake? Yeah, it is, but it's for a helluva lot more than that too."

Chloe looked at him and knew he was telling her the truth. She felt the burden that she'd been carrying ease up, as if it had been lifted off her shoulders. "So, what are they doing now?"

Shadow said, "Setting a trap."

"Is it dangerous?"

Shadow shrugged. "Everything is dangerous to a point. Is this dangerous like a mission? No. They should be able to go, set the trap, and come back without anyone ever knowing a thing about it."

She felt relief sweep over her. "Thank you for telling me."

Finn said, "We're just gonna hope that we don't get our asses kicked for doing it."

Chloe kept her thoughts to herself. "How long have you all been together?"

Finn said, "You can assume from watching us work together that it's been a long time. Some of us knew each other before we became a team, and some of us didn't. Chloe, we like you. All of us do. But if we take out Snake, you're going to have your freedom back, with some qualifications to keep us safe. That means that you shouldn't know more than the bare minimum and that's to keep you and us protected. We'd like to be able to talk to you freely, but if we do, you wouldn't ever be able to leave. I'm sure it's not worth it for you."

Chloe felt like she'd been stabbed with an icy blade. And yet, he was right, wasn't he? What could be more important than getting her freedom back? And why didn't the thought make her feel good? Shadow watched her silently, reading the thoughts as they passed across her face. He hoped against the odds that there would be an end to this that made sense.

Chloe chased them off after dinner and took care of the kitchen herself. Shadow carried the trash out and took a walk around, checking to make sure that nothing was out of place. There was a farm gate across the driveway nearly to where it opened onto the road and it had a sturdy padlock on it. More importantly, there was a surveillance camera mounted unobtrusively in a tree and trained on the end of the driveway. When they all went up to their rooms, everything was locked up and secured for the night and there were no disturbances. Not a soul knew where they were, not even the people they worked for.

Two days went by, and then Finn got a message from Jax, letting him know that they were starting back. Chloe had wandered the house for those two days, thinking about looking through things for information that could help her get free, but in the end, she told herself that she shouldn't do it, considering the cameras that were mounted everywhere. She knew plenty of places she could have looked without anyone ever knowing, but something kept her from doing it. She told herself that she was a fool, but she still didn't do it. Then she told herself that it was much more important to gain Jax's trust than to find out some tidbit that wouldn't really solve her situation. She just couldn't go sneaking around.

She wrote about it in the journal she had continued to keep ever since the day Jax had given her the laptop. She wrote about the plan to look through everything while Jax was gone and about how she'd been unable to go through with it. She wrote about the strange reaction she'd had when Finn had talked about getting rid of Snake permanently so that she could have her freedom. And she wrote about the fact that her life before had become like a dream she'd had once, like it had never been real and what *was* real was her life as it had been since she'd met Jax and his crew.

When Finn told her that Jax had started back, she knew she was running out of time to search for clues, and when he let her know that he and Shadow had to make a run to the building supply store, she had the perfect chance. She assured them that she would be fine while they were gone. Shadow gave her a phone that she could contact them on and they went on their way, locking the gate on their way out. Chloe watched them drive away and then, her heart pounding with anticipation, she went to the office. She didn't really know what she was looking for, but she assumed that she would know if she found it. All the drawers in the office were locked, both file cabinets and desk. She took a hairpin and worked carefully at the desk drawer until she was rewarded with the turn of the lock and she pulled the drawer open, holding her breath.

She looked through the paperwork she found there, careful to put everything back the way she had found it. Nothing jumped out at her; it was mostly receipts and expenditures from their recent move. It occurred to her that there might not be any paperwork regarding the missions that Jax's crew carried out. A paper trail would be a bad thing in their case. In the third drawer she searched, she finally found something that looked important. There was a letter that had been kept for a long time. It was printed, not handwritten, and it had no return address and no signature. It acknowledged hiring Jax to lead the group known as Elite 6 and stated that the group was to perform under top secret procedures. The document stated that Elite 6 would be supported by the home base whenever possible, but if any mission went wrong, they would be on their own. Home base would disavow them and deny any knowledge about their operations. It was to be a lifetime agreement and when the day came that operations could no longer be carried out, Elite 6 was to disappear from the United States, never to be heard from again.

Chloe felt chilled as she read the document and she shivered at the feeling it gave her. They would be deserted if things went wrong for them. No wonder Jax was being so careful about security. She carefully replaced the document and went on through the rest of the drawer. Then she found the manila envelope that she had been paid to deliver to Jax. Her hands trembling, she took it out of the drawer and sat staring at it for a long time. She started to open it, then stopped, afraid of what she would find. With a deep, shaky breath, she finally pulled a single page from the envelope. The page was headed "Marked for Elimination." There followed a list of six names, Axel Keller, aka Jax, Finnegan McGregor, aka Finn, Michael Thomas, aka Shadow, Cooper Garrity, aka Coop, Simon Clay, aka Slade, and Nicholas Dolan, aka Joker. At the bottom of the page it said, "Start the Countdown."

That was what had been given to her to deliver to the group. No wonder they had been ready to take drastic action. Their identities were supposed to be top secret. Who the hell was Snake and why was he out to kill them all? Her blood ran cold as she realized what a dangerous thing she had been sent to deliver. Jax had told her the truth; the man who sent her was perfectly comfortable with sending her to her death. And he was obviously determined to see Jax and his whole crew dead. She could have—should have—been dead the night she showed up at Jax's door. Only the fact that he took control of her and kept her prisoner, had saved her. She carefully returned everything to the drawer and closed and locked it. Then she went to the two-drawer file cabinet that sat beside the desk. It only took seconds to get it open.

There wasn't really much in the file cabinet. She leafed through the few folders that were stored there and didn't find much that caught her eye. Until she found a folder simply marked Snake. She opened it and found a list of names under the heading Snake's Organization. None of them meant anything to her. She turned to the second page and found a death certificate for a man named Ivan Vasiliev, aged twenty-two when he died. Cause of death was multiple gunshot wounds. She couldn't find anything that explained his connection to Snake; maybe he was part of the organization. Next were a number of pages of notes about surveillance of Snake and his organization. The dates told her that some of the surveillance had been done recently, since she had become an unwilling part of Jax's group.

Chloe did some more looking, but didn't find anything that made sense to her, so after a look at the clock, she closed and locked the drawer, checked to make sure everything was where it belonged, and left the office, turning the light off as she went. She still had plenty of time before Finn and Shadow were due back, so she went to the barn and tried the door. As expected, it was locked up tight and she went back to the house and up to the bedroom. She looked through Jax's drawers and found nothing but clothing. She got the same results when she looked through the things that were hanging in the closet. With a sigh that was mostly relief, she ended her search. She had learned a little, but nothing that she could use to escape; and after what she'd found in the manila envelope, she didn't know if getting away was a good idea. In fact, she wondered how badly she even wanted to escape, at this point.

Chloe sat down with her laptop and wrote in her journal, not about her search of Jax's office, but about her mixed-up feelings. Then she went back to the story she'd been writing and lost herself in it for a while. When she heard the truck pulling up to the barn, she realized more time had gone by than she'd thought. She went to the kitchen and looked out the window at the two men unloading things from the truck. They laughed and joked as they worked and she wondered how they could be so carefree when they'd basically signed their lives away to work in the Elite 6. They were bound forever, until their superiors decided that they were done with them and then they had to disappear. She shivered at the idea and wondered if they'd be set free while they were still young enough to build lives of their own. What kind of organization did they work for?

Jax pulled in late in the afternoon two days later, and the four men were greeted by Finn and Shadow as they piled out of the SUV that Jax backed up to the barn. They thumped each other on the back and insulted each other with plenty of laughter, while they unloaded the back of the SUV and popped open ice-cold beers to fortify themselves. It took only minutes to unload, with all six of them doing it, and they gathered around the back of the SUV to discuss how the trip had gone.

"Everything went as planned?" Finn asked.

Jax nodded in satisfaction. "All ready to go. Shadow, did you plant those seeds?"

"Sure did. Sent it out as internet chatter. Both groups should have gotten wind of it by now."

"Good. Let's hope it works the way we planned." Jax was casting surreptitious glances at the house now and then and Shadow grinned at him.

"We're finished out here," Shadow said. "Why don't we go on in the house? You guys must be hungry."

Joker said, "I'm fucking starving. Jax wouldn't even stop for sandwiches today."

Coop said, "Yeah, I don't know what the big hurry was; you'd think he had a curfew."

Slade elbowed him and said, "Yeah, I know what the hurry was."

"You guys are assholes," Jax said and headed for the house.

Chloe was in the kitchen. She looked up as Jax came through the door and took a deep breath. She struggled to keep her face impassive, but a smile broke through anyway. Jax crossed the kitchen in three long strides and snagged her around the waist, pulling her against him for a deep, lingering kiss until she made a little humming sound in the back of her throat. He let her go just as the rest of the crew trooped through the door.

"Shit," Jax muttered. "It's as bad as having a bunch of kids."

Joker said, "Damn, something sure smells good."

Chloe grinned at him. "Beef stew and apple pie." She slid a large pan of biscuits into the oven and said, "Twenty minutes and the biscuits will be done."

"Damn, I love your biscuits," said Coop, laying a hand on his heart.

Slade was passing out more beer and he handed one to Chloe. They talked through dinner and long after dessert, clearly satisfied with how their mission had gone. By the time Jax and Chloe were able to go up to bed, Jax was itching to get his hands on her. He went to the shower, and when he came out, Chloe was sitting on the bed in nothing but an oversized t-shirt, and the room was lit by a single, small lamp. As Jax dropped his towel and joined her on the bed, she switched off the light and he gathered her into his arms.

Chapter 11

The next afternoon, the crew gathered around the TV in the den and began watching the news. Shadow had a computer monitor set up on the coffee table and there was a satellite view of their last base building.

"Anytime now," Shadow said tensely.

Just a minute later, they watched as the building exploded in a burst of flame, dust, and debris. It didn't spread out to the surrounding buildings or onto the street, but imploded, coming down upon itself.

"Bingo!" Shadow said, and a cheer went up from the crew.

Jax was watching intently and he said, "Damn, Joker, that was good work. The buildings on either side don't look like they're even touched."

Joker said, "Hey, I know my stuff. That's why I got this job."

Jax laughed. "Can't argue with that."

It wasn't long before police vehicles started arriving, along with the fire department. It took only minutes longer for the first news van to show up. And about then, Jax's phone rang.

"Yeah... no, it's news to me. I'll turn it on and wait for it."

He listened for several minutes. "No, that's even less of a good idea now. Keep me informed." He clicked off the phone and said, "That was Gunner, letting me know that our last base building just exploded. He wanted our location."

Finn looked at him strangely. "He should have known that security would need to be ramped up even further."

"Yeah, he should have."

Shadow was typing away on his laptop. "There's a lot of chatter going on. From Gunner's group and from Snake's."

"Good," Jax said in satisfaction. "Let them go after each other."

"Here it comes on the news," Coop said.

They watched the coverage of the explosion, first responders making sure that the fires were put out. Their job was unusually easy, for such a large explosion. Chloe walked in to find them all intent on the TV screen.

"What's going on?" she asked.

Jax looked at her and said, "Our last base building just blew up."

Chloe gasped and said, "It blew up?"

"Sure did," Coop said.

"Was anyone hurt?"

Slade said, "Nope. Not even the surrounding buildings were hurt."

Chloe stared at them and then said, "That's what you went to do. You blew up your own building."

Jax said, "It would be better for you not to ask questions."

"Am I wrong?" Chloe asked.

He didn't answer.

Shadow said, "Boss, there's activity at Snake's compound. Looks like they're ramping up their security."

"Interesting. I wonder what's happening at Gunner's office."

"As you know, we can only watch the street there, but I'm

keeping an eye on it."

Half an hour later, Gunner left the building, accompanied by his two top men. The three of them got into a sleek black Escalade and started down the street. Shadow watched intently until, two hours later, he saw the Escalade again.

"There they are, at the gate to Snake's compound."

"Son of a bitch," Jax said softly. "They're actually going there, in person?"

Shadow nodded grimly. "Looks that way."

They had forgotten that Chloe was still there, watching and listening.

"This isn't good, boss," said Joker.

"No, it isn't."

Coop asked, "What's our next move?"

Jax sighed heavily and said, "I don't know. That's going to take some serious thought."

Slade said, "So Gunner knew exactly what was going on when Snake sent Chloe with that envelope. How deep does this go?"

Jax said, "That's what we have to find out. If it goes as deep as I think it does, what's their reason? We've got plenty of action left, and if we didn't, we could just be retired."

Finn said, "It was always a fifty-fifty deal—if they'd let us retire or not. That's why we needed to be prepared."

"You're right about that," said Jax. "We're prepared, but we're going to have to be real careful."

Shadow, watching the screen, said, "Damn, I wish we could listen in."

"You can forget that," said Jax. "There's no way we can get close enough to do that."

Finn said, "Don't be so sure of that. If we can get to some-body in Snake's organization, we could get a bug in there."

Jax said flatly, "Nobody in Snake's group is going to turn on him. They're way too scared of him for that."

"We don't have to turn him. Just get a chance to walk past him on the street," said Finn.

Shadow said, "They've got one guy who makes a run to town several days a week. He sends messages, picks things up, does general errands."

"Have you gotten a good look at him?" Jax asked.

"Yeah. I saved an image of him." Shadow punched some keys and said, "Here he is."

Chloe had walked closer to them and she gasped and said, "That's the guy! That's him!"

Jax looked sharply at her. "That's what guy?"

She was shaking. "The guy who hired me to deliver the message, that's him."

"Are you sure?"

She said bitterly, "You bet your ass I'm sure. I'd never forget his face."

Jax said, "We need to ID him. We need to know everything about him."

Shadow was already typing. "On it, boss."

Jax walked over to Chloe and took her by the arm, walking her out of the room.

"What are you doing?" she asked.

"You don't need to see and hear what's going on in our operation."

"Why? Who am I going to tell? I'm a prisoner here, remember?"

He scowled. "You're a prisoner for your own safety. And the less you know about this ugliness, the better off you'll be. It has nothing to do with you."

Chloe gave an incredulous laugh. "Bullshit, Jax, it has everything to do with me. I was used to set all of this in motion. I think I *need* to know what's going on, for my own safety. For example, do Snake and Gunner know I'm here? Or am I supposed to be dead?"

Jax stared at her, clearly struggling. Finally, he said, "We think that they're assuming you're dead. But they have no way of knowing for sure. If you had showed up to pick up your money, they would have killed you then. That's why I couldn't let you leave."

A chill shuddered through her, but she said, "And don't you think they want to know for sure?"

"Yes. Yes, we think that's why our security was compromised. But we need to know which one of them is behind it. We never expected to see Gunner and Snake actually meet in person. They're bitter enemies; if they're working together, we need to know that."

Chloe said, "B-but isn't Gunner supposed to be one of the good guys? I thought... I assumed he was part of the government. A secret part, but still a part."

"He is," Jax said bitterly. "There are no good guys in this business. The best I can say is every mission we've ever carried out was against a target who deserved what they got. And, Chloe, if you want to go back to your old life someday, you can't know the details of what's happening with us."

She stared at him for a long moment and then said, "It's too late, Jax. I can't unhear what I've heard and I can't unknow what I've learned since I've been with all of you. There's no way to keep me out of it because I'm at the center of it. The more I know, the better equipped I'll be to protect myself."

"How are you going to protect yourself, Chloe? You can't, not against these people. They're ruthless, they won't stop until they accomplish what they want. That's why we have to take them out."

Chloe raised her chin stubbornly. "Then let me be part of it. Let me at least know what I'm up against when something happens. Teach me things that will help me. I'm not helpless."

Shadow said, from behind Jax, "She's right, boss. It'd be

better to equip her with some knowledge and skill than just to keep her here like a sitting duck. At least she can learn some basic self-defense and how to hide and melt into the background. At least she can know the faces that present the danger. It couldn't be worse than knowing nothing."

Jax let out a sigh of pure frustration. "Dammit, I don't like this! It's too dangerous."

"It's dangerous no matter what we do. Knowledge won't make it more dangerous. I've got an ID on the guy who hired Chloe."

Jax said, "Let's have it."

Shadow said, "Come back to the computer."

After a moment's hesitation, Jax said, "Come on, Chloe. You might as well see this."

They went in and sat down at the computer monitor. Shadow had put the surveillance footage up on the TV screen and the guys were watching it. Coop said, "Here comes Gunner's Escalade."

Shadow said, "Okay, if they go directly back to home base, it's going to take them about two hours. Chloe's guy is Dimitri Volkov, works for Snake and does pretty much anything and everything. I'd say it looks like Snake trusts him as much as he does anybody. Volkov was a close friend of Ivan and he's stuck close to Snake ever since Ivan was killed."

Chloe recognized the name Ivan and asked, "Who's Ivan?"

Grimly, Jax said, "Ivan Vasiliev was Snake's son. He was a target of one of our missions several years ago."

Chloe said, "Oh, my God. You killed Snake's son?"

"We did, and he was a monster who needed killing. Of course, Snake has been out for vengeance ever since. Ivan was his only child and now Snake has no one to pass his legacy down to. So, he hates us with a passion."

"Dimitri has a thing for fast cars. Snake makes him take a couple of thugs with him when he goes to run his errands, but now and then he sneaks out by himself to take a drive. He also has a thing for American women and he frequents the brothels whenever he gets the chance. He has a reputation for hurting them, but he pays well, so they don't turn him away. I'm sure they don't dare turn him away, either."

"Does he do anything on a regular basis?"

"He does. He goes out on Mondays and picks up a package from one of Snake's drug runners. Must be someone Snake doesn't trust to anyone else because other thugs make the other pickups. That's the one thing that he does every week like clockwork."

Chloe was listening with a horrified fascination. It was a world she'd never glimpsed before and it was terrifying. "What are you going to do?"

"That's what we have to figure out," Jax said. "Shadow and Coop think it's possible to get a bug into Snake's compound, so we could hear at least some of what goes on there. We've got to find out just what's going on between Gunner and Snake."

Chloe shuddered. "I don't understand how someone who's supposed to be working against these kinds of people can team up with them."

"It's possible that Gunner is working on some sort of plan to bring Snake down, but it sure doesn't look that way. That's why we have to know for sure." Jax studied the face on the computer screen.

"What will you do if Gunner turns out to be part of it?"

Jax said grimly, "Then all hell's going to break loose."

Shadow sat back and said, "What *are* we going to do if that's the case?"

Finn and Slade were listening to the conversation while Coop and Joker kept a watch on the TV screen, split between live news coverage and the surveillance footage of Gunner's home base.

"I don't know, I really don't," Jax said. "Let's talk about what we can't do. We can't just run. Gunner has at least some limits on what he can do, but Snake has no boundaries at all. We have to take out Snake and his organization. We can't take out Gunner's group; they're too well disguised as the good guys. If we have solid proof, we could take it higher up the government ladder, but it's a tossup whether they'd help us or put us down. The best thing we could do with it is hold it over Gunner's head. But it's going to have to be damn good evidence for that to work."

Finn said, "If we could ID the bunch who showed up at our last mission, that might be enough. If there's the connection we think there is."

"Yeah, you're right," Jax said. "Any progress on that, Shadow?"

"No," Shadow said, frustrated. "It's a dead-end everywhere I go."

Finn said, "Remember that woman who helped us with an ID a few years back? The one from Russia, the hacker?"

"Yeah," Shadow said. "That's a good thought. I'll get in touch with her right away."

"Good. We need a break. Coop, I've got a job for you."

"Yeah, boss? What is it?"

Jax said, "You're going to teach Chloe some basic survival skills. Make sure she knows how to watch everything, how to hide, how to make herself unseen. And how to handle a weapon and some basic self-defense."

Coop looked surprised. "Okay, boss."

"You start tomorrow. And don't go easy on her."

"Got it."

"Boss, what if we sent something to Dimitri, something he'd keep around. We could put a device in it and activate it by remote control," Shadow suggested.

"They'd sweep anything that was brought in," Jax said.

"Yeah, but if it's not activated yet, they won't find it. If they do regular sweeps, they'll find it eventually, but if we could get their conversations for a while, we might get something useful."

"Okay, what do you suggest we send?"

Finn said, "A scale model of a car. You said he has a thing for fast cars. They make some really nice ones, the type of thing you'd put on a shelf to admire."

Jax said, "It's worth a try. Do it."

"We'll make it look like it came directly from the seller, like somebody ordered it for him," Shadow said.

"Good."

"Boss," Joker called, "Gunner's pulling into home base."

Jax turned his attention to the surveillance footage and Shadow switched it to full screen. They got a good view of Gunner's face as the Escalade turned off the street and into the driveway. Jax swore under his breath. "What the hell are you up to?" he muttered. They were in so far over their heads; if Gunner really was working somehow with Snake, it would be a miracle if they survived it.

Shadow said, "I sent a message to Irina Petrov. It'll be a while before she answers. She'll have to check us out again and verify who she's talking to."

"You sure we can trust her?" Jax asked, even though he knew the answer.

"Her survival depends on it too, so we don't have to worry about her. If she agrees to help, we'll be able to trust her."

"Okay. Shit, what a day." Jax rolled his shoulders, trying to relieve a little of the tension.

Finn said, "Well, we've got more of a plan than we had yesterday, so that's progress."

"Let's just hope something comes of it. Chloe, come with me." Jax led her out of the room. She followed him up the stairs to the bedroom and he closed the door behind them. He sat down in a chair and pulled her over to stand in front of him. "I want you to understand exactly how shaky this all is. If Gunner is working with Snake, we're in way over our heads. We're going to be fighting for our lives and the odds aren't in our favor. If there was a place I could send you, where you'd be safe, I'd do it in a second, but there isn't. So, when Coop teaches you what he's going to, you need to work at it as if your life depends on it; because it does. Maybe now you understand why I needed you to learn to obey me without question."

Chloe raised an eyebrow and said, "I'm not a child."

"Really. I'm not sure you've learned that lesson. It's more important now than ever and you *will* obey me, you understand?"

"Why did you kill Ivan Vasiliev?"

"It was our mission," Jax said simply. "Ivan personally butchered over a dozen young girls after he used them for his own pleasure. He was only a young man and he was evil through and through."

"Is his father the same way?"

"His father is worse. So, you understand how important your obedience is?"

"Yes, I guess so. But I'm not a child and I'm not stupid. I don't need to be ordered around and expected to obey just because you'll spank me if I don't."

Jax let out an exasperated breath. "That's not why. If I tell you to do something, there's a reason for it and the reason is undoubtedly connected with keeping you alive. So, you have to be prepared to obey without question."

Chloe said, "In that type of situation, I'll definitely listen to you."

"I can see you haven't tasted the last of my belt."

"Why don't you have a little faith in my ability to make a sensible decision?"

"I never said I didn't. But my job is to protect you and I don't need you making it any harder. So, make up your mind that obedience is important to you. It could be what saves your life."

"This is all crazy," Chloe muttered. "What are you going to do if you receive another mission?"

"I'm not sure. We'll have to make that decision when the time comes."

"But if you think Gunner is working with Snake, you can't go off on a mission that Gunner assigns to you. That would be stupid!"

"What would you suggest? We can't let Gunner know that we could be onto him. And I can only hold him off for so long. He's already asked twice where our new location is."

"Well, give him a fake location, the opposite way from here." It sounded reasonable to Chloe.

"And then, when he finds out we're not there, he'll know we're on to him. Game over. The best I can do right now is refuse to tell him on the grounds that security was compromised and we don't have the answers yet as to what happened."

"So, what you're really saying is that you have to find out fast, so you can do something about it before you end up trapped." Chloe felt chilled as she said it. "You're saying you're running out of time."

"Now you've got it." Jax gave her a grim nod. "So, I don't have time to waste, getting you to behave. Don't test me."

"All right." She gave her assent, although she gave it reluctantly. Jax pulled her onto his lap, his arms wrapped around her and she turned her face up for his kiss.

He twined his fingers in her hair and said roughly, "I'm not prepared to see anything happen to you."

Chapter 12

Coop was teaching Chloe a few maneuvers that would get her free of someone who got hold of her and would disable someone who attacked her. She did well at getting loose from him; she was quick and slippery and she had a way of ducking down low and slipping out of his grasp. Going on the attack was harder for her, but she was determined and she learned quickly. He taught her how to fade into a crowd, slipping in behind someone so that nobody would actually get a good view of her. He taught her things to look for, danger signals that would warn her off before it was too late. By the time they finished for the day, Chloe was exhausted, dripping with sweat, and sore all over. She stood in the shower, letting the hot water stream down over her back and wondering how she would survive learning to survive.

When she went back downstairs, moving stiffly, she found Jax and Coop in the kitchen. Jax handed her a cold beer and said, "Coop says you show some promise and you worked hard at it. Work harder tomorrow."

She felt a little rush of temper and snapped, "Yes, sir, boss!"

"And lose the attitude," he said mildly. "I'm ordering dinner tonight. You've done enough for today. Come with me."

Chloe followed him, glad that she didn't have to deal with dinner for them all. He led her out of the house and to the barn, Coop trailing behind them. When she stepped into the barn for the first time since it had been an empty building, she stopped in her tracks, stunned at what she saw. It looked like an ultra-high-tech facility, like something you'd see in a movie. There was equipment of all kinds, computers, large monitors, and electronics that Chloe didn't recognize. There were work-tables, and a large array of weapons hung on the wall at one side. At the back was what Jax explained was a sound-protected, two lane shooting area where they could keep their marksmanship sharp. Opposite the weapons wall was a set of shelving that held what looked like electrical supplies. Joker had put the bombs together there that took down their old base building.

"We discussed it and decided that since you already know more than I ever intended, it would be safer for you to know it all. Well, all that we can share with you."

Chloe's eyes were wide, unable to take it all in at once. Looking at the tools of their trade, she had a clear under-standing of just how dangerous their world was. This was no movie set; it was all too real.

Jax said, "Tomorrow, you'll repeat what you worked on today and you'll learn to shoot."

"I know how to shoot," Chloe said, not taking her eyes off the sight in front of her.

Jax and Coop exchanged glances. "You do?" Jax asked.

"Yeah. I had a friend who bet me that I couldn't do it, so I got a gun and learned. I beat her at target practice every time."

"What kind of gun did you buy?"

"Nine-millimeter, semi-auto handgun."

Coop was trying to hide a grin. Jax said, "Good. You'll be a step ahead of where I thought you'd be."

"I've been wondering something," Chloe said.

"What's that?"

"Your missions are done in secret, aren't they? Like, there's some kind of a cover story to conceal who did it, right?"

"Yes," said Jax with a frown. "What are you getting at?"

"Well, when you killed Ivan, wasn't that mission kept secret too?"

"Yes, it was a well-planned operation."

"You said that Snake has been out for revenge ever since. If the mission was secret, how did Snake know that your crew did it?"

Jax said, "He didn't know at first. When I said he was out for vengeance, it was against whoever was responsible. Then, about a year ago, he found out somehow and we heard through internet chatter that he was hunting us. Our entire existence was a secret up to that point, but we heard enough to know that he knew about us. Then, of course, he sent you."

"So how did he find out?"

"We don't know. That's part of what we're trying to uncover now. That's part of why we became suspicious of Gunner in the first place."

"Would it have to be Gunner himself? Could it be someone who works for him?"

Jax said, "If Gunner is working on a plan to bring Snake down, then it could be someone in his own group who leaked the info to Snake. And that would put Gunner in just as much danger as we're in."

Chloe let out a long breath. "Geez, could it get any more complicated?"

"Never say never."

Shadow showed Chloe some of the things that they were

monitoring with their sophisticated computer equipment and showed her the car they would be sending out the next day to Dimitri Volkov. It was an exquisite diecast model of a sports car that Chloe couldn't begin to identify and Shadow had already put the listening device in it, so expertly that it couldn't be seen from any angle that he turned the car. They were packing it in a box that had been prepared to look like it had come all the way from Italy, from an anonymous sender. They knew there was a good chance that it would be destroyed once it got to Snake's compound, but they hoped that Dimitri would find it too hard to resist.

Chloe got a tour of the whole building, peppering her guides with questions as they went. It was frightening, but fascinating and she was a little in awe at the extent of their operation. "Did you have all this at the old base?" she asked.

"No, this is a considerable expansion of what we had there. But it was necessary, given the things that have happened lately. Even Gunner couldn't argue with that." Jax was determined to find out the truth, but he still hoped that Gunner hadn't gone to the dark side. It was hard to fathom that kind of betrayal.

Shadow said, "I got a message from Irina Petrov. It's a go. I sent her the pictures and she's going to see what she can find."

Jax said, "I thought she might turn us down."

Shadow replied, "She hates Snake as much as we do. I knew she'd help if there's a chance we might take him out."

"Good. That means she'll work her ass off on it."

"Exactly."

"Who is this Irina Petrov?" Chloe asked.

"She's a Russian computer hacker, formerly a spy. She's for hire, but she's picky about who hires her."

"Why does she hate Snake so much?"

"Before she became a spy, when she was a young girl, she was in Snake's hands. He was still in Russia back then and he snatched her off the street. She had a family then, and he took her away from them and did what he always does with young girls. But Irina managed to escape him. In retaliation, he killed her whole family. She was picked up by the Russian SS and trained as a spy. I've never heard anything but rumors about how she managed to be released from service, and some of the stories are pretty wild, but she did and then she went underground and that's where she stayed. Like I said, she's for hire, but only for those who meet her standards, and she's expensive." Shadow told the story with more than a little admiration for the woman.

Chloe felt as if she'd stepped into an alternate universe. "All of this sounds like a movie, not like real life."

"Unfortunately, this is a real part of life. Fortunately, most people never have to be exposed to it," Jax said darkly.

The next day, Chloe trained in the barn, while the rest of the guys carried on various tasks, including getting the model sent to Dimitri Volkov. The following day, they watched on the computer monitor as it was delivered to Snake's compound. All they could do was wait, until it had been long enough to be safe to activate the listening device. Chloe finished her training for the day with some time in the shooting lane, where Coop was impressed with her ability. On the third day after sending the car, Shadow activated the bug and settled down to listen, hoping for results. There was nothing for a long time, but then he straightened up, looking alert, and listened intently. He grinned and gave them a thumbs up, then put it on a speaker.

There was some background noise and then a voice clearly said, "You want me to take care of it tomorrow?"

"Yes. Get rid of her and make sure that she's not found. She didn't even last a month," the voice was thick with disgust.

"He gets out of control more quickly than he used to. He used to enjoy them for a while before he started that."

"That's not our business. He can do what he wants and we do what we're told."

"True. But he's going through a lot of girls."

"You want to tell him that?"

There was a sharp laugh. "No, I'll just do as I'm told."

"Good decision."

"Let's go have a drink."

And the bug went silent. Jax said, "That's good work, Shadow. Maybe it'll get us something useful."

"I'm setting it up to record whenever there are voices. We can't sit here and listen twenty-four hours a day."

"Good. Anything from Irina?"

"Not yet. I'll hear from her when she has something."

Chloe said, "I've been wondering about something else. What would Gunner get out of working with Snake? Wouldn't it be risking everything for him?"

Jax said, "Yeah, that's part of what doesn't add up. That's why we think it may be someone in his organization, working behind his back. It took Gunner a long time to get where he is and he'd lose everything if he is found out. The risk is just a lot higher than any reward I can think of. Unless Snake has something on him, something important enough to make him take the risk. I don't know what it could be."

"Maybe you need to have a discussion with Gunner."

Jax shot her a keen look. "I've been thinking that myself. What do you think, Finn?"

"I've been thinking the same thing," Finn said.

"Time for a trip. But I'm not driving this time. I'll fly to that little airstrip in Ohio, then rent a car and go from there. And I won't contact Gunner until I get to Ohio."

"Are you going alone?" Finn asked.

"No, I'll take Slade. Shadow, you keep on with surveillance, Coop, you keep on training Chloe. Finn, you're in charge. Joker, Shadow's going to need another set of eyes."

"You got it, boss." There were nods all around.

Jax said, "And tonight, we're getting pizza. Joker and Coop, you take care of that. I'm going to make travel arrangements. Slade, you come with me. Chloe, you're off duty."

"I'm just going to finish setting up this recording before I go in," said Shadow. "I'll link it to my laptop so I can check on it from the house."

Finn said, "I'll stay here with you. You can show me how to access it too."

They all went their separate ways and Chloe went directly up to the shower. It had been a long, exhausting day again, but she felt good too. By the time they gathered in the kitchen, Jax had his travel arrangements made. They would leave in the morning. Coop and Joker got back with the pizza and they all talked while they ate.

"We'll plan on staying over for a night, depending on when we can see Gunner and what we discover. We don't have any time to waste, and you guys keep me up to speed on anything that happens here." Jax was itching for some action. "I'm going to do my best to be able to meet Gunner in private, where none of his guys are around us."

Shadow said, "It's time for something to happen. I've got that feeling."

"Man, your feelings are usually right on," said Joker.

Coop said, "Let's hope this is one of those times."

"Shit, remember the time he had a feeling those California girls were really into us?" Slade asked.

They all broke up laughing. "Yeah, that feeling wasn't so right on, was it?" Finn poked fun at Shadow. "I thought they were going to kill us before the night was over."

"One of them almost *did* kill Slade!" Joker was laughing almost too hard to speak.

Jax shook his head at them. "You'd have thought they

hadn't seen women in ten years," he said to Chloe. "They were like a bunch of high school kids."

Chloe had to laugh too. "I guess when you work hard, you have to play hard."

The guys cheered for her. "Yeah!" said Slade. "She gets us! We deserve to play hard."

Jax rolled his eyes. "You had to encourage them, didn't you?"

She laughed at him and said, "I'll bet you played hard too."

"Now and then," Jax admitted with a grin. "And I guess we *were* on a break."

Jax and Chloe went upstairs soon after they were all finished with dinner and Jax packed a bag with what he needed for the next couple of days. When he was finished, he sat down in the chair and beckoned to her. She walked over and he pulled her down onto his lap and put his arms around her waist.

"I need you to listen to Finn while I'm gone."

Chloe rolled her eyes at him and said, "I am *not* two years old, Jax."

"I didn't say you were. I need to know that you're being careful. To the best of our knowledge, there is nobody who knows we're here and that's the best thing we've got going for us right now. But you still have to keep your guard up. That's what I mean when I say I want you to listen to Finn. If anything weird happens, you'll need to do whatever he tells you."

Chloe was silent for a moment, then said, "I can do that."

"Good" He buried his face in her neck and just held her for a minute. Then he stood up and carried her over to the bed.

"What are we doing?" Chloe asked softly.

"You look amazing when you're working those self-defense moves." Jax said as he pulled off his shirt.

"I do? Exactly how do I look?" Chloe asked, cupping her breasts in her hands.

"Hot. You look amazingly hot." He stripped off his jeans and then knelt over her on the bed.

Chloe ran her tongue across her top lip and her eyes grew smoky as he leaned over to brush her lips with his. Her tongue darted out and licked his lips and he gave a low growl and moved in for a deeper kiss. She nipped his lower lip lightly and then sucked it into her mouth, swirling her tongue over it and then opening her mouth to let him in. His tongue probed her mouth and his teeth grazed hers as their tongues danced together. His hands were on her breasts and he found the rigid tips with his thumbs and forefingers, rolling them and pinching them, making her moan. He slid his hands under her sweater and pulled it off over her head. The bra followed the sweater and then he had her bare breasts in his hands. She bit his lip and he pinched her nipples until she gave a little hiss of pain. He squeezed and kneaded the firm, round orbs, pulling and twisting the swollen nubs as he did.

His mouth left hers and a trail of fiery kisses rained down her throat and to the mounds in his hands and she felt his lips burn the sensitive skin around the tender teats until he fastened his mouth over one, sucking and licking it until she arched her back and gripped the back of his head, pulling him closer. He bit the rosy tip hard enough to make her cry out in protest and squirm in pleasure. He cupped his hands under her breasts and squeezed them together, turning his head back and forth to worry both nipples with his teeth and tongue. He could feel Chloe wriggling under him and he realized that his cock was rigid and straining toward her, eager to take her.

"Jax," Chloe gasped. Waves of aching pleasure were

washing over her and there were electric-like shocks prickling at her spine.

Jax pulled at her jeans, unfastening them so he could pull them down over her hips and off, flinging them to the floor. Chloe stretched beneath him and he took her wrists in one hand and held them above her head. His other hand explored her body, stroking her tender, aching nipples and down the taut muscles of her belly to cup her pelvis in his hand, grinding his palm against the vee between her legs, where he could feel the wet heat of her arousal through the thin silk of her panties. She struggled to get free, but he held her firmly and pulled down her panties, pulling at the soft down between her legs, teasing her. She felt like her body was on fire with need, every nerve ending sparking with desire. There was no way to get enough of him, as he kept holding back, teasing her until she was panting with the longing for more.

Jax straddled her, trapping her legs between his so she couldn't part them and he lay down on her, kissing her eyelids as she squirmed, his iron hard cock lying against her belly, his balls pressing against her crotch.

"Oh, God! Jax, please—"

"Please what?" he asked, nuzzling her neck.

"Please, please."

"Tell me. Please what?"

"Please, I need you."

He shook his head. "Not good enough. I want you to tell me what you want."

"I want you… I want you to fuck me!"

The ache was engulfing her, she felt every inch of her skin begging for his touch. Her pussy was dripping with desire, swollen with need and finally he rolled off her and pulled off her panties the rest of the way. His hand went to her crotch, his fingers stroking her slick, swollen folds. She cried out at the intensity of her reaction to his touch. She arched her back as he thrust two fingers into her and pushed deep into her tight, hot center. His thumb found the hard little bud and swirled around it while he pumped his fingers into her, making her cry out again. She was so wet, so hot, he marveled at her. When he pulled his hand away, she made a little cry of protest, feeling bereft. Her legs fell open and she arched her pelvis up at him.

With a hoarse cry, he plunged into her as deeply as he could, sinking the full length of his cock into her tight, hot depths. He withdrew almost completely and thrust again, pumping into her, barely able to hold onto his control.

Chloe rose to meet him and they rocked together in a fierce rhythm, their bodies slapping together, trying to get even closer to each other. Chloe felt the climax building, the pressure in her groin growing, the flame burning hotter and hotter and just when she was almost there, he pulled away.

"No. Not yet," he panted.

He turned her over and pulled her to her knees, then knelt behind her and pressed against her puckered little rosebud. She cried out in protest at the feel of him pushing into her and then in pain as he forced himself in, through the tight ring of muscle and deeper inside. The pain was blinding and he filled her so that she didn't know how it was possible to take him in. Then the pain began to mingle with the pleasure that was blossoming, an exquisite blend of excruciating pain and growing pleasure. He was finally in, the entire length of him, and she moaned at the intensity of the mingled sensations. He pulled back and then thrust forward, gently at first, then with growing force, and as her pleasure grew, she rocked back against him until they were slamming together, his balls falling heavily against her swollen pussy.

Chloe was shaking with the force of the ecstasy sweeping over her whole body and she felt the feeling growing, building until it had to explode. Her heart was pounding and her legs were trembling uncontrollably.

"Oh… oh… oh," she moaned, unable to hold back.

The orgasm swept over her, a fierce climax that shook her body with shudders as her powerful muscles contracted over and over, rocking hard against him until he couldn't hold back any longer and he emptied his seed into her with spasms of the ultimate pleasure. They shuddered together, quivering with the aftershocks of their union and weak from the intensity of it. They collapsed on the bed, wrapped in each other's arms, and lay there, panting until their breathing and their hearts slowed. Eventually, they could move enough to go to the shower together and they played in there until the hot water ran out and they had to get out.

Chloe stood in the bathroom and dried her hair, her whole body glowing with satisfaction. For that time, the time they had spent together in bed, she hadn't had a single thought for the danger that was lurking so close to them. But now, those thoughts crept back and she had one overwhelming thought; they had to find a way out of this, a way to safety. Jax had told her that she was going to belong to him and she knew now that she did.

Chapter 13

Chloe was jittery while Jax was gone and she tried to keep her mind off it by working hard at the training that Coop was giving her. She worked until she had no more to give, then she showered and cooked dinner. Joker insisted on taking care of the kitchen after dinner and she was grateful, finding that she was nearly nodding off by the time she had eaten. The next morning, after breakfast, she went to the barn dressed to work and found Shadow typing away with an intent look on his face. There was an intense atmosphere in the barn; Finn, Coop, and Joker were all gathered around the computer behind Shadow and she knew something important was happening.

"What's going on?" she asked softly.

Finn motioned for her to come closer and he said, barely above a whisper, "Shadow is talking to Irina. I think she's made some IDs."

Chloe sucked in a breath and said, "Oh my God, that's really big, isn't it?"

Finn nodded, looking grim, and said, "And Jax is waiting

for Gunner to get back to him with a meeting place and time. He's going to see him privately, away from his office."

"That's what Jax wanted, isn't it?"

"Yep, and it could be a good sign. It could mean that Gunner has suspicions about someone in his organization. I really don't want him for an enemy."

Shadow was typing furiously on his keyboard and then he waited, finally nodding with satisfaction, and signed off. He turned to look at the rest of them and said, "I've got the IDs. Irina is done. She said she's not having any more to do with this and she wished us luck."

Chloe felt a chill. "That sounds bad," she said.

Shadow looked grim. "It ain't good. But knowledge is good; it's the only thing we can use to figure out our next steps. Jax should have an interesting meeting with Gunner."

Finn looked impatient. "So, who were they? Did she ID them all?"

"She did. I just need to decode this message. Give me a few minutes."

Finn said, "Okay, I'll check the audio from Snake's compound." He went over to another laptop and checked the link for the bug they had planted. He put in an earbud and listened intently for a few minutes. When he finished, he sat down with Coop and Joker and said quietly, "There's some more conversation between Dimitri and two others, unknown but not Snake. There's more rumbling about Snake and the girls. He seems to be making his guys nervous. It must be bad or they wouldn't even dream of saying anything critical of him."

Shadow looked up and said, "I've got the names." They all looked expectantly at him and he said, "All of them were Russian assassins. To lose all of them in one night, had to have been a big blow for the Russians. That's why Irina won't have any more to do with it."

"Is that within Snake's authority, to call them here?" Finn asked.

Shadow was shaking his head. "It might be, with permission from Russia. He would have had to give them a powerful reason for needing us taken out. More than just vengeance for his son. What did you hear from our bug?"

Finn repeated it again and Shadow looked thoughtful. "I wonder if Snake is becoming a liability for Mother Russia."

Joker said, "His operations all take place here, though. If he's causing trouble, it's here in the United States."

"Yeah, but he still answers to people in Russia; he's not on his own here. I think he goes on as if he *were* an independent operator, but they still call the shots when it comes to something big." Finn was thinking out loud.

Shadow said, "Plus, there's the fact that if too much attention is called to an increase in missing girls, it brings unwanted attention to the Russians. And if Snake is wasting them, not selling them like he's supposed to, then he's losing money for Russia."

Chloe was staring at them in horror. "Where do these girls come from? Are they Americans?"

Finn said, "No, they're kidnapped and shipped here to be sold. They come from Russia and a number of other countries. So, Russia has a big stake in what Snake does here."

Chloe said, "Russia, as in the *government* of Russia?"

"No, at least not in any official sense. The Russian underground, or mob, if you will. Although I'm quite sure that there are Russian officials involved in it," Finn answered.

"Oh, my God, that's horrible." Chloe was deeply shocked.

Coop was thinking hard. "So, we have to figure out what reason Snake would have given his higher-ups to get them to okay the assassins if it was Snake who was behind that."

Shadow said, "I'd like to go back to the idea of Snake becoming a liability to Russia. We know exactly what they'd do if they made that determination; they'd kill him. But they'd want it kept quiet because they wouldn't give up the operations here. They'd replace Snake with someone they could trust. What if Snake asked for assassins to take us out and they figured they could get rid of us. They have to know that we're after Snake, and then the assassins could go and take care of Snake. They tie up the loose ends, us, and get rid of Snake all in one night. And they would know that our deaths would be covered up by our people."

Joker said, "But we took out all their assassins and Snake is still alive and well."

Coop said, with a dark look, "And now we've crossed the Russian underground."

They sat in silence, taking that in for a minute. Finally, Finn said, "We'd all better hope and pray that Gunner is still on the good side. We'll never get out of this if he's in on it too."

Shadow said, "You know, there's one thing that doesn't make sense in all this."

Coop said sarcastically, "What? Only one?"

Shadow grinned and said, "You guys didn't have a lot of trouble taking out these assassins. Were they really assassins, or something else? Real Russian assassins are good, just like ours are good. For that many of them to be taken down that way, I don't know, it doesn't add up."

Finn grumbled, "Yeah, the one who shot me must have been pretty good."

Shadow chuckled at him, and Coop said, "You're right. They couldn't have been the Russian elite. For one thing, they didn't really have a plan. They just barreled in there and started shooting at us. That's not the way assassins work."

Shadow said, "I need to do a deep dive on those guys now that I have the IDs. I'm on it."

Finn said, "I can work on that too. We'll split them up and start digging."

Coop said, "Come on, Chloe. I figure in another couple of days, you'll be beating my ass."

She laughed a little and got up to follow him, glad to have the activity to keep her mind off everything she had just heard. Joker went to the computer monitors and they all went to work.

By the end of the afternoon, Chloe was tired, but exhilarated; she was getting over the sore muscles she'd had the first few days and getting noticeably stronger. She and Coop stopped to check with Finn and Shadow, who were making slow progress.

"We're having to start with these guys as children and try to trace their lives. They all seem to have come from the same area in Russia; in fact, they were in school together as children. It looks like they were brought up and trained from a young age for something, but they couldn't have been primarily trained as assassins. We'll figure it out."

Chloe went on to the house to shower and start dinner and Coop did the same, offering to help her in the kitchen. They soon had dinner in the oven and Coop went back to the barn while Chloe sat down with her laptop to do a little writing. She found it hard to concentrate, her mind going back to everything that had been happening and wondering how it was going for Jax. She finally put the laptop away and poured herself a glass of wine. She sat at the table, just thinking and sipping her wine, and she found herself reliving the last night she'd spent with Jax and the feel of his hands on her. Her belly crawled with heat and she knew that she would never get enough of him. She craved him, craved his touch, whether it was tender or rough, either way, it satisfied a need within her. She felt more alive when she was with him than she'd felt in her young life before she met him.

When the others came in, they had news; Jax and Slade would be on their way back in the morning. They should arrive sometime in the afternoon. Jax hadn't told them much about his meeting with Gunner, saying that he would explain it all when they got there, but he had said that he was optimistic. Chloe immediately felt better, knowing he was on his way back soon and she would be in his arms the next day.

Their bug had picked up some more conversation between Dimitri and an unknown person, more of the same uneasy talk about Snake and the girls. They seemed to be growing more concerned and the important part of the conversation had been when Dimitri had said, "This is the third time in ten days. I don't want to keep making this run; it's only a matter of time before they find something and then the heat's going to be on. I don't want to get caught with this mess."

The other person had spoken sharply to him and Dimitri had grumbled, "Yeah, you can say that. You're not the one having to do it. You need to do something." Then they had left the room and there was no more to be heard.

And in the morning, the news broke that the bodies of two young girls had been found in a deep pond in the area where Snake's compound was located. It was a sickening story; the bodies had been defiled and autopsies were being performed immediately. Long before Jax got back, there had been a news conference with the local chief of police, who released the information that the girls had been sexually violated and tortured for hours before they died. They hadn't been identified yet, but they were apparently in their early teens. It was a horrifying story and Chloe watched the news with tears in her eyes, sickened by what had been done to the girls. Later in the day, a third body was discovered and it immediately became an even bigger story.

They were all in the barn when Jax and Slade arrived. The two men walked in to find them all hard at work and they all gathered around the tables where Shadow and Finn sat at the computers.

"Let's fill each other in," Jax said. His eyes searched until he saw Chloe approaching with Coop and his eyes met hers briefly. He didn't pay attention to the men around him but reached out and pulled her against him for a quick kiss.

Slade had a briefcase, which he opened and pulled out a folder, handing it to Jax. Jax said, "I can verify that Gunner is after Snake and in full support of us. He has a leak in his organization and he's setting a trap for him, probably right now. We're going to concentrate solely on taking down Snake and we have Gunner's backing. He has heard from sources in Russia that the powers there are not pleased with Snake and they're ready to be rid of him."

"We have a theory on that, boss," said Shadow. "Irina ID'd the men who showed up to crash our mission and they're reportedly Russian assassins. But that doesn't add up because we just took them out too easily. They had no plan; they just rushed in and started shooting. They couldn't have been real assassins."

"Was Irina giving you the truth?" Jax asked.

"Yeah, I'm sure it was the identities those guys lived by, but it's fake. We've been looking into them and there's some pretty strange stuff in their backgrounds. They were all from the same town in Russia and they were all very close to the same age. They attended the same school as boys and apparently, they were being trained in some kind of program; what it was, we haven't figured out yet."

Finn said, "And there's a lot of uneasiness in Snake's organization. Apparently, he's been escalating his treatment of the girls he samples before he sends them on to be sold and they haven't been surviving. Dimitri is grumbling that he doesn't want to make some kind of run for Snake anymore, because it's getting too hot, he's afraid of getting caught. And this morning, the news broke that two bodies of young girls were found in a pond. I'm guessing that's the run that Snake sends Dimitri on, to get rid of the bodies. They're in their early teens and they were sexually violated and tortured to death."

Jax whistled. "Shit, that would make Russia unhappy with him. They don't need careless behavior over here, especially if it could be connected with them."

Coop said, "From what Dimitri said, this has been going on for a while; he said Snake is wasting a lot of girls."

"That's ugly, really ugly," mused Jax. "No wonder Russia's unhappy with him. So, tell me what else you've come up with."

Shadow said, "Well, nothing for sure, but we were speculating that maybe Russia sent these guys primarily to get rid of Snake, but they figured they could take us out first and be rid of some loose ends. But we took out all the men they sent."

Jax said, "So we need to know more about the guys they sent. You're right; real assassins would have had a plan and probably would have killed us all. I don't know why they would have sent guys after us without a plan, but maybe they thought it was going to be easy. They know very little about us. Before Gunner's leak, they didn't know anything."

Joker said, "I know one thing. If those guys had been real assassins and we killed them all, Russia would be after us like white on rice."

"And there's no chatter that indicates that," Finn said.

"They must have been expendable," Jax said thoughtfully. "I wonder what their next step will be with Snake."

"I don't know, but the heat is on now, and I wouldn't be surprised if they find more bodies."

"Have you heard anything from Snake's compound since the news broke?" Slade asked.

Finn said, "No, but I was about to check again."

Shadow said, "I'll log on from here and we can all listen."

Shadow switched on the recording and there was some muffled background noise before they heard Dimitri's voice. "Shit, shit, shit! All I did was follow orders!"

Another voice said, "Your orders were to be sure they couldn't be found. So, you didn't follow orders. You botched it; you botched it bad."

Dimitri sounded desperate. "It wasn't my fault. He's out of control; there were too many. I did the best I could."

The other voice was disdainful. "You're not a stranger to this business; you know how it works. You're the one responsible for them getting found."

Dimitri's voice was fierce. "That's bullshit! He's responsible; he's the one killing them."

"You're a fool, Dimitri. You should have made sure this couldn't happen. Do you think he's not in deep shit now? Now Russia has a problem, and what do you think they're going to do with him? You think he's going to let you get away with what you did?"

"I've got to get out of here," Dimitri said desperately.

With a laugh, the other man said, "You can try. I don't hold out much hope for you but do what you want."

There was a sound of rushed footsteps and something banging and then Dimitri muttered, "Grab what I need and get out."

A moment later, there was a short, startled cry and then a horrible, gurgling sound that went on for way too long. Then there was a heavy thud and the unknown man said, "Idiot. Did you think he was going to let you run? Anton, get rid of this."

There were some sounds after that but no more conversation, and the men around the computer looked at each other knowingly. Jax said, "Well, that's the end of Dimitri. Now, what's going to happen to Snake?"

Chloe was horrified; she had just heard a man being murdered. It was a nightmare. She shuddered and kept silent.

Jax sighed heavily and said, "I have a burner phone to communicate with Gunner privately. I'm going to have to let him know." He sent a text to Gunner and received one back within a couple of minutes. "Gunner said they heard the news about the bodies being found, and it's no surprise that they eliminated Dimitri. Snake's future just got very shaky."

Slade said, "By the way, our location is still a secret. Gunner said he didn't want to know; that way, there is no chance of his leaker letting that out before he gets caught in Gunner's trap. That should only take a day or two, but Gunner agreed that it's an extra layer of safety if our location is unknown."

Finn said, "That's good to know. And another way to know Gunner is solid. I'm glad to know it; he was the last guy in the world we needed as an enemy."

"Agreed," said Coop. "Now we need a plan."

"That's what we're going to be doing tomorrow, coming up with a plan. We've got a shitload of information to coordinate and study and then we need a viable plan. It's time to put an end to this shit." Jax was fiercely determined. He looked at Chloe, who was still pale and still. "Chloe, I know you didn't want to hear what happened, but keep in mind that he was the guy who sacrificed your life to deliver that message to us. If we hadn't kept you with us, he would have killed you."

Chloe shuddered again and said weakly, "I'm not sure that's helping."

"Come on, you're going to be okay. Guys, I think it's time for a drink all around."

Finn opened a drawer and pulled out a bottle of excellent whiskey and a stack of disposable plastic glasses. He poured whiskey for all of them and they passed them around.

Jax said, "Here's to putting an end to this butcher."

They all drank together and the whiskey warmed Chloe and brought a little color back to her cheeks. They talked a little more while they finished their drinks and toasted Gunner for sticking to the right side.

Jax said, "We've got a few hours left before we need to get dinner. Let's organize our facts and coordinate the things that belong together. Tomorrow, we all work on coming up with a plan. Coop, you and Chloe too."

"Okay, boss," Coop said with a nod of approval.

The recent events had made them all draw together, the feeling that it was them against a great evil bringing them closer to each other. They worked together, discussing, organizing, floating ideas, and approving them or shooting them down. That evening, they all prepared dinner together, creating a huge taco bar and gorging themselves, washing tacos down with Finn's pitchers of margaritas. They even cleaned everything up afterward, putting away the leftovers and poking fun at each other. There was a huge battle coming and they were preparing themselves for it their way, strengthening their bond and their resolve.

Chapter 14

The next day brought an unexpected development. Snake had disappeared sometime during the night and not a soul at his compound knew anything about what had happened to him. There was a lot of conversation between people at the compound and they had nothing but speculation. Had the higher powers gotten him? The consensus among Snake's organization was that they would have made an example of him, not done it quietly and secretly. So, the next most likely thing was that he'd made a run for it. Which left them in a panic, not knowing what they should do to try to save their own skins. There were still everyday tasks that needed to be done, collecting from their drug dealers, selling girls, collecting from their loan sharks. A man named Ilya stepped up and began giving orders to the others. There was a slight objection, but he gave a sort of speech, telling them all that their best chance was to carry on in the way that Snake's superiors would expect. If they could keep the operation going and the money flowing, they would be proving that they were capable of carrying on without Snake and they would be safe from reprisal from Russia. It made sense, so the others accepted his authority and went about business as usual.

Jax sat back, looking impressed. "Shadow, see what you can find out about this Ilya. And Snake's on the run now. See if you can find anyone he would go to for protection or some kind of help."

"On it, boss." Shadow turned to his computer.

"I need to speak with Gunner," Jax said. He went to his desk and got on the phone. He was there for some time and when he rejoined them, he was smiling grimly. "Gunner has received a message from Russia to inform him that Snake has been labeled for elimination. He has no backing from anyone in Russia and if something happens to him, there will be no reprisals from Russia."

Finn looked impressed. "That's the first time I've ever heard anything like that from them. They usually like to take care of their own dirty laundry; they'd consider it interference if we took him out, even if it was what they wanted to happen."

"Gunner said they called Snake a mad dog that needs to be put down. They regret the trouble he caused over here and they hope it's over now."

Slade snickered. "Yeah, they hope he gets his head blown off, rather than getting caught and arrested. That could cause them some major headaches."

Jax said, "It could. I'm sure they've got people on their way to take over the operation or decide if it needs to be shut down. They won't want to shut it down, but they might feel that it's not worth the risk."

"You really think they might do that?" asked Joker.

"I don't know. I guess it depends on a lot of things. For example, if more bodies are found, I think there's a good chance that they'll cut it off. They can't afford to have it become public knowledge."

"That wouldn't make anything that's already happened right, but at least it wouldn't continue," said Coop.

Jax said, "Well, the bottom line is that's to be left to the police and FBI. Our orders are to concentrate on Snake; capture him if we can, take him out if we can't. Gunner has passed on information about Snake's operation to the authorities and he says it's out of our hands now."

"Suits me," said Slade. "I'm not a policeman."

"Good thing," said Coop. "You already like doughnuts too damn much."

Slade punched him on the arm and said, "Asshole."

"Do you think Snake's got any chance of getting back into favor with Russia?" asked Joker.

Jax shook his head. "No, I think he went too far. If they're coming all the way from Russia to make a decision on his operation, then they want him dead and out of their hair for good. I imagine he's been a problem for a while."

Finn said, "Couldn't happen to a nicer guy."

Shadow said, "Snake has past associations with a few people in Brighton Beach and in California. But I don't think he can go to any of them; I can't imagine they'd be willing to help him, knowing he's marked. If he goes to anyone, it's going to have to be on a personal basis and I haven't found any personal connections yet."

"Do we know anything about what kind of resources he has?"

"I've got a search going for bank accounts. You know how that goes. I'm sure he salted away an offshore account somewhere; don't they all?"

Chloe asked, a little timidly, "Does this mean we're safer now, with Snake running away?"

Jax said, "No, until we find him and take care of him, we have to be on our guard even more. Snake is the kind of sick guy who will want to carry out his strongest wish, to get revenge on the people who killed his son. He might just run for his life, but we can't rule out that his final goal will be to get us."

Chloe's heart sank. She was suddenly desperately weary of it all and wished with all her heart that she'd never taken the job of delivering that envelope. She was sick of being afraid, sick of being trapped, sick of not being in charge of her own destiny. Then she looked at Jax and felt that stirring that she always felt when she looked at him. Maybe what she was really sick of was the two of them living under the pressure of constant danger. She had a moment of utter clarity and the thought struck her, *he is my destiny*. Her energy came surging back and she straightened her shoulders and finally felt ready to face whatever was to come. With Jax, not alone, with her destiny.

Jax had seen the emotions play across her face and he wondered what she was thinking. Just then, Shadow said, "Got the bank accounts. One in the Caymans and one in the Bahamas. I guess he likes warm weather and sandy beaches." He gave a whistle. "Damn, he did a good job of providing for his retirement. There's a lot of money there."

"Give me the numbers and I'll pass them on to Gunner," Jax said. "He can decide what to do about it."

"Jax, what about looking into Ivan's personal associations?" Finn suggested. "As far as we know, Ivan was the only person Snake ever really cared about; maybe there's someone Ivan cared for who Snake would contact."

Jax said, "It's a long shot, but worth checking out. Was there a woman in Ivan's life?"

Finn said, "It's hard to imagine, knowing what he did to all those girls, but how many sickos like him carried on a normal home life with someone who had no idea who they were really with?"

"That's true. Did we ever delve into Ivan's personal life when we carried out that operation?"

"We must have. It's normal background, part of the package we put together for every job."

Shadow said, "We did. He had a wife and a home in Brighton Beach. She had no idea what he was up to and we never had to go to his home or have any contact with her. They had no children. He divided his time between his home and Snake's compound. She believed he traveled for work. We had a good cover for the whole operation and it was ruled an accident. So, unless Snake had some contact with her and told her the truth, she never found out what Ivan really was."

"Find out what you can about her now," said Jax.

Shadow nodded and went back to his computer.

Chloe worked for several hours with Coop and the work of the day went on. Later in the day, she showered and took care of dinner. She was just walking into the kitchen after her shower when Jax came in looking for her. He put his arms around her and kissed her, gently but deeply, making her sigh and melt into him.

"God, you smell good," he said, burying his face in her hair. "Are you okay? This has been a lot of stress. You want me to order dinner tonight?"

She hugged him hard. "No, it's going to feel good to do a normal, everyday job like cooking dinner. I'm fine. Some of this has been hard to hear, but I'm really okay."

"You know what I'd like to do once this is all over?"

She shook her head. "No, what?"

He said, "I'd like to go back to the island. Lie on the beach, cook over the fire, go to town and order from the food trucks, buy beer from Andre. Make love in that pretty little bedroom and sleep with the sea breeze coming through the window."

Chloe's eyes were dreamy. "That sounds like heaven."

He leaned down to kiss her again. "Let's do it."

"You promise?"

He kissed the end of her nose and said, "I promise."

Chloe went about cooking dinner with a smile on her face and an island in her heart. When the crew came in, they were talking about Shadow's research into Ivan's wife. She still lived in Brighton Beach, in the same house she'd shared with Ivan. She kept to herself and there wasn't a lot that Shadow had been able to find out about her, but they knew where she was, at least.

Jax said, "Someone has to go check her place out and watch to see if Snake shows up there."

"I'll go," said Finn. "I'll take Slade with me. It could take a while."

"Yeah," Jax mused. "It sure would be nice if we could get an idea where he is, but I don't know any more efficient way to find him. Did anyone else pop up that he could go to?"

Shadow said, "I found mention of a brother, but I haven't gotten too much yet. I'll dig into it again after dinner, see what I can find out."

"Okay." Jax wasn't looking forward to an all-night work session, but it looked like it was going to happen.

Chloe spoke up. "Let's have dinner with no talk about Snake or the Russians. Tell me a little about how you all ended up together."

The guys looked at each other and Jax nodded. It was a good idea to take a break. "Well, Finn and I were in the Army together before this group was ever thought of."

"Really? What did you do in the Army?" Chloe asked as she passed the salad bowl on.

"We were badass Rangers," Finn said with a grin.

"Yeah, we served together for six years. Then we'd had enough. We left the Army and went to work for a private contractor doing basically the same things we'd been doing, but for a lot more money." Jax speared a pork chop and passed the platter on.

Joker said, "I was in the Army too, but I was in bomb disposal. It doesn't take too long to have enough of that and I got out after four years. I tried working for a private contractor, but the bureaucracy was just suffocating and I quit. Then I went to work teaching self-defense classes. There wasn't any money in it but it was a lot more satisfying. I ran into Slade one day, we'd known each other in the Army for a short time, and he brought me to meet Gunner."

"Gunner snagged me right as I was leaving the Army," said Slade. "I didn't have any idea what I could do after the military and I liked the sound of what he was proposing, so I was in." He piled mashed potatoes onto his plate and reached for the gravy.

"What about you, Coop?" Chloe asked.

"Gunner contacted me after Slade told him about me. I was in tech school with Slade; we used to hit the gym at the same time and we got to know each other there." Coop grinned and spooned green beans onto his plate.

Shadow said, "And I didn't know any of these assholes before this group formed. Gunner was responsible for putting it all together and training us. It was two full years before we carried out our first mission."

Chloe said, "How long ago was that?"

Jax said, "Eight years. We're having our tenth anniversary soon."

"What's the longest you've ever gone without having a mission?"

They all said together, "Five months."

They laughed hard and Coop said, "It was the longest five months I've ever lived through. Just waiting, day after day, with nothing happening."

Joker said, "Yeah, it's kind of a good thing because there's nobody evil enough to need our services, but damn, we needed some action."

"That's when we met the girls from California who tried to kill us," Slade said.

Chloe was laughing at them.

Finn said, "We were so bored that one night we went out for karaoke."

Coop was overcome with laughter and Joker punched him in the arm and said, "Hey, I enjoyed that."

Coop said, "Yeah, everybody else did too. Chloe, he didn't sing anything but Elvis songs and he danced too."

Chloe giggled at the mental image of Joker impersonating Elvis. Jax said, "It took two of us to drag him out of there. He thought he'd found himself a new career."

Joker looked affronted and said darkly, "You guys don't know good music when you hear it."

"Shit, man," said Slade, "don't you remember the applause we got when we hauled you out of there?"

"They were cheering for me," Joker insisted.

"Yeah, for you leaving," Coop said and Slade high-fived him.

Jax drawled, "We had to get you out of there; I was afraid the bar was going to fine me for bringing you in there."

They all hooted with laughter and Joker flipped them off and helped himself to another pork chop. Loftily, he said, "I'm never singing for you people again."

Finn said, "Mission accomplished."

Jax grinned as he looked around the table at them. They needed to burn off some of the stress they'd been under and they didn't have the luxury of taking a break now, so he silently thanked Chloe for setting the guidelines for their dinner conversation. After they'd wiped out the pork chops and mashed potatoes, Chloe brought out a triple layer choco-late cake, and the guys gave her a cheer.

"Damn, that looks good," said Coop.

"I'll put on some coffee," said Jax.

Coop said, "I need a glass of milk with that."

"Yeah, me too," said Slade.

The rest opted for coffee, thinking about the fact that they were going to continue working after dinner. When they were finished, Jax said, "Okay, you guys, Chloe outdid herself with this dinner. You guys handle the cleanup. Chloe, I need to talk to you for a few minutes."

She followed him upstairs and as soon as he closed the door behind them, he swept her into his arms. "That was a good move you made, telling everyone no shop talk during dinner. Everybody needed a breather."

"I'm glad," she said, "but I was honestly just thinking that I needed a breather."

"That's okay. Your instincts were right on. We're going to go back out to the barn after the kitchen is clean. We're probably going to work through most of the night. If you could keep the coffee coming until you're ready for bed, I'd appreciate it."

"I can stay up and keep you in coffee," Chloe said.

"I don't want you to stay up all night. When you get tired, start one last pot and then go on to bed. We'll be fine, it's nothing new to us."

"Okay," Chloe said, thinking that she'd do what she wanted to. "I'm glad everyone had a good dinner and some good conversation. And I'm probably going to have dreams about Joker impersonating Elvis."

"They'll be nightmares," Jax promised her with a grin. He gave her a long, probing kiss and she made that little hum in the back of her throat. He pulled away with an effort and said, "We'll have to continue this later."

"Promise?" she asked with a sultry smile.

"Oh, you bet your ass. Feel free to come out to the barn if you're bored."

"We can't do this in the barn," she teased him.

"We could, but I prefer not to have an audience." Jax laughed at her.

"Okay, don't work too hard."

"If we find something important, it'll be worth it."

Chloe made several trips to the barn with coffee and she baked a batch of cookies and took them a plateful of them, warm from the oven. They were deep in concentration on what they were working on, so she delivered her goodies quietly and left them alone. She meant to keep it up as long as they did, but sometime after two a.m. she gave in to her exhaustion and put on a final pot of coffee before she went to bed. She woke briefly when Jax crawled into bed, not long before dawn, and went promptly back to sleep.

Chapter 15

Finn and Slade were packing their bags and leaving for Brighton Beach. They would find out what they could about Ivan's wife and then fly back. They would also be listening to the heavily Russian neighborhood gossip if they could. Finn was fluent in the Russian language and Slade could get by. They both took fake IDs from their collections of false documents, with credit cards that matched the IDs and the usual things they would carry in their wallets. Joker was driving them to the airstrip and he would pick them up when they got back. They took burner phones with them and they would pick up weapons from a contact in New York after they landed and rented a car. It was a familiar routine and one they were comfortable with.

Once they were gone, Jax sat down with Shadow and asked, "Anything new?"

"I know that Snake does have a brother. His name is Luka Vasiliev but after he got to the US, he had it legally changed to Lucas Vale and he goes by Luke. He wanted to wipe out all ties to Russia and Snake gave up on making him part of his operation many years ago. They had no contact with each other, as far as I can find, once Luke had his name changed. He lives in Arizona and works in real estate. He's been moderately successful and lives a quiet life."

Jax asked, "Wife and kids?"

Shadow said, "A son and a daughter, both have nice careers in business, both college graduates. The wife divorced him after the kids went to college, but they stayed on friendly terms and they see each other for holidays and so on."

"So, if Snake is desperate for a place to go, that's a strong possibility."

Shadow nodded. "Definitely. Luke wouldn't like it, but he might help him just to avoid problems for his family. Which we know Snake wouldn't hesitate to threaten him with."

"On the other hand, Snake will know that we'd find out about this connection. It wasn't that hard, was it?"

"No, not at all. Luke never hid his past, he just wanted to end it."

"We'll have to follow up on it. Coop and Joker can go. That leaves us to hold down the fort."

Shadow frowned. "We could wait until Finn and Slade get back."

Jax shook his head. "They could easily be gone a week or more. We can't afford to wait."

"I don't like us being all split up. What about using someone from Gunner's group?"

"I thought about that, but it's Snake. We know more about him than anyone else and I can't see sending someone we don't really know after the worst enemy we've got."

Shadow sighed. "Yeah, you're right. But I still don't like it."

"I don't like it any better than you do, but I don't see any other choice. We'll just have to watch our backs and they'll have to do the same."

Shadow nodded toward Coop and Chloe, who were working at hand-to-hand combat on a mat in the middle of the barn. "She's getting pretty skillful. She's quick and getting stronger all the time."

"Good. The better trained she is, the better I feel. She's a damn good shot, too."

Just then, Chloe made a quick move and flipped Coop to the mat, pinning him in one smooth, fluid motion. Joker let out a yell and a whistle and Shadow and Jax grinned as Coop picked himself up and high fived his student. Chloe was flushed and grinning with pride and she gladly accepted the bottle of water Coop handed to her. Jax beckoned to them and they walked over to join him, with Joker following behind them, still poking fun at Coop.

Shadow filled them in on what he'd found out about Snake's brother and Jax said, "I need you two to go to Arizona and see what you can find out. Things are hot for Snake; his picture is plastered all over the place now and he needs to go into hiding, or better yet, get out of the country. We need to get him before he does that, or we might never get him."

"Okay, boss, when do you want us to leave?" Coop asked.

"The sooner, the better. As soon as you can get your things together, I'd like you to get on your way. I'll call the airstrip and they'll be ready for you. You can drive the Jeep and leave it there. You can take your weapons on this flight; they won't be searching you or your bags. When you land, you'll be out in the desert and they'll have a car for you. Luke lives on the outskirts of Apache Junction, about an hour from where you'll be landing." Jax got up and said, "I'll get you some cash."

Coop went straight to the shower and then packed quickly and clattered down the stairs, where Joker was ready and waiting. They had their IDs, Jax gave them plenty of cash, and they looked eager to go. Both of them were casually dressed in jeans and boots. Coop wore a short sleeved, white pullover that showed his muscular build and Joker was in a faded denim shirt with the sleeves rolled up. Joker was shorter than

Coop, but powerfully built, with sandy, tousled hair and a neatly trimmed beard. Chloe suspected that they had no problem picking up women when they got the chance.

"Watch your backs and don't try to take Snake before you talk to me."

Joker raised an eyebrow and said, "If we've got a clear opportunity, don't we need to take him down?"

"If you can do it safely and without collateral damage; you'll have to use your own judgement. It'll be justified. The Feds want him alive, but if it's between him getting away or taking him out, you take him out. We can't let him get out of the country."

"Got it."

Shadow said, "I'll send texts to both your phones with names and addresses you'll need."

Coop said, "Good. We'll let you know when we land."

Chloe handed Joker a bag of the cookies she'd made and he gave her a loud, smacking kiss on the cheek and made her giggle. "You guys be careful," she said, hugging them both. She stood with Jax and Shadow and watched them drive away, unable to shake the feeling she had that bad things were coming.

Jax's phone vibrated and he read the text from Finn letting him know that they were in New York, had their car rented, and were on their way to Brighton Beach. They would get rooms and then pick up their weapons before they went to locate Galina, Ivan's wife. They planned to find a neighborhood bar where they could get something to eat and listen to the local gossip. Shadow sat down at the computer to search for cameras near Luke Vale's house. It was in a subdivision, so there were no traffic cams, but the houses were nice ones and likely to be protected by home security systems that might provide him with some looks.

"Boss, I've got cameras on Luke's place." Jax hurried over

to join him and Shadow nodded at the monitor. "The house across the street has a front door cam that picks up a view all the way to Luke's front door. And the next-door neighbor has one on his fence that gets a side view of the back yard and a partial view of Luke's back patio doors. The one across the street also has one on the garage that shows Luke's garage. You really gotta love home security systems."

"That's good work, Shadow. We're going to have to take turns watching for activity."

Chloe was standing behind him and she said, "I can take a turn at that. If I see anything, I just call you guys, right?"

Shadow and Jax exchanged glances. Jax said, "Yeah, as a matter of fact, that would be a real help."

"Let me watch. And you guys can keep on working at other things. I don't know how to do what you guys do, but I can watch this screen until something happens."

Shadow said, "Let me set you up on this monitor over here. That way, I can keep working at mine but we're right here if you see something." He moved over to the next table and pulled up a split screen that showed all three views of Luke's house. "This monitor is bigger, so you'll get a better view of what's going on. You want some coffee or anything?"

"Just water would suit me fine," Chloe said and Jax brought her a bottle.

"Just speak up if you need anything," Jax said, resting his hand on her shoulder for a moment.

She gave him a quick grin and then turned her attention to the screen. An uneventful hour and a half went by and then Chloe straightened up and said tensely, "A car just pulled into the driveway."

The two men joined her and watched as the garage door slid up, the luxury car pulled into the garage, and the door slid back down. A minute or so later, the front door opened and a man stepped out. He was dressed in business attire, though he had loosened his tie and unbuttoned his top button. He looked up and down the quiet street before he stepped to the mailbox beside the door and pulled out his mail, leafing through it before he stepped back inside and closed the door. And that was all the activity there was to see for another couple of hours.

Jax walked over and said, "Chloe, why don't you take a break for a while? I'll take a turn watching, you stretch out the kinks."

She wanted to insist that she could keep watching, but she needed the break. She was stiff and her eyes were tired, so she got up and stretched, saying, "Okay, I'll go to the house and have a little break and I'll make us some sandwiches and bring them out."

Jax said, "That sounds good. We'll have a beer with them."

Shadow said, "Now you're talking. I'm going to take a quick break too, boss."

Chloe and Shadow walked into the house together and Chloe went into the downstairs bathroom while Shadow went up to his room. When he came back down, Chloe was in the kitchen, busily taking the fixings for sandwiches out of the refrigerator.

"Do you need help with anything?" Shadow asked.

"Nope, I'm fine. But my stomach just growled. I didn't realize how late it was getting."

"Yeah, you get into this kind of stuff and time doesn't seem to mean much after a while. Well, I'm going back out; just give a yell if you need anything."

Chloe turned on the little TV in the kitchen while she worked, feeling that the house was just a little too quiet, and listened to the news. When she was finished, she loaded a tray with the plate full of thick roast beef sandwiches and a bowl full of fruit, along with paper plates and napkins. She switched off the TV and carried her tray out to the barn. It was beginning to get dark and she stood for a minute, looking around at the shadowy landscape. She shivered a little and reminded herself that there were surveillance cameras and security alarms all over the property that would alert them if there were ever an intruder. But she was glad to go inside to the light and warmth and company of Jax and Shadow.

Shadow looked at her and groaned. "Damn, you don't know how good that looks. You said your stomach growled and made me realize I'm starving." He went to the cooler and pulled out three icy bottles of beer and they settled at the end of the table where Chloe had watched the monitor. Shadow turned it so they could watch while they ate and there was silence for the first minute or two while they helped themselves to sandwiches.

Finally, Jax swallowed the bite he was chewing and said, "I heard from Coop. They landed about an hour ago and they're on their way to Apache Junction. And Finn and Slade located Galina's house and sent us the address so Shadow can look for cameras. They're at a neighborhood bar now getting something to eat and hoping to hear some of the local gossip."

"Wow. There's a lot going on, isn't there?" Chloe commented.

"Yeah, there is. Let's just hope we get a lead on Snake."

"And fast. This needs to be finished," said Shadow.

"Agreed. And when it is, we're going to have another break. And after that, we can get back to business as usual."

Chloe gave him a little smile, thinking of his promise to take her back to the island. It was still light in Arizona and she caught a flicker of movement in Luke's back yard. He stepped out to the part of the patio that they could see in the camera view and opened the lid of the fancy gas grill sitting there. They watched him go about lighting and scraping the grill and then closing the lid to let it heat up. He went back into the house and returned a minute later with a plate that held a thick steak and sipping a glass of red wine. They watched him put the steak on and talk on his cell phone for a bit, nothing unusual for a warm evening for a man alone. He took another call before his steak was finished and then he disappeared back into the house. But just a minute later, he reappeared with a tray that held his steak and a bowl of salad, along with utensils and a fresh glass of wine. He sat down at the table under the shelter of an umbrella and ate his dinner outside.

"Is this the kind of thing you guys do all the time?" Chloe asked.

"This is the kind of thing we do way too much of," Jax said with a nod.

"Yeah, surveillance sucks but it's a necessary evil," said Shadow. "It's really tedious, except for brief moments when something is actually happening."

"Wow, and people think it's all action," Chloe said.

Jax laughed. "There's a whole lot more surveillance than there is action. But that's not a bad thing, if you really think about it. Action means violence."

Chloe was sobered. "That's true. How do you do it?"

"It's our job," Jax said simply. "It's what we know and what we do best. And we know that our targets are some of the most evil people there are, so that makes a difference. They're people who will never be touched through normal legal channels. They're never going to get arrested and sent to jail. There's never been a target who didn't deserve what they got."

"And you're sure of that?"

"We are. It was a condition of us agreeing to form the group in the first place. All other means of getting them had to be exhausted or clearly impossible and there has to be no doubt about the things they've done and the fact that their evil is going to continue."

"Do you ever get tired of it?"

Jax said heavily, "Yeah, we get tired of it. It's hard, it's hard mentally; it wears you down. That's why we have to take the breaks that we do, we have to refuel, get ourselves back. And that's why Gunner has no objection when I tell him that we need a break."

Shadow said, "Every one of us has had times when we wanted to walk away, never be part of this group again. But we can't; we know that and we're lucky that we have a boss who keeps a finger on it and knows what we need."

Jax said, "But what's going on now with Snake is not business as usual at all. It's something we've never faced before, having him after us. And it's all because of the leak. He never knew a thing about us before that happened. So, we have to get this resolved."

Chloe said hesitantly, "It feels like something bad is coming, like there's something dark all around us."

Shadow slid his chair over and ran through a security check. "Everything's secure, no alarms, no breaches."

Chloe looked relieved and Jax said, "I know what you mean. It's weird to have so many of us gone and to be so spread out. It makes things feel strange, like things are so far from normal that something has to be going wrong. But it's going well with no problems so far."

Chloe said, "Yeah, it *is* weird to have them gone. Maybe that's all it is."

"Take a look. Coop and Joker just went by Luke's house."

Chloe sat up straight, her attention riveted on the monitor. "That was them?"

"Yep." He looked at his phone as a text came in. "They're parking down the street a little and watching the house. After dark, they'll plant some electronics so they can get a look inside."

Shadow said, "And they'll relay it back to us so we can look too."

"Wow. That's kind of cool."

Jax laughed at her. "You want to be part of our group?"

She snorted at him. "I think I already *am* part of your group."

Shadow laughed. "She has a point, boss."

"Yeah, I guess she does."

"That was delicious, Chloe, thank you," Shadow said, draining his beer.

Chloe said, "You're absolutely welcome. I'll put these sandwiches in the cooler. If you get hungry again, they'll be there."

Jax selected a bunch of grapes from the bowl and popped one into his mouth before he went back to his spot beside Shadow. "Are you good watching for a while again?"

"Yep, I'm fine."

"Shadow, why don't you go catch a few hours' sleep? We're going to have to take shifts out here; there's too much that has to be watched."

"Will do, boss. I'll be back in three hours."

And so, the night went on, with all of them watching and sleeping in shifts.

Chapter 16

Finn and Slade heard some interesting, hushed talk about Snake and his situation from the locals in the bar, but there was nothing that indicated he'd been in Brighton Beach for a long time. The general consensus seemed to be that people were savagely pleased to see Snake take a tumble from his position and they expected that he would be hunted down and killed. There was not a bit of sympathy expressed for him. Snake had clearly wronged many of his own people. Next, they turned their attention to Galina. They watched her comings and goings and it was obvious that she lived a quiet life, going to work every day at a commercial bakery, leaving at exactly the same time and arriving home every afternoon at the same time, except on Wednesday, when she stopped at the market and carted her groceries home in a little wheeled cart.

Finn approached one of her neighbors while she was at work and pretended to be an old acquaintance there to look her up. The neighbor was glad to talk but had little to tell. Galina lived alone, didn't have a social life to speak of, went to work every day, and minded her own business. The neighbor did say that she went to the library on Saturdays and she was a prolific reader. So finally, Finn and Slade went to her door after work and approached her directly. When she answered the door, a look of terror crossed her face.

"Who are you?" she asked fearfully.

"We're not here to do you any harm," Finn said quickly. "We just wanted to ask you a few questions."

"Did he send you?"

"Who do you mean?"

Her mouth remained stubbornly shut.

Slade said, "If you mean Viktor Vasiliev, then, no, we're no associates of his."

Galina's face was white as a sheet. "I don't have anything to do with him. I haven't seen him in many years and that's the way I like it."

"You have no contact with him at all?" Finn asked.

"No. Never. Now leave me alone; I have nothing to say to you."

She stepped back and closed the door firmly. Finn and Slade looked at each other and Finn said, "I think she was telling the truth."

"Yeah, me too. There's nothing here for us to find. Let's go."

After he contacted Jax, he got the okay to leave Brighton Beach. "Let's go home," he told Slade.

Things were quiet in Arizona as well. The only activity that had taken place at Luke Vale's house was when his daughter stopped by to visit him. But after the sun set, Coop thought he saw a movement in Luke's back yard.

"Joker, are you watching the video from inside the house?"

"Yeah, he and his daughter are just watching TV."

"I just saw something in the backyard."

"Shit! Someone just came in through the patio doors. He's in the shadows, I can't see him clearly."

But then they heard the newcomer say, "Hello, my brother. It's been a long time. No, no, don't get up. Stay right where you are."

Luke's voice was strained. "What are you doing here?"

"Your brother comes to visit after all these years and that's what you have to say?"

The woman gasped at his words. "Brother? Dad, what is this? I never knew you had a brother."

"Tsk tsk, Luka. You didn't even tell my lovely niece about me? One would almost think you don't even like me."

"What do you want, Viktor? I have a little money in the house. I don't know what else you could possibly want from me."

Snake sneered at him. "I don't need your money. You and your daughter are going to get me across the border and then you can go on your way. That's the only thing I need you for."

Coop and Joker were moving, quietly gathering weapons and silently leaving the car and creeping toward the house. They got to the window on the side of the house, where they had placed the video camera and saw that Luke and his daughter were on their feet. Snake had a gun on them and Coop signaled to Joker to go through the front door while he went in the same way that Snake had. They were both wearing earbuds and, on Coop's countdown, they burst into the house.

The three inside had moved through the kitchen and were headed for the door to the garage. Snake immediately grabbed the woman and held her tightly against him, backing toward the door.

"Put your weapons down," he snarled. "I'll kill them both."

Coop said calmly, "Okay, take it easy. Nobody has to get

hurt." He slowly sank toward the floor but as he set down his gun, Joker took a step to the left and chaos ensued.

Snake shoved backwards through the door after his brother and shots rang out. The woman Snake was holding screamed and went limp and he dropped her and slammed the door shut as he bolted through it. Joker rushed to the injured woman and they could hear the garage door sliding up and then the squeal of tires. As Coop made it through the doorway, the fancy car shot out of the garage and down the driveway. He ran after it, but it was too late. The car fishtailed, but quickly straightened and raced down the street. He rushed back into the house, swearing as he went.

"How is she?" he asked tensely.

"Not good. We need an ambulance fast."

Coop was already dialing 911 and when he finished the call, he dialed Jax and filled him in quickly. Jax said, "I'll get the police and FBI on it. Hopefully they can stop them. Stay with the girl. At least we know where they're headed. Are the police there yet?"

"No, nobody's here yet."

"Well, they will be. Don't say any more than that you were after Snake and he escaped with Vale. I'll get you out of there and then you go directly to the airstrip."

"Got it." Within an hour, they were in the car and headed to the desert.

Back at the barn, Jax clicked off his phone and sighed. Gunner had stepped in to get the Arizona police to let the two men go. "What a fucked-up mess. Our job is going to get a whole lot harder if Snake makes it across the border."

Chloe said, "Mexico will cooperate, won't they?"

"That's not the problem. He can take off through those South American countries and just vanish without a trace. I just hope the Feds get him."

"How's the woman? What's her name, anyway?" Chloe asked.

"Her name is Ruth Pinedo. She's married to a city council member there in Apache Junction. She's in surgery and hopefully she'll make it. The shot that hit her was from Snake's gun and that's a good thing for us. Plus, it puts more heat on Snake. I can guarantee that local police want him bad."

But Luke Vale knew the area well and he knew of a quiet place to make the crossing, and by morning, Jax had to accept that they had made it into Mexico. There was a massive information campaign going on to try to locate him, but there were no reported sightings. Two days after they had run, Luke's car was found, abandoned, with blood in it, and a few hours later the body of Luke Vale was found in the desert. His daughter, Ruth, made it through surgery and was expected to make a full recovery, but she was heartbroken at the loss of her father. All they could do was wait and hope that someone spotted Snake eventually and reported it. Gunner told Jax to take his team on a break and forget it for a while.

"Hey, guys, Gunner wants us to take a break now and I think he's right. Morale is pretty low and there's really nothing we can do as far as Snake is concerned. I think we need a break and after it's over, we'll be back on mission status. What do you think?"

Slade said moodily, "Yeah, I'd like to forget all this shit for a while. I vote yes."

Joker and Coop agreed and Finn nodded. "I think that's a good idea."

Shadow said, "I'm with you guys, but I wanted to point something out. If Snake gets to the point where the heat's off some, he's still going to want revenge for Ivan. That hasn't changed. I can't imagine a normal person in his place daring to come back into the States, but Snake isn't a normal person and I'll bet he'll try again."

Jax considered what he said and nodded slowly. "You're right. Especially now that he's lost his whole organization, I'd be willing to bet he's going to blame that on us too."

"Hell, he'll probably blame us for the fact that he "had" to kill his own brother." Joker looked disgusted as he said it.

"You're probably right," said Coop. "He's a real nutjob."

"So, I think we're rid of him for now, but eventually he's going to come after us." Jax looked savagely eager at the idea of facing him again.

"Next time he's not walking away," Coop said grimly.

"So, we're going to shelve the topic of Snake for the time being. Where do we want to take our break? Snow or beaches?"

"Shit, boss, we're going to get plenty of snow right here when winter comes," Joker said. "Definitely beaches."

There was a chorus of agreement and Jax said, "Okay, beaches it is. We don't usually go to the same place twice, but I really liked the island."

There was another chorus of approval and Coop said, "Oh, yeah. Great food, cold beer, warm water, lots of pretty girls. I'm for that."

"Everybody good with that?"

They were more than good with it; they were enthusiastic.

"Okay, I'll make the arrangements and we'll leave on Monday."

The island was just as good as they remembered it and they were all rejuvenated by their time there. Jax and Chloe spent a lot of time walking and talking and making love in the balmy breezes. But for Jax's part, the conversation only went so deep. He still didn't talk about himself or his past, even though Chloe tried to get him to tell her. He would clam up or change the subject, shrugging it off with a joke. So, she took what she could get, and she rarely thought about leaving the group anymore. Sometimes it seemed as if her entire life had been with them.

Their break went by way too quickly and they found themselves on a plane back to Montana. But they were all better for the time they had spent on the island and went back to work training and honing their skills when they got back. Shadow still watched for any sign of Snake, but there was nothing. Finally, the day came when Gunner contacted him with an assignment. Jax sent Chloe to the house while he presented the mission to his team. They started their preparations and were busy putting their background information together for the next couple of days.

Jax walked into the house looking for Chloe and found her sitting with her laptop in the den. He sat down beside her and said, "What are you working on?"

"Just writing some thoughts right now," Chloe said. "What's up?"

"We're going to be flying to our mission location; Gunner is sending his plane to the airstrip for us and we'll be gone for several days. I'd like you to come with us."

Chloe looked surprised. "Why?"

"I just don't like the idea of leaving you here alone for that long. I need the whole team together on this one and I'd rather know that you're in a cushy hotel room than here by yourself. You can read, shop, whatever you want, to keep yourself occupied, and you'll be safe."

Chloe said slowly, "All right. Can I take my laptop?"

Jax hesitated, his eyes searching her face. "What will you do with it?"

"It would be a good time to write, with not much else to do. I'm not going to run, Jax. I thought you'd have realized that by now. Although the world is probably safe enough for me now, I have nothing to run to. But it would be nice to get up in the morning and decide what I want to do without getting permission from anyone."

"You mean from me."

Chloe shrugged. "You *are* the one who locked me in and told me I can never leave. It's not that I want to leave, I just want the freedom of making my own choices."

"It's not really that I expect you to run. What I don't know if you understand is what could happen if you start surfing the internet, or send some emails; once you're out there, you can be found by someone with even just adequate skills. And if you're found, then we can be found." Jax was doing his best to be honest with her.

She looked a little startled. "I didn't really think about it that way. I know you're right about having a presence on the internet. If you just type in my name, you'll probably find me from before I walked into your world."

"I'm sure that's true."

"Then I give you my word that I won't sign onto the internet while we're gone. I'll work just as I do here."

"And when we get back, I'll see what Shadow can do about setting you up with an internet identity as Brynn Kelly."

Chloe's face lit up. "He can do that?"

"Yes, I'm sure he can. If he can make it safe for you that way, then I have no objection."

Chloe set her laptop on the table and threw her arms around him, kissing him passionately. "Thank you, Jax. It would honestly open up the world for me."

He kissed her again and thought that he would be willing to do just about anything to see her react this way. Finally, he drew away and said, "So that's settled. We're finished with the background and setting up our plan now, so we'll be ready to go in a few days."

"I'll be ready," Chloe promised, still smiling.

The next few days, it seemed like the pace of Chloe's life had picked up, become more stimulating. She finally decided that it was because she had plans and things to look forward to. The story she was writing was coming along nicely and once she finished it, she wanted to try to find a publisher who would accept it. The idea was beyond exciting and she thought that Brynn Kelly made a perfect pen name. She laughed a little at how she was getting ahead of herself, but she still felt a thrill of excitement when she thought about it. She packed for the trip she would be taking and Jax let her know that they were going to New Mexico so she could decide what to pack.

The team felt good about the upcoming mission. They had researched everything thoroughly and there were no mysteries complicating this one. It would be pretty straightforward and a natural gas explosion would be blamed for the death of the butcher they were after. He had run from his own country after he'd been directly responsible for the savage deaths of an entire village. He was the black sheep of an enormously wealthy family and their influence kept him protected. As long as it was judged to be a tragic accident, the family would be relieved to have him gone. He was so confident in the protection of his family that he didn't even bother to have a bodyguard or more than a rudimentary home security system.

The plane that Gunner sent for them was a luxuriously appointed private jet and they flew in comfort and loaded their equipment in the two SUVs that were waiting for them at the airport. They had reservations at an excellent inn in downtown Taos. Chloe was wildly excited about going there; the sightseeing would be wonderful. Jax gave her an extra stack of cash, even though she'd barely made a dent in the cash he'd given her back when Shadow gave her the identity of Brynn Kelly. She was traveling as Brynn Kelly and she had insisted that the guys call her that in the days leading up to the trip.

Brynn was wide-eyed as they drove to the hotel, gazing at the picturesque town and she was charmed when the inn where they would be staying was designed to look like a natural part of the town. Their room was spacious, spotlessly clean, and had a real wood burning fireplace that was ready to light. She was eager to explore the town the next day. They planned to be there for three days and she would be on her own for most of that time. And it turned out that she kept so busy seeing the sights that she barely opened her laptop. She bought some souvenirs and drank in the history of New Mexico and the art that the community was filled with.

On the evening of their second day, the crew went back out after dinner, and in the morning, the whole town was abuzz with the news of a house just outside of town that had exploded during the night. There was one person killed, found dead in his bed, and the preliminary report stated that it appeared to have been caused by a gas leak. The man who lived there was something of a recluse, although he was apparently a member of a wealthy family from Brazil. The crew checked out of the inn, spent a few more hours in Taos, then boarded the jet and flew back home. The entire mission had gone exactly according to plan and Jax felt like his group was back to normal, finally.

Chapter 17

There was a lull in the action after the crew returned to their base. They had spells of actual boredom and there were poker games and arm-wrestling tournaments as well as a few nights out on the town to try to keep them busy. Jax set up a horseshoe pit along one side of the barn and Slade was soon named the horseshoe expert. Shadow set up a social media presence for Brynn Kelly, and Chloe spent several days reading her history and background over and over until she was familiar with it. She thought back to the early days with Jax, when she had vowed to gain his trust, although then it was with an ulterior motive of finding a way to escape. Now, she had to admit to herself that she had no desire to escape. She shied away from the word "love" but she knew her feelings for him were deep and intense.

Jax came into the bedroom one afternoon, where Chloe was putting away her freshly folded laundry and said, "So Shadow tells me that he set up a social media identity for you and you've studied it until you're comfortable with it."

"Yes, he did. I know how to answer questions as Brynn Kelly."

He looked at her intently. "Chloe, can I trust you? Really trust you?"

She gazed at him for a long moment. "When you first made me a prisoner, all I thought about was finding a way to get free. I decided that the only chance I had was to make you trust me. The strange thing was that in the time it took to try to get you to trust me, *I* learned to trust *you*. I don't know exactly when it happened, but it did. I learned that what you told me about the danger I was in was all true and you really were protecting me. And it's not that I'm unable to look out for myself, but your world is a whole new level of danger that I knew nothing about. I know a lot more now; enough to know that I *need* your protection. So, yes, you can trust me. I would never do anything to bring more danger to any of us."

He gazed at her for a little longer and then nodded. "Okay. Then here is your internet password. Shadow has a list for you of all the things he set up, usernames and passwords. He'll give it to you whenever you ask for it."

"Can I ask you something?"

He looked wary but said, "Okay, go ahead."

"You said once to me that you had no idea if your mother could cook. Didn't you ever know your mother?"

He was silent for a minute and then he gave a sort of frustrated laugh. "What the hell made you think about that?"

"I don't know, it's just always bugged me."

"My mother ran off when I was two years old. And my old man made sure I heard about it, over and over. The only good family I had when I was a kid was my Aunt Nola and she died when I was twelve. I took off not long after that and I've been on my own ever since then."

Chloe's heart ached for him. No wonder he was so private. "Your mother was a fool."

It took him by surprise. "Well, I never knew her, not when I was old enough to remember, so it didn't hurt me any."

Right, Chloe thought, *it didn't hurt you at all.*

"Thank you for the password," she said with a warm smile, reaching up to kiss him.

"You're welcome," he murmured. "I'd like to continue this, but I've got some work to do yet."

"Okay. I'm making spaghetti and meatballs for dinner. I should get back to the kitchen."

"The guys are going to go back to taking their share of kitchen duty while things are slow like this. So, you'll have some more free time."

"Thanks!" She flashed him a brilliant smile and they walked down the stairs together.

A few days later, Chloe was sparring with Coop in the barn when she heard Shadow give a sharp exclamation. Jax turned toward him with a questioning look.

"I've got something important, boss," Shadow said tensely.

Jax rolled his chair over next to him and said, "What is it?"

"I found a record from a hospital for Galina Vasiliev. It wasn't in Brighton Beach; it was several hours away."

"What kind of a record?"

Shadow looked at him and said, "A birth record."

"Ivan and Galina had a child?" Jax was shocked.

"The baby was born eight months after Ivan was killed. And it was a boy."

Jax whistled. "Holy shit. And I'm guessing that Snake never knew this."

"That would be my guess, too. It's not hard to imagine that Galina didn't want him having anything to do with her son."

"No, couldn't blame her for that. What did you find about the kid?"

Shadow said, "So far, nothing. He'd only be, what, four years old? He's not even in school yet."

"Finn," Jax called and beckoned him over. "Did you and

Slade see any evidence of a child when you were checking out Galina Vasiliev?"

Finn looked surprised. "No, not at all. Nothing in the house or yard and we watched her go back and forth to work and her normal errands. There was never a kid."

Slade had come over to join them. "Maybe something happened to him."

Shadow shook his head. "If he died, there would be a death certificate."

Chloe and Coop came over to the group and asked what was going on. Jax explained it and then asked Chloe, "What do you think a mother would do in her shoes?"

"If she knew what really happened with her husband, what he did and how he died, she wouldn't want Snake anywhere near her child. She wouldn't want him to even *know* about him. If she had to, she would send him away if she felt he would be safer that way."

Coop raised an eyebrow and said, "Send her own baby away?"

Chloe nodded. "Yes, if she thought that's what she had to do to save him. It would be a sacrifice for her, but a mother will do anything to protect her child."

Jax's face was impassive. "We need to find out."

Shadow and Finn exchanged glances. Finn nodded and said, "If Snake found out he had a grandson, that would be enough to make him risk coming back into the country."

Jax nodded. "It would. Finn, you and Slade need to go back to Brighton Beach. Look for neighbors who have been there a long time, as long as Galina has. See if anybody remembers anything about a baby. Dig up everything you can before you talk to Galina. Make a trip to that hospital and see if you can find out anything else there. Maybe there's a nurse who remembers her. Four years is not that long. There's got to be somebody who remembers *something.* I'll get a plane arranged at the airstrip."

Half an hour later, the two men were ready to go. Jax drove them to the airstrip, so he could talk to them some more on the way. "We're going to be looking hard for any sign of Snake while you're gone. Once we find the kid, we have to figure out how to let Snake know about him. I don't think he'll be able to resist coming after him. He thinks there's nobody to carry on his name. He'll have to try to claim him."

"What are we going to do after we find out everything we need, boss?" Slade asked.

"Then we're going to set a trap," Jax said grimly.

"You sure it's worth it to let him know about the kid?" Finn asked.

"Worth it to get Snake? You bet your ass. And to make sure the kid stays safe, we can't fail. Taking Snake down is the only way in the world that kid will be safe."

Finn knew it was the truth. His phone vibrated and he answered it. When he hung up, he said, "That was Shadow. Gunner got his leaker. His office is all clear now."

"That's good to know," Jax said. He pulled into the lot at the airstrip and went inside with his men. "Everything ready?" he asked the guy at the counter. At his nod, Jax said, "You guys be careful and stay in touch. We'll do the same." He waited until their plane was in the air and then started back to base.

Jax walked into the barn to find a bustle of activity. Shadow was busily sending messages to every contact he had, urging them to listen and look, and to let him know immediately if they saw or heard anything about Snake. Joker and Coop were cleaning guns and Chloe was apparently in the house. Shadow nodded at him and Jax sat down beside him.

"How's it going?" Jax asked.

"Just planting seeds and looking for sprouts. I'm giving

every contact I've got a little push to get them to look and listen a bit harder. You might want to go talk to Chloe. She was kind of upset when you left."

Jax looked bewildered. "Upset about what?"

"I think she gathered from the conversation that you're planning to use the kid as a lure for Snake."

"Shit," Jax muttered. "All right, I'll be back." He went to the house, where he found Chloe in the kitchen, banging pots and pans and not accomplishing much. "What's going on?"

She whirled around and pointed a finger at him. "You tell me. Are you really planning to use that little boy as a lure for a murdering monster?"

Jax's temper rose quickly. "That's not exactly the way I'd put it and it's not really your business."

"Not my business?" Her voice rose indignantly. "The monster who wants all of us dead is not my business?"

"Dammit, Chloe, of course Snake is your business in that respect. But what I have to do to get him is not your problem."

"How could you? How could you put a little boy in danger to get what you want?"

Now he was pissed. "It's not to get something I want. And, for your information, the only way that little boy will *ever* be safe is if Snake dies. As long as his so-called *grandfather* is alive, that kid is in danger. Snake has to go so that little boy can live a safe and free life. And be back with his mother, where he belongs."

"But... but to *use* him as bait. It's just wrong!"

"You know something, Chloe? You just told me a few days ago that I could trust you and I accepted that as it was given. Maybe you ought to have a little trust in me and my ability to do what needs to be done and do it without collateral damage. Collateral damage is something I can't stand. It's something I do everything I possibly can to avoid. Once in a while, an accident happens, like what happened to Ruth Pinedo. But that was Snake's bullet, not ours, that struck her. So, a little trust from you would be damn nice."

He left her staring after him, her mouth open. She felt a little bit ashamed of the things she'd said to him, but what else was she supposed to think? He really was going to use a little boy for bait, wasn't he? She thought back over what he had said and realized that he hadn't really spelled it out that way. But she couldn't imagine what else he could be planning. When her head began to ache, she had to stop thinking about it. She found comfort in cooking and made a pot full of potato and bacon soup. She refused to let herself think about the fact that it was one of Jax's favorite things.

When everyone came in at the end of the afternoon, Chloe was subdued, going about her business without saying much. It was dark when Finn called to let Jax know they had arrived in Brighton Beach and checked into a hotel. They would start their search first thing in the morning. After dinner, Coop and Joker took care of the dishes and Chloe went upstairs early. When Jax finally went up, he found her huddled in the chair, hugging her knees and wearing her pajamas.

She said, "Jax, I'm sorry if I jumped to conclusions about what you're going to do. You didn't actually say you're going to use him as bait. Just, please don't let him get hurt, please!"

He gave her an unsmiling look and said, "Nothing is going to happen to him. Or to his mother. But Snake has to go."

Chloe gulped and said, "Okay. If you say nothing is going to happen to him, then I believe you. I don't know what you're going to do, but I have to trust you to keep them safe."

Jax gave her a long look and then said gruffly, "The soup was damn good."

Chloe smiled a little. "I remembered it's one of your favorites."

"Yeah, I thought you did." He went to the shower and

Chloe turned off the light, leaving only the little bedside lamp on, and crawled into bed.

Jax came out clad only in a towel and tossed it over the laundry hamper before he got into bed beside her. He put his arms around her and she snuggled close, breathing in his clean, manly scent and laying her head on his muscular chest.

"What happened to your pajamas?" he asked softly.

"Mm, I decided I didn't need them," she murmured as he stroked her hair and then lifted her mouth to his.

He kissed her, gently at first, then probing deeper into her sweetness, his tongue playing lazily with hers. She felt the familiar heat crawl through her belly and the tightening of her nipples and her pussy. Her skin tingled as he stroked her throat with his fingertips and traced a languid line all the way down, between her breasts, shivering across her belly and then tugging lightly at the down between her legs. A shudder ran down her spine and gooseflesh was raised on her bare skin, all over her body. Jax kissed her shoulder and her eyelids, nuzzled her ear, and nibbled at her earlobe, making her shiver with delight. Her entire body was humming, vibrating with little quivers of pleasure, and she felt the trickle of her feminine juices between her thighs.

When Jax kissed the inside of her wrist, she whimpered at the heat that washed over her. He nipped at the tender skin there and she squirmed as her body responded. She felt like tiny sparks of electricity were jumping off her skin at every touch and the hard, tender tips of her breasts ached for his touch, his mouth. He was driving her mad with his light, teasing little touches, nibbles, and gentle pinches. She squirmed, straining toward him, but he went on with his teasing. Just when she thought she'd die if he didn't touch her engorged breasts, he fastened his mouth over one rosy teat and suckled hard. Her back arched and she moaned at the heavenly sensation. He obliged her by cupping the other breast in his hand and rolling the tip between his fingers and thumb. Chloe gasped at the shockwaves that ran through her, from those tender, swollen teats, down through her belly and straight to her aching pussy. The muscles in her groin were clenching, burning for him, and she was dripping her sweet juices. She thought incoherently that it wasn't possible to go on this way without having him inside her.

He turned her over and trailed a burning line of kisses down her spine and then he smacked her bottom sharply, bringing a little gasp of surprise from her. He smacked the other cheek, and her back arched, to bring her bottom up to meet his slaps. He spanked her for a few minutes and the pain was pleasure, building and building, until she craved the spanking, craved the heat in her reddening ass. And when he stopped spanking her, she felt a sharp pang of disappointment, but then he turned her back over and her legs fell apart, her pussy burning and aching with frantic need. He kissed the hollow at the top of her thigh and she whimpered wordlessly her need for him. His tongue darted out and licked at her belly button and she wriggled mindlessly, unable to reach his rigid shaft. He lowered his head and nuzzled her pubis, his breath burning her swollen folds. His tongue darted out again and circled the tender bud of her clit and she cried out, begging for more.

Jax slid a finger between the slick, tender folds, stroking and exploring while his tongue teased her clit. When he pushed two fingers into her tight, hot channel, she cried out again and her heels drummed the mattress as she finally reached his steely member and her fingers wrapped around him. He inserted another finger and thrust deep into her and she stroked the full length of him, squeezing and rubbing her thumb over the soft, velvety head. She kept it up until he moaned, thrusting against her hand. His cock was aching, longing to be buried deep inside her and when he pulled his hand away, she flipped him over on his back and straddled him. She rubbed her hot, wet pussy up and down his iron hard shaft and finally settled down on him, sinking down until he filled her. Then she rose slowly up and sank down again, over and over, gradually quickening the pace until she was riding him hard and fast. He clutched her tender, heated cheeks and pulled her down harder and her arousal grew, filling her with urgency, growing until she knew it had to explode. Her thighs were quivering, her pussy muscles were clenching, and she couldn't stop the orgasm. Her vision exploded with flashes of light, as if there were fireworks going off in the room, and her pussy clenched with strong spasms as the climax rocked her with shudders of pure pleasure. Chloe bit her lip hard to contain the scream, quivering and shaking.

Still, she rode Jax until he arched his back, grinding against her and he exploded with his own climax, emptying himself in her sweet, hot center, pulsing and throbbing with his release. The room spun around them and they shivered together, shaken by the power of their coupling. Jax knew he would never get enough of her, he wanted her endlessly; every time he looked at her, his cock ached with desire for her. He'd never felt anything like it in his life and he never wanted to let her go. Chloe felt a powerful wave of tenderness wash over her and she knew she would be his anytime he wanted her. It wasn't within her powers to resist him. He was everything she wanted and she knew she was truly his. They lay there together for a long time until they began to grow cold and Jax pulled the blankets up over them. Without words, they drifted on the aftermath of their lovemaking until they were finally asleep.

Chapter 18

Finn and Slade hit paydirt when they went to the hospital where Galina had given birth. They were able to look at the birth certificate after showing their false FBI IDs and they found that Galina had filled it out completely, including the father, her husband, Ivan. Maybe she had thought it might be useful to her someday but, in any case, she had filled it out correctly. She had named the child Nikolai. With some more questioning, they found a nurse who remembered Galina. The nurse had been in the labor and delivery and remembered that Galina had been alone and had been completely stoic until her baby was placed in her arms. Then she wept, great wracking sobs until the nurse had to take the baby so Galina could cry herself out.

The nurse said, "It was so sad. She said her husband had died in an accident just a few months before and her son would never know him. It was funny, though, she didn't cry then. In fact, she looked strange… kind of *victorious* when she said the baby would never know him. She left the next day, still alone. She took a taxi. Poor woman."

Finn and Slade thanked her and then drove back to

Brighton Beach. It was time for Galina to be at work, so they slipped into the house and searched for evidence of a child. The only thing they found was a single photo of a little boy. Written on the back, was Nikolai, age 2. They left the house and went to find some neighbors to talk to. It took a couple of hours, but they finally found one woman who, after a few questions, said that she did have a vague memory of a baby at Galina's house. She assumed someone was visiting and she said it wasn't very long until there was no baby there anymore. No one else had any memory of a child at Galina's and they finally exhausted all the neighbors. Next, they went to the personnel offices at the place where Galina worked and again showed their fake IDs and asked to see Galina's employment file.

The woman in the personnel office had to check with her supervisor, who came out to talk to them. "Is there a problem? Has Galina gotten into some kind of trouble?"

"No, not at all," Finn assured her. "There was a possible distant relative who inherited an estate that had been confiscated by the government. It's being released now and we have to locate everyone who might have a claim to the money."

The supervisor looked at them strangely and said, "Isn't that an odd kind of thing for the FBI to be handling?"

Slade said, "Not in this case. It was an FBI case that resulted in the seizure, so we're responsible for closing it out too."

"Oh, I see," said the woman. "Very well. Sonia, go ahead and give them the file and show them to the empty office so they can go over it privately."

In going through the file, they discovered that Galina kept medical insurance for her son, Nikolai, who resided with her mother, near Syracuse. She also named him as her life insurance beneficiary and Finn made a note of the address of Galina's mother. They returned the file when they were finished and stood on the sidewalk a few minutes later.

Finn said, "Looks like we're going to Syracuse."

Slade said, "I'll drive, you call the boss."

Jax put Shadow on the task of looking up Galina's mother and let Finn know that they hadn't uncovered anything on Snake yet. "Let me know what you find," he said as he hung up.

It only took a short time for Shadow to say, "I don't know who this woman is, but she's not Galina's mother. Galina's parents both died in Russia and then Galina was brought here by an uncle. She was only sixteen then and she lived with her uncle until she married Ivan. The uncle went back to Russia to stay a few years ago."

Jax said, "Interesting. The mystery gets deeper and deeper."

Chloe was listening and she said, "Poor Galina, this is terrible. Her husband was so evil that she had to give up her baby to keep him safe from his own grandfather. It's awful."

Jax said darkly, "Yeah, it's way past time to put him down like the mad dog that he is."

Chloe had to admit he was right. Everyone would be better off with Snake dead. "Where are they going now?"

"To the address they got for Galina's mother. It's in the Syracuse area. It's going to take them at least four hours to get there." Jax called Slade back and relayed the information Shadow had found. "Be careful. Shadow's looking up the address now to try to get info on who really lives there."

In just minutes, Shadow said, "Bingo. The property is owned by Jed and Mary Decker. Jed Decker passed away five years ago and his wife, Mary, still lives there. She's fifty-two and has never remarried. Their house was paid off and Jed had a life insurance policy that pays the bills and Mary picks up some extra money by writing a couple of columns for the local newspaper. Household stuff, you know. She works from home and emails her columns to the paper. Just like Galina, she lives a quiet life. Anyway, there's nothing threatening there for Finn and Slade to worry about."

"Okay, I'll let them know."

Shadow turned his attention back to the computer and, a few minutes later, he exclaimed, "Shit! Boss, somebody reported a sighting of Snake!"

Jax turned quickly to him. "Where?"

"Bolivia. The posters all say he's to be considered armed and dangerous and if spotted, just report it."

Jax thought for a bit. "You think it's for real or someone just thinking they saw the guy from the poster?"

"Hard telling. If we get another report, I'd say he's really there."

"Shadow, see if you can find anyone who Snake could still consider loyal to him. We don't need to contact him, we just need a name that Snake would believe."

Shadow smiled. "I think I get where you're going with this, boss."

Jax gave him a grim smile in return. His voice was quiet but fierce when he said, "We're going to get this son of a bitch."

It was a lot harder task to unearth someone who could be loyal to Snake than to find the owners of a house in New York, but Shadow set to work.

Slade parked on the street under a big shade tree a couple of houses down from the one they were looking for. It was a neat, well-kept Craftsman style home with a wide front porch and flower beds along the front of the house, with more big shade trees in the yard. There was a white picket fence around the backyard, and looking through binoculars, Finn could see a swing set and a wading pool. They watched for a while and a mail carrier walked up to the porch to put the mail in the box beside the door. But the door opened and a cheerful looking woman stepped out. The mail carrier handed her the mail and they talked for a minute before he went on his way with a last wave at what was most likely Mary Decker. A few more minutes went by, and they heard the bang of a door, then a little boy ran into the back yard, followed by the woman they'd already seen.

"Aunt Mary! Will you push me?" He was running to the swing set and Mary laughed and followed him.

They couldn't hear her answer, but they watched as she pushed him on the swing, with him constantly shouting, "Higher! Higher!"

Finn was snapping pictures and finally, he said, "Well, should we go talk to her?"

Slade said, "Might as well. We're not going to get much else sitting here."

They got out of the car and walked up to the house, ringing the bell at the front door. When there was no answer and they could still hear the little boy shouting and laughing, they walked around to the backyard. The woman froze when she saw them and quickly stopped the swing and bent down to tell the little boy something. He ran immediately for the house and went inside.

Mary walked over to them cautiously. "Who are you? And what do you want?"

"We need to talk to you," Finn said. "Are you Mary Decker?"

"No, no, no. That's not how this is going to go. Who are *you?*"

"I'm Jack Fox and this is Robert Maxwell. We're with the FBI. If you'll step closer, we'll show you our IDs."

She looked them over for a few seconds and then walked closer. They both offered their IDs and she studied them carefully before she spoke again. "Okay, next question; what do you want?"

"We need to ask you some questions about Galina Vasiliev."

Panic crossed her face immediately and she struggled to regain her composure. Her voice trembled when she said, "I don't know any Galina Vasiliev."

Finn said gently, "We know that's not true. We're not here to cause any trouble for her or you. We're here because we need to help. That little boy deserves to live with his mother and be safe and secure. That's our job."

She stared at them and tears filled her eyes. "I don't know if I can believe you. It could be a trick."

"Can we go inside and talk? We'll tell you what we know and what we plan to do."

She hesitated for a full minute and then nodded her head jerkily. "Okay." She opened the gate and let them in, then led them into the house. The little boy looked up, his eyes wide and scared.

"Don't you bother my Aunt Mary!" he snapped fiercely.

"It's okay, Nicky. I let them in."

He walked over to her and hugged her legs, giving the two men the evil eye.

Mary said, "Why don't we all sit down? Nicky, you go get yourself a cookie from the cookie jar and then go play in your room."

He started to argue, but she gave him a look and he scowled and said, "Okay. But if you need help, you just call me."

"I will, I promise. Now go on."

After he trudged away, Finn said, "We know that Galina is Nicky's mother and we have a pretty good picture of why he's living here. It was more important to her to keep him safe than to have him with her. It was a helluva sacrifice on her part. We know all about why Nicky's in danger and we know how to make sure that he's safe for the rest of his life."

"How can you do that? There's only one way that could happen and it's impossible."

Finn said, "No, it's not impossible. It's our job, our mission. The subject we're after has been responsible for unspeakable acts of violence and normal law enforcement procedures are useless against him, as you know. There are people who can't be touched by the law and he's one of them."

The look on her face told them that she knew damn well that was true. "So why are you talking to me? What does any of this have to do with me?"

Slade said, "We had to find Nicky. We have to make sure that he's in a safe place and protected when we make our move."

Her face was full of doubt and suspicion at his words. "He was safe here until you showed up."

Slade said, "The two of you are in hiding, aren't you? He can't be with his mother because it's too risky. In another year, he'll be school age. What happens then? He'll be in the system, which means he can be found."

The struggle on her face showed that she had been thinking about exactly that. "I could homeschool him," she said weakly.

"So, he doesn't have friends, or sports, or any of the normal things kids do. And you'll still be hiding and living in fear. There's only one way to put an end to it all."

She still wasn't convinced.

Finn asked, "How long have you known Galina?"

"Ever since she came to the States. Her uncle brought her here and they lived near here. We became best friends right away, even with the age difference between us. She was such a sweet girl and so happy. When she met her husband, she was swept off her feet. But after they were married, everything changed."

Finn probed gently. "How did it change?"

"He would go away a lot; he told her the traveling was part of his job. When he would come back, he would be… different. Sort of wild, *exhilarated,* I guess would be a good word. He would be insatiable, for her, if you know what I mean. It scared her; he would hurt her during sex. It got worse and worse and, one day, she overheard him talking on the phone to someone, bragging about what he did to young girls. From that day on, she was terrified. When he died in that accident, it was the best thing that ever happened to her, until later, when she found out she was pregnant.

"At first, she was upset about having *his* child. But she made up her mind that the baby would be just as much hers as his, and there was no reason he had to be like him. She was positive from the beginning that she would have a boy. And she took good care of herself and she was happy. And then she found out who Ivan's father really was. And she knew right away that if he found out about the baby, he would take him. She started right then, making plans to make him disappear so that he would have a chance to be safe. It broke her heart, but she had to send him away."

Finn studied her for a long minute. "It wasn't an accident that took Ivan." He said it quietly but firmly.

Mary's eyes widened in shock and she sucked in a sharp little breath. "You? That was you?"

"Now do you believe that we want to protect Nicky and his mother?"

"Oh, my God. It's really true."

"It is. Now we need to take all three of you to a safe place. We have to go get Galina and we need you to help us convince her. Pack a bag for yourself and for Nicky and we'll get you out of here."

She looked around helplessly. "But this is my home."

Finn said, "When this is all over, you'll be able to come back. You'll be able to do what you want and go where you want without fear. And Galina and Nicky will be able to do the same. Doesn't that sound good?"

She sighed wearily. "It sounds like heaven. All right, I won't be long."

They heard her talking to the little boy and in a short time, the two of them walked in with their bags. They had her lock up her house and she parked her car in the garage, retrieving Nicky's car seat, then locked the car too. A minute later, they were all in the big black SUV and starting the drive to Brighton Beach. Slade sent a text to Jax and let him know what they were doing. It was late when they got to Galina's house and Nicky had slept in the car for a couple of hours. When they went to the door, it took a long minute for Galina to answer it. She was obviously looking at them through the peephole and Finn held up his ID.

"What do you want?" she asked, speaking from behind the closed door.

In answer, Finn motioned for Mary to step in front of the door and they heard a muffled cry before the door was thrown open. Galina's face was full of fear as she looked wildly at them.

Finn said quickly, "We're not here to harm you; we need to talk to you."

She stepped back so they could come in and she couldn't take her eyes off her son, gazing hungrily at him. "What's going on? Why are you here?" she asked Mary.

Mary said, "Let them explain."

Nicky raised his head and stared at Galina. "You're the

lady my Aunt Mary tells me about. She said someday I would meet you. She shows me your picture."

"And you're Nicky," Galina said unsteadily. "Your Aunt Mary tells me about you too. She told me that you're a smart, brave boy."

"I am!" Nicky declared.

They settled the little boy down in the living room to watch cartoons, turning it up a little on the loud side, and the adults moved to the kitchen to talk.

Galina listened to what Finn had to say and then she turned her attention to Mary. "Is this what they told you?"

Mary nodded and said, "Exactly what they told me."

Galina turned a fierce gaze on Finn and said bitterly, "So you want to use my son as bait for Viktor! That's what you're really saying, aren't you? And while you're at it, you'll be using me too and probably even Mary."

Finn gave her a level look. "You will all be protected. At all costs, you will be protected."

"You don't know what you're dealing with. Nobody has ever beaten the Snake. He's ruthless and willing to do any kind of evil thing necessary to get what he wants."

"He doesn't have the power now that he once had. He stepped over the line and Russia has put him on the list to be eliminated. His organization has been taken from him and he's on the run. We have to get him to come back to the United States."

"If Russia has put him on a list, then let Russia get him. Leave us out of it."

Finn leaned forward and said, "Russia will not care about collateral damage to any of you. They won't lift a finger to protect you. If they feel the easiest way to get him is to give you up, then that's what they'll do. Our boss despises collateral damage and so do the rest of us. We are your best hope."

Galina pressed her fingers to her forehead and sat silently

for a long minute. "You haven't given me any choice, have you? May you all burn in hell if anything happens to my son."

Finn said steadily, "Nothing will happen to him; you have my word. Any of us won't hesitate to put our own lives on the line to make sure of that. Now pack a bag and be quick about it."

Chapter 19

Slade drove to the airstrip and Finn sent a text to Jax. *On our way to the airstrip with all three subjects. Will text again when we get in the air.*

Jax told his men, "They got them. They should be in the air within two hours. Shadow, any progress on that name we need?"

Shadow said, "Still looking, boss. Snake is a very unpopular man, it seems."

"That's not hard to believe. He killed his own brother, for God's sake. But we need a name, and we need it badly."

"I'm looking back to when Snake first got to the US, before he got an organization underneath him, when he actually needed help from people."

"Good, there has to be someone whose word he would believe."

But when the time came to go to the airstrip to pick up the group, Shadow was still searching. Jax went to talk to Chloe before he left.

"Chloe, Finn and Slade are landing soon and they have

Galina and her son with them, the woman who's been raising the boy, too. He doesn't know that Galina is his mother and I suspect that she won't tell him until after she knows Snake is taken care of. It would help if you could try to make them feel more comfortable about being here. They're probably going to be suspicious and scared, especially Galina."

Chloe gave him a long, searching look. "I'll do my best," she said finally. "Do you know exactly what you're going to do? How you're going to go about this?"

Jax said, "That's something I can't talk about now. Every operation is top secret and this one has to be the best kept secret that ever happened, for everyone's sake."

"All right; I'll do what I can." She felt a pang of disappointment that he wouldn't confide in her. And she still felt nervous about the whole thing, wondering exactly how Jax was going to go about getting access to Snake.

"Thanks. I'll be back as soon as I can." He left without kissing her, sensing her mood and not wishing to answer any more questions.

When Jax got back, he brought the two women and the little boy directly into the house to introduce them to Chloe. All the men knew that while they had "guests", Chloe would be known strictly as Brynn Kelly. They all went by their nicknames, so they weren't concerned about spilling their real identities. Chloe had practiced at it enough that she had learned to react naturally to being called Brynn. Galina and Mary looked weary and apprehensive and Nicky gazed around with wide eyes at the largest and nicest house he'd ever been in.

Chloe greeted them all with gracious words and a quiet smile. "Welcome to our home," said Chloe. "If you need anything at all, just ask me. Let me show you around a little."

She showed them around the house and then led them upstairs. Joker had moved into Coop's room and cleaned out his for the guests. The room had two twin beds and they had moved a portable bed in as well. Fortunately, the room was spacious.

"I hope you're okay with sharing a room. If not, one of the guys can move out to the barn. Just say the word and we'll move things around."

Galina said quickly, "No, we'd rather be together."

"Okay, good, I thought you might." She showed them the bathroom and the closet where fresh towels and linens were kept. "We want you to be comfortable while you're here."

Galina said softly, "There's nothing comfortable about this. But we'll keep up the show for Nicky's sake. And *nothing* had better happen to him."

Chloe gazed at her steadily. "We don't want anything to happen to *any* of you. That's the whole point of all of this. And when it's over, you'll be free."

There were tears in Galina's eyes and she whispered fiercely, "You'd better be telling the truth!"

Chloe couldn't blame her for her feelings. She would be just as upset if she were in the other woman's shoes. "Feel free to use the library or the den whenever you want. The library is stocked with all kinds of books and there are a ton of movies to watch. We'll have dinner at six; maybe you'd like to rest or just relax for a while before that."

Galina waved her off and said, "We'll be fine."

So, Chloe walked out and down the stairs, hearing the door close firmly behind her. She went to the kitchen and started dinner, thinking about the woman upstairs. She couldn't imagine what it had been like to give up her own child in order to keep his life safe. Jax and his men *had* to be successful in getting rid of Snake permanently. Her skin crawled at the thought of him and the evil he had done. It had to end.

Nicky came clattering down the stairs and Chloe smiled,

thinking that at least he had lived a safe and happy life so far. Mary followed him into the kitchen and looked at Chloe hesitantly.

"Galina is resting. Nicky wants to watch a movie and he swears he's terribly hungry."

Chloe smiled. "I think growing boys are always hungry, don't you? And what is your favorite thing to eat, Nicky?"

"Pizza," he said promptly, "and then peanut butter and jelly. And chips."

"Well, we don't have any pizza in the house, but I can fix you right up with peanut butter and jelly. Here, Mary, I'll show you where things are so if I'm not around and he needs a sandwich, you go right ahead and help yourselves."

Nicky chattered while Chloe got out a paper plate and showed the pantry to Mary, grabbing bread and peanut butter and handing it to Mary. She hoped to get her to relax a little by having her join in with making Nicky's snack.

"Nicky, could you get the jelly out of the refrigerator? There's grape and strawberry, which do you like the best?"

"I like grape, that's what Aunt Mary gives me."

"I like grape too. And when I have a peanut butter and jelly sandwich, I like a glass of milk with it. How about you?"

He nodded vigorously and as Chloe finished spreading peanut butter on a slice of bread, she pointed to the cupboard above the coffee pot and asked, "Mary, could you grab a glass from that cupboard? And thank you for getting me the jelly, Nicky."

"That's a big jar of jelly," he observed solemnly.

Chloe laughed. "That's because all those guys have big appetites. And guess what? They have to take their turns working in the kitchen too. If I do the cooking, I don't have to clean up the mess."

Nicky looked impressed. "That's cool. Aunt Mary has to

do it all. Except I have to put my dishes in the sink. Once I dropped a glass in there and it broke all over the sink. So, Aunt Mary got me a stool so I can reach better."

Mary had relaxed enough to say, "I did, because you aren't going to get out of doing your share just because you're short."

Chloe laughed and said, "I love that logic. Would you like something to snack on, Mary?"

"That bowl of fruit looks awfully good," she answered after a second's hesitation.

"Please, help yourself."

Chloe handed the plate with the sandwich and potato chips on it to Nicky and he set it on the table and then seated himself there. Mary got him a glass of milk and then she chose a fat orange from the bowl and sat down with him, taking a napkin from the holder on the table. The atmosphere had lightened considerably and after they had eaten, Mary took Nicky to the den to find a movie.

"The remote controls should be right on the coffee table in there," said Chloe. "Yell if you need any help with it."

A few minutes went by and then Mary came back into the kitchen. "Can I help you with dinner?" she asked.

"Sure, I'd love to have help," Chloe said. "I'm making chicken and noodles and mashed potatoes. What's Nicky's favorite kind of vegetable?"

"He likes corn the best, but he'll eat most kinds of vegetables. It was one of the things I got him used to when he was really little. I didn't want him to grow into a picky eater, so he learned to try everything I offered to him. Then, if there was something that he really didn't like, he didn't have to eat it again. So, he likes most things."

"That's really smart. We usually have a salad along with whatever else we're having. I wasn't kidding when I said those guys have big appetites."

The two women worked together companionably and just as they were finishing up, Galina came into the room. "Where's Nicky?" she asked tensely.

Mary said, "He's watching The Lion King in the den. He had a snack first; he said he was starving."

Galina looked upset. "I don't... I don't even *know* him," she said.

Chloe said, "That can all change now."

"No, it can't! Nothing can change until this gets done. And I'm not going to believe it can get done until it actually happens. I can't take any stupid chances."

"But you can still spend time with him and get to know him, without telling him everything," Chloe pointed out.

"But even if it really does happen, how can I ever explain it all to him?"

Now Mary spoke up. "We get through this first and then we'll figure it out. He's young, he'll adapt and he'll understand, especially when he gets older."

Chloe said, "That's all we have to do for dinner for the time being. Will you ladies join me for a glass of wine?"

Mary said, "That sounds wonderful. I'd love to."

Galina hesitated but finally said, "All right, yes, that sounds good."

Chloe grinned and said, "We can take it to the den and watch a little Lion King with Nicky."

Galina said hungrily, "That sounds even better."

They joined the little boy in the den and sipped their wine while they watched the movie with him, although Galina watched him much more than she watched the movie. She relaxed a bit as she spent time with her son and he chattered away to her without a bit of shyness. He even made her laugh several times and Chloe smiled as she watched. But when the men came in for dinner, Galina stiffened up immediately and it was obvious just how deeply her distrust and fear ran. She was silent through dinner, although Nicky loved talking to them all. Coop and Joker were assigned to kitchen duty and it wasn't long after dinner when the effects of the traveling caught up with Nicky and the two women took him upstairs to their room. Jax and Chloe went up next so they could talk over the day.

"How are they doing?" Jax asked.

"Nicky's fine, as you could see for yourself. Mary has already relaxed a lot; I think she'll be fine in a couple of days. Galina is scared to death and worried about how she's going to handle everything. She doesn't really believe that you're going to be able to pull this off and she's literally afraid for their lives."

Jax said, "Shadow's trying to find someone who Snake would trust, or at least believe, if he heard that he had some information. But he's not having much luck and we need it."

"So, what else do you have going on?"

"If we don't find someone whose name we could use to plant some information, then all we can do is wait and hope someone spots him and then we can find a way to get him to come back into the country."

Chloe stared at him. "Jax, that sure sounds a lot like you're still planning to use that little boy as bait."

He gave her a stony look. "I am not planning to put that kid in any kind of danger."

"But you're going to try to let Snake know about his existence, aren't you?"

"There's no other way to get to Snake. He has to come back to the States for us to be able to get him."

"And you really don't think that's enough to put Nicky in danger?"

"No, I don't. He's never going to get near the kid. Where do you think he'll go? He'll go to Brighton Beach. He'll think that Galina has him and he'll go there looking for her. Nobody at all knows about us being here. Not even Gunner knows where we are. This is the safest place in the world for those three people."

Chloe was shaking her head. "I don't like this, Jax. Isn't Russia after him? Why not let them take care of their own dirty work?"

"Because Russia wouldn't hesitate for a second to use Nicky and Galina to get Snake. And they wouldn't give a shit about sacrificing them to get it done. They wouldn't think twice about it."

Chloe shivered. "God," she whispered, "that's so evil."

"Yeah, it is," Jax said grimly. "This is one ugly business. In fact, all our business is ugly. And that's another reason we have to put an end to Snake. It's not just for Nicky and Galina, it's for you. The only way for you to be free of this shitty life we lead is for Snake to be dead and gone. Then you can finally have your life back."

Chloe's heart sank to the pit of her stomach. "You want to be rid of me?" she whispered.

Roughly, he said, "It's not about what I want, Chloe. It's about you and your life, your freedom. I had to keep you safe and the only way to do it was to keep you with me. But if Snake is dead and his organization is destroyed, then there's nothing holding you here anymore. You can do what you want, make your own decisions. My life is right smack in the middle of evil things every day. You don't have to live with that. Not if Snake is gone."

The idea of walking away from him took her breath away and a searing pain stabbed her in the heart. She turned away so that he wouldn't see the tears that sprang to her eyes and Jax watched her, his own heart turned to stone. It was going to kill him to watch her go, but he had no right to keep her. He was not worthy of her; he'd done things that he could never bear to admit to her and she deserved better. He was no better than the people he hunted, he just happened to stand on the right side of the fence while they were considered to be the evil ones. The fact that his actions were "justified" just wasn't good enough. It was ugly and dangerous and she deserved much better. Once she was gone, his heart would be dead, but she would be safe and she could live her life without his shadows hanging over her head.

"I'm going to take a shower," Jax said heavily.

When he closed the bathroom door, she drew up her knees and wrapped her arms around them, lowering her head to her knees. She was filled with pain. He didn't want her to stay once Snake was gone. She thought the loss might kill her and she didn't know any way to make him change his mind. When he came back out, he was dressed in clean clothes.

"I'm going out to the barn for a while. I've got some work to do."

Chloe stood in the shower for a long time, the tears pouring down her face as the ache in her heart refused to subside. It was late when he crept quietly into the dark bedroom, where she lay in bed, still wide awake. He got into bed and sometime much later, she finally drifted into a restless sleep. When she woke in the morning, he was already up and gone and she got dressed mechanically, her head aching. It was early afternoon when she finally saw him as the guys came in for lunch and all the conversation was superficial.

Several days passed that way and Chloe began to feel a slow burn that got a little hotter each day. She thought about the past few months and decided that she wasn't going to let him make her leave. She had a mind of her own, she was a grown woman, and she could make her own choices. Feeling better and stronger, her attitude changed and she got her old sassiness back. One evening after dinner when Jax made his move to go back out to the barn, she waited a few minutes and then followed him out there. He was the only one in the barn and she locked the door behind herself when she went in. He was seated at the computer, staring at the screen, and she walked up behind him and put her arms around his neck.

"Shit! You scared the crap out of me! What are you doing out here?"

"Well, you don't seem to want to come to bed with me at night, so I came out here to talk to you," she said.

"I've been busy," he hedged.

"Yeah, you look busy; you're just sitting there staring at the screen. How long has the same thing been on it?"

"What exactly is it that you wanted to talk about, Chloe?"

She pulled out a chair and sat down beside him. "I want you to tell me more about your life, about you, about what you do that seems to weigh on you so heavily."

He shook his head and said firmly, "I'm not going to do that. You don't need to know those things."

"Oh, really? It seems to me that you know pretty much everything about me, but your life is one big fucking secret. We've shared some of the most intimate things that a man and woman can possibly share, but you won't tell me a damn thing about your life? That doesn't cut it, Jax, and I'm not having it. You're going to talk to me."

She had balls, he had to admit that. "Chloe, it's best for you not to know—"

"Just stop it! I'm not five, I'm a grown woman. I've seen enough to have a pretty good idea of what you do and it hasn't scared me off yet. Now, I'm not asking you to tell me your entire life story right now. Start with one thing. The only thing you've told me was that your mother ran off when you were little and you never knew her and apparently your father was a shit. I thought you were going to start letting me into your life then, but you clammed right back up and didn't tell me any more. Tell me, Jax. Tell me what happened after your aunt died and you went off on your own. You said you were only twelve. Tell me."

He looked at her face, at the earnest warmth in her eyes, and he wavered. Could she really live with the man he was? Slowly, he said, "We lived in Texas. I had to find a way to eat, a place to sleep, so I latched onto one of those traveling carnival outfits. I did shit work, like cleaning up animal shit and putting up and tearing down rides. It was hard fucking work, but I got fed and I could always find a place to sleep out of the weather. There was this guy, and he decided he liked the looks of my ass and he was going to have what he wanted of it. The foreman hated that kind of shit and he beat the hell out of him and then he took me to the sad clown's trailer. He told him to take me in and look out for me and that's where I spent the next two years."

"My God," whispered Chloe. "You were just a kid."

Jax looked away from her and wondered why the hell he was talking. He was crazy to tell her about his life; she was bound to hate him if she knew the things he'd done. But he went on.

"Yeah, well, by the time two years were up, I was a whole lot smarter kid. I learned to be a pretty good pickpocket and I hid my money and saved it. And when the sad clown, Arnie was his name, died, I was done with the carnival. It was time to move on. I took my money and Arnie left a little box with more money in it, so I was set for a while. I found a ranch that was willing to take me on for next to nothing, but it was honest work and they let me sleep in the bunkhouse in a real bed. I tried to keep to myself and just do my work, but they hired a new man and he didn't like me any. He picked at me and picked at me, and one day I walked into the bunkhouse and there he was, going through all my things. It wasn't much but it was everything I had and he just looked at me and reached into the bottom of my duffel and pulled out the little box that had my money in it."

Jax wouldn't look at her. His face was hard and his eyes were haunted. "I just snapped. I never made a sound, I just went after him and it shocked him so much that I knocked him to the floor and started pounding his head on the floor. He was a lot bigger than I was, so it didn't take too much for him to start pounding the shit out of me. A couple of the other guys came in to see what was going on and they pulled us apart. The foreman told me to pack my stuff and hit the road and he said he'd hold the other guy for twenty-four hours before he made him hit the road. The rule was no fighting and no exceptions. So, I stuffed everything back in my duffel and left. I don't know if they really held him for twenty-four hours, but he caught up with me the next day. When he started beating the crap out of me, I grabbed a rock and I hammered him in the head with it. After the third time I hit him, he didn't move again. So, I was fifteen years old when I killed my first man."

Chloe was silent for a minute. "So, you killed a guy who was beating you up; do I have that right?" He didn't answer and she said, "So the way I see it, he had it coming. You think maybe he would have just roughed you up a little and then left you alone?"

Startled, Jax said, "No, he was going to kill me."

"Well, then, I'd say you did the only thing you could under the circumstances. Jax, you were dealt a really shitty hand. Nobody deserves to have to hit the streets at the age of twelve and take care of themselves at that age. Look at you now. What you do is tough, I know that, and it has to weigh on you, but you made it to a place of leadership. And you're not a thug. You do something that our government has decided they need for the safety and security of our country. I don't know a lot of details, but I think I've got that right, don't I?"

Jax finally looked at her and he nodded slowly. "I guess you do. It's not something a normal person can live with, knowing what we do."

"Well, then," she said briskly, "I guess I'm not a normal person. Now come on, it's late and we need to go to bed."

He stared at her, then rose without a word and went with her.

Chapter 20

J ax stopped spending his evenings in the barn and Chloe was glad to have him back in their bed. But the tension was growing as Shadow failed to find the name they needed and there were no more reports of Snake being spotted. Galina was restless and she made it clear that she didn't believe they would ever be able to be rid of Snake. She was increasingly resentful that they had carried her away from Brighton Beach and the hidden life she had created for Nicky. Chloe went out to the barn one day and listened to the frustration of the team. She was there when they were thrown a crumb as another person claimed to have seen Snake in Bolivia.

"That's enough to make me believe that he's really there," Jax said. "Now we've got to come up with that name."

Chloe said thoughtfully, "I wonder if Galina would know of someone who was friends with Snake or Ivan."

Jax went still and stared at her. "It's sure worth asking. Chloe, she might take it better if you talk to her. She's pretty unhappy right now and it's getting worse. If you can get her to see that this might help us bring this all to an end, maybe she can come up with something."

"I suppose I can try. What am I trying to find out?"

"We're looking for the name of someone who was friends with Snake or even Ivan, maybe someone who worked for them but didn't have any conflicts with them. If she can remember anyone Ivan mentioned, all we need is the name. Shadow can find out if it's someone we can use. We won't be contacting them; we just need a name."

Chloe looked mystified. "I don't understand what good that will do."

"It's how we're going to try to lure Snake back into the country and keep Galina and Nicky safe."

"All right, I'll see what I can do."

Chloe thought about it for a while, trying to think of the best way to approach Galina. She decided that honesty would be the most likely way to reach her. After lunch, she went to the den where Nicky was watching another movie and the two women were with him.

"Galina, could I talk to you for a little bit?" Chloe asked.

Galina looked at her for a moment and then nodded curtly and got up to follow her. Chloe took her to the library and closed the door, then motioned for her to sit down at the conference table. "Jax thinks he knows where Viktor is. There have been two people who have reported seeing him in Bolivia."

Galina sucked in a breath and asked, "What are they going to do about it?"

"They are going to try to lure him back. And they want to take him in Brighton Beach, so that he will never be anywhere near you and Nicky. There is nobody outside of us who knows that any of us are here, not even Jax's boss. It's been kept secret since we came here so that Viktor would never have a way to find us."

"Why are you telling me this?"

"For one, because I think you have a right to know what's happening. And also, because we need something from you."

Galina's eyes narrowed. "What do you need from me? What could I possibly do to help?"

"The men need to know if you can think of anyone at all who Ivan mentioned, someone who he was on good terms with, perhaps someone who worked in the organization or a friend."

"And this is important why?"

"I don't honestly know how they're going to use the name. I only know that they're not going to try to contact the person; they just need the name."

"That doesn't make any sense."

"It's best that their plans remain secret; it's safer that way," Chloe said.

Galina sat there thinking for a long time. "I can't think of anyone Ivan didn't look down on. He had contempt for the people who worked with him or for him, and he had only bad things to say about them. And I'm sure that his father was the same way. I've researched him during these years since Ivan died, and he is pure evil."

Chloe's heart sank. "Think hard, Galina. Even if you don't think it's someone important or on good terms with him, the guys will research the name and find out if it's what they need."

Galina shrugged helplessly and thought some more. "I have heard Ivan mention the name Grisha. I don't think I ever heard his last name, though."

Chloe wrote it down. "They still might be able to figure it out. Anyone else?"

"I remember that he talked about someone he called a mule. I didn't know what he meant by it. Let me think... Pyotr, Pyotr Baranov."

"That spelling is beyond me, would you write it down?"

Galina wrote the name down and sat there frowning for a few minutes. Chloe probed gently. "Is there something else?"

The other woman hesitated before she said, "There was only one person Ivan talked about a lot and that was a woman. He had a relationship with her for years. He used to tell me how much more of a woman she was than me. He threw her up in my face a lot. Ivan was an ugly, ugly man."

Chloe shuddered. "That's terrible; I'm so sorry you went through all that."

"Her name was Svetlana Drozdov; I'll never forget it. I used to wish that he would just stay with her and stop coming home. But he always came back. I'll write it down."

"Thank you, Galina. If you think of anyone else, will you let me know?"

Galina's eyes were dark with venom. "If it means that Viktor will die, I'll do anything I can."

"I'll take these names to the barn and they'll get right to work checking them out."

"I'm going back to my son."

Chloe hurried out to the barn and told Jax and Shadow about the conversation. Shadow took the names and got busy on his computer. Sometime later, he leaned back with a look of guarded satisfaction. Jax saw the look on his face.

"You got something?"

"Grisha was a dead end. Even with no last name, it looks like the only Grisha connected with Snake's organization was a low-level errand boy. He's still hanging around the area where Snake operated, hoping that the organization will rise again and he'll be able to work for them. Pyotr Baranov was exactly what Ivan called him, a mule. His job was moving things and he went back to Brighton Beach to work for the organization there. If we can't do any better, there's a chance we could use him, but I think the woman is a better bet. She's quite the woman, apparently. She was involved with both Ivan and his father and they both knew it. She was clever enough to keep them both interested and she found ways to be useful to them both. It seems that they were both fascinated by her. She latched onto one of the Russians who came to clean up Snake's mess; the one who was in charge, of course."

Jax said, "Is there any indication that she's in touch with Snake?"

Shadow shook his head. "No, she's sticking pretty close to the Russian, at least for the time being. Snake doesn't have anything to offer her. He's on the run, living in a shithole, and she likes men who can give her the good life. But I'm willing to bet that Snake would be interested if he thought she was contacting him."

Jax said thoughtfully, "Or he could think that it's a setup, the Russians trying to draw him out."

"It's possible. But she had a pretty good hold on him while he was still king of the hill."

"Then let's try it. I'm getting sick of waiting and everybody else is too." Jax gave the okay.

"We have a rough idea of where in Bolivia he might be, so I'll send out a series of messages that will travel down the grapevine, hinting that Svetlana is looking for him. Once the word has spread, I'll place a couple of classified ads, keep them running for a few days. We know he'll be watching for classified ads; they have communicated that way for a long time. Once he's on the move, I'll just have to watch for signs of him, but we know he'll look for Galina in Brighton Beach."

There was an excited little buzz among the guys as Jax and Shadow filled them in on the new developments. They were all ready for action and ready to bring their enemy down once and for all. Jax made a phone call to Gunner and they talked at length about the situation. Gunner agreed to plant some hints in his circles, ones that the Russians would be monitoring. Word would spread quickly and Shadow sat back to watch.

After nearly a week, they agreed that it had been long enough for the hints to spread, and Shadow prepared a classified ad for Bolivia's newspapers and its radio classified ad program. The ad read *Looking for Viktor regarding grandson. A secret was kept from you. Svetlana.*

Jax stared at the text that Shadow brought to him for his okay. "That's not exactly subtle," he said. "You think he'll buy it?"

"I don't think he'll be able to resist it," Shadow said. "There's nothing at this point in his life that he would want more than having his name continue. It's the only thing he has a claim to."

"I agree," said Finn. "He's lost everything else. If he knows Ivan had a son, he's going to want him."

"Okay, do it," Jax said. "How soon will it run?"

"It should be running tomorrow, the next day at the latest. I'm going to run it for two weeks."

Finn asked, "Did you say that the mule went back to Brighton Beach?"

Shadow said, "Yeah, he's working for the bunch there."

"We need to find a way to let him find out that Galina had a baby, just in case Snake tries to contact someone who can verify the rumor."

"That's a good idea, Finn. Can you do it?" Jax asked Shadow.

"Shouldn't be a problem," Shadow said. "Just drop a rumor and it'll spread."

"Do that too." Jax felt a grim satisfaction that they were finally doing something.

"On it."

Finn said, "As soon as the ads are up, we should all be at

the computers monitoring all the internet chatter we can. There's never an end to what we need to comb through."

Jax nodded. "That's exactly what we'll do. And two of us will sleep during the day and monitor at night."

Finn said, "I'll do that and Coop can work with me. He's a night owl anyway."

Coop nodded his agreement and a few minutes later, Shadow said, "Okay, everything's set. Now we wait and watch."

The tension continued to rise as they kept vigil over the internet chatter, listening carefully; it was tedious work and required them to keep a sharp focus for hours at a time. After four days of watching and listening, there was finally a break.

"He's on the move," said Slade. "He was spotted getting on a bus, one of those ones that travel all night. He's going northwest."

Joker asked, "You think he's going to try to travel that way all the way to the States?"

"I'd say he'll take what he can get without using an ID or passport. He can't cross the borders by car and he needs to stay under the radar. If I were him, I'd want to stay out of Brazil, too," Shadow said.

Coop said, "He might even be able to take some flights. As long as he has money, he'll be able to travel."

"That's one thing he did have, money," Jax said morosely. "We need to find someone to monitor in Brighton Beach. Maybe we need to be watching the mule, Pyotr. Snake is going to need someone to help him once he gets to the States."

"That, we can pull off," said Shadow.

"What about putting some cameras on Galina's house?" asked Joker.

"I'll get Gunner to set it up. If we can get a bug into Pyotr's place, we might catch him communicating with

Snake." Jax was thinking out loud. "What do we know about Svetlana, besides what Galina told us?"

"She's with that Russian, I'll see if I can find out where he is now." Shadow turned back to his computer. Half an hour later, he said, "Bingo. The Russian has moved to Brighton Beach and he's recruiting people to take up Snake's operations. He's living in an apartment there, pretty deluxe, and he has a woman with him. That's got to be our girl, Svetlana. We need some more surveillance planted."

Jax said, "Give me the details and I'll get Gunner on it."

By dinnertime, a lot of things had fallen into place and they stood a decent chance of being able to know when Snake hit United States soil. By morning, they had eyes and ears in Pyotr's apartment, the apartment Svetlana was staying in, and Galina's house. They started the routine of around the clock surveillance and Chloe didn't see much of them unless she delivered food to the barn. Snake was spotted in Columbia two days later, at an airfield. Jax had Gunner contact the airfield and get the destinations of their latest flights. There was one that left in the right time frame, destination Honduras.

Shadow said, "If he keeps finding flights, we've got a path to follow. Is Gunner tracing what he does after he lands in Honduras?"

Jax nodded. "He is. Snake will be landing late tonight and the next flights out will be in the morning. If he keeps taking flights, he'll be in the States by Saturday. Slade, Joker, Finn, I'd like you to get to Brighton Beach. We'll keep watching and as soon as we've seen enough, we'll join you there. Take all the equipment you need."

Finn nodded and asked, "You're going to leave the women and kid here alone?"

"I'm going to give Gunner the phone number that I leave with Chloe and give her his. Shadow can set up a link between

Gunner and the surveillance camera on the driveway so Gunner can watch for trouble. He's also going to show Chloe how to monitor all the surveillance cameras."

Finn asked, "So Gunner knows our location now?"

"Yes. His leaker is in prison and Gunner is our safety net for the women and the boy while we go after Snake. If anything weird happens, Gunner can get men from local sources out here in a hurry. I'd still rather not have them staying here alone, but I think all the bases are covered."

Finn protested, "I don't like leaving them here alone, either. We can get by one man down. Coop and Chloe have worked and trained together a lot. Why not have him stay here and protect them?"

"Coop, what do you think?" Jax asked.

"I hate to miss the party, but I don't like leaving them here alone, either. I'm okay with staying."

Jax studied him for a minute, then shifted his gaze to Finn, who gave him a slight nod. "Okay," said Jax, "Coop, you stay here. It does seem like a better plan and it would take a load off my mind."

"You got it, boss," Coop said.

The three men packed efficiently and Jax drove them to the airfield, going over their plans several times on the way. He waited until they were in the air and then headed back. When he got to the house, it was nearly time for dinner. He went inside and filled Chloe in on what was happening and then told her he was going to the barn to relieve Shadow for a while.

"I'll bring you out some dinner," Chloe said, giving him a kiss.

"Why don't you bring out dinner for both of us and we can talk about all this in more detail?"

"Okay, I'll do that. Mary's been helping me with dinner. I'll let her know we're down three men and that I'll be having dinner with you."

When Chloe got to the barn with her tray, Jax took it from her and set it down, then swept her into his arms for a deep, probing kiss. She melted into his arms with a little mew of pleasure.

"Things are really starting to happen, aren't they?"

Jax said, "They are. Let's sit down and eat, and we can talk about everything. But something smells damn good; what is it?"

Chloe took the dome off the tray to reveal barbecued pork chops with mounds of steak fries and a fresh, tossed salad.

"That looks as good as it smells," he said as they seated themselves and filled their plates.

"We're going to keep watching and when it looks like Snake is getting closer, Shadow and I will take off for Brighton Beach. Coop is staying here with you. Shadow's going to be showing you things about how to watch the security cameras and, of course, Coop can do that too. I'm leaving you a phone with Gunner's number in it and I'm giving your phone number to him. He's going to have a link to the surveillance system here and if any of you see something weird, you call each other right away. If anything happens and you need help, Gunner will get it to you fast."

"How soon do you think he could be in the States?"

"Could be as early as Saturday. He's hopping flights out of little airstrips, which gives us a path to watch. He should be getting on a flight in the morning; Gunner will verify it for us."

Chloe fretted a little. "So, Gunner knows where we are now. And you're sure that the leak he had was caught?"

Jax nodded. "Yep, he has very quietly been put in high security custody and he's not getting out for a very long time, if ever."

"God, I hope everything goes smoothly."

"You and me both, baby. We need this monster to be gone forever and everybody can live safely, without another thought for him."

"It's hard to imagine," Chloe said, nibbling on a fry.

"It's been a long time coming, but it's going to happen."

Both of them thought about what was going to happen to them once Snake was gone, but it wasn't the time to talk about it.

Chapter 21

The atmosphere in the barn was one of intense concentration; Chloe was learning everything she could about monitoring the surveillance cameras and being ready for every possibility. She and Coop had a good bond after all their training together, and she trusted him to give her the best guidance if something unexpected happened. They worked well together and understood each other. As Jax watched them together, he felt good about the decision to have Coop stay back with the women. Coop had also rounded up a softball and mitt and spent some time teaching Nicky how to pitch and catch. The little boy had a serious case of hero worship for the big, tough assassin. On Friday, they knew it was possible for Snake to hit American soil by Saturday morning, and Jax and Shadow prepared to leave.

Chloe walked into the bedroom, where Jax was putting clothing into his duffel bag. "When are you leaving?" she asked.

"Two hours," said Jax. "All the arrangements are made. Can you think of anything I haven't covered with you?"

"No, Jax, you've been over things several times; I can't

think of anything you haven't covered. And you know that if something unexpected happens, it won't be something you were able to predict."

He shot her a frustrated look. "That's not helping."

She smiled faintly. "I know, but it's true, isn't it?"

"Yes. That's why I don't feel ready. Dammit, I hate leaving you here."

She looked suddenly serious, almost angry. "You just make sure you do your job and leave that little boy with a safe life!"

"That's my job, isn't it?"

Her eyes flashed at him. "Yeah, it is, and I'm betting that you don't usually go into a job with this many misgivings, do you?"

He looked frustrated as he muttered, "No. The stakes aren't usually this high."

"Well, you're the best, aren't you? Who's better than the Elite 6 Assassins?"

His head shot up and he stared at her. "Where did you ever hear that name?"

Chloe's cheeks turned pink and she said, "I don't... I didn't—"

"Didn't what? I've never told you that."

She stood staring at him for a few seconds, then said defiantly, "I saw it in some paperwork."

"What paperwork? There's no paperwork lying around with that name on it."

"It was before... before I knew I could trust you. I was just looking for something—"

"Looking for what? Something you could use to get away? Is that what you did, went sneaking around to find something you could use?"

"Jax, it was before. Before so many things changed. I didn't know, I didn't feel what I do now."

It was like a curtain came down over his eyes. "Well, don't

worry, Chloe. I'm going to carry out this mission and then you'll be free to go. You'll be safe and you can go back to a normal life."

"Jax, stop it. That's not what I want."

"And yet, this is my life and it's never going to change. You were right; you deserve to get away from it all." He turned and zipped up his bag and then walked around her and out of the room.

She stood there, feeling her heart shatter. She had never felt so cold or alone in her life. When he closed the door behind himself, she sank down on the chair and covered her face with her hands, so shaken that she couldn't even shed a tear. He'd been so cold that it terrified her. It was a long time before her trembling legs would hold her and she walked numbly down the stairs, where the house was empty and silent. They were all outside, loading things up and kidding around, getting ready to go. Even Galina and Mary and Nicky were out there. But Coop shot a look at her, knowing that something wasn't right.

Jax spent the last hour tersely going over things with Shadow and Coop and largely ignoring Chloe. Then they were loading into the SUV and pulling away from the barn-yard. Jax never offered her a word or a look. The two women took Nicky in for some lunch and Coop walked over to Chloe.

"What the hell's going on?" he asked.

She looked miserably at him. "I did something. It was a long time ago, when I still thought I needed to find a way to get free. I looked through some paperwork in the office. It wasn't much; everybody was gone except Finn and Shadow and I didn't even try the whole time you were all gone, even though I felt I should. I just couldn't. Then, when I knew there were only a few more hours, I sort of panicked and went look-ing. But after that, things changed. I learned to trust him; hell, at that point, he didn't trust me, either. It didn't mean anything and I never would have tried to use it, even if there was a way to."

"Shit. You're the first person I've ever seen him trust, except for us."

There was a hitch in her voice as she said, "He's never going to forgive me, is he?"

Coop was silent for a moment before he said, "Hey, never say never. I've never seen him care for anyone like he does for you, either."

"But he just left, without a word or a touch, not even a look."

"He needs some time," Coop said. "It's a crazy, tense time. He'll get over it when all this is done."

She looked at him through unshed tears. "You really think so?"

Coop nodded firmly. "Yes, I really think so." He sincerely hoped he was telling the truth.

Jax was in a foul mood as he drove to the airstrip. Shadow tried to speak to him several times before he gave up and lapsed into silence. It had been obvious that something was wrong between Jax and Chloe before they left and it was clearly something big. Shadow sighed and had the thought that this kind of distraction was the last thing they needed. Well, Jax was a professional and he'd just have to get over it.

Once they were on the plane, he tried again. "So, boss, what the hell kind of argument did you have with Chloe?"

"I didn't have any argument with Chloe." Jax snapped the words and turned to look out the window.

"Um, it was obvious that there was a problem. There's no use trying to say there wasn't."

"Drop it," said Jax.

"Well, now, I'd like to do that. Under normal circumstances, I'd be glad to. But we're about to take on the biggest and hardest mission we've ever had. You obviously are upset and you don't have your head where it belongs. So, spit it out, we'll talk it over, and you can do your job the way you should."

"Shut the hell up, Shadow. This has nothing to do with you."

Shadow's head jerked toward him and he said grimly, "Oh, yes, it does. How many times have you laid down the law to us about having our heads in the game? You're the man in charge. If your head isn't right, you put us all in danger. So, you spit it out or we'll cancel the whole mission."

Jax knew it was an empty threat, but he also knew that Shadow was telling the truth. "All right, then, here it is. She accidentally spilled the fact that while we were away on a mission, she went sneaking through the office and looking at paperwork to see what she could find out about us. She was trying to find something she could use to help her get away."

"What did she find? And how did you know that she did it?"

"She knows we're the Elite 6 Assassins. And none of us ever mention that name."

"That's it? She didn't find out anything more than that?"

"She broke into a drawer and sneaked through the paperwork."

Shadow cocked his head and thought. "Geez, boss, what would you do? She walked into something that was no fault of her own and she's been held prisoner ever since. In case you couldn't tell, there's been quite a change in your relationship with her in the past few months. Do you think she just should have accepted the end of her life as she knew it and accepted you being her master for the rest of her days? Really? Isn't it kind of natural to try to escape?"

Jax shifted uneasily. Defensively, he said, "You know I

couldn't let her leave. She would have been dead in a matter of hours."

"Yeah, I know that. I'll bet you could have gotten that across to her in a number of different ways too. I get that you don't like her breaking into the files, but maybe you should cut her a little slack. It's not hard to see that things have changed in how she feels. Hell, boss, it's obvious that she trusts you and loves you."

Jax felt his anger slip a little. "You really think that?"

Shadow laughed. "Shit, boss, everybody knows that."

Jax thought it over and finally said grudgingly, "I guess I'd probably have tried to find a way to get away too."

"You think? If you're smart, you'll get this job done and go back and apologize to her."

Jax looked shocked at the idea. "Apologize…"

"Yeah, I know you've never done it before, but there's a first time for everything, right?"

"Shut up and give me a beer."

Shadow grinned and rummaged in the cooler. "Just do it. It'd be really stupid for you to blow things with her."

Chloe and Coop kept a close watch on the surveillance system. Shadow had set up alarms that would be triggered by any breach of security, so that they didn't have to keep a constant watch, but they still did a lot of watching. Galina's nerves were stretched thin and Mary tried to keep her occupied spending time interacting with her son.

On Saturday, Jax's group got word that Snake was on what would be his last flight toward the States, expected to land in a remote airstrip in the desert of Mexico. From there, he would have to travel on the ground in order to cross the border without being detected. They knew they had at least twenty-four hours before Snake could get near Brighton Beach, but they began the watch anyway. Shadow called Coop and passed the information on. Coop was irritated that Jax didn't make the call himself and doubly irritated that he didn't take a moment to talk to Chloe.

"Why didn't the boss make this call?" he asked. "What the hell is he doing?"

"Still pouting," Shadow said cheerfully. "Tell Chloe that everything is going according to plan and Jax will talk to her soon."

Coop laughed. "Will I be telling her the truth?"

"Yep, guaranteed."

"Okay, be careful."

"Always," said Shadow, then he broke the connection.

A little of the strain left Chloe's face when Coop told her what Shadow had said and Coop was glad he'd told her. "I just can't wait until this is all over," she said with a sigh.

"You and me both. But we're on the home stretch now. A couple more days, and it'll be finished."

Gunner sat in a meeting, bored as usual when he had to attend those kinds of things. Down the hall, a man walked briskly into Gunner's office, carrying a file folder. He sat down at the desk and logged onto the computer. He worked there for a few minutes, then opened the folder and made some notations and shut down the computer. He was long gone when Gunner left the meeting and returned to his office.

In Brighton Beach, the surveillance was going as usual, long and tedious. But even through the tedium, there was an undercurrent of excitement. They had gotten word that the plane Snake was on had landed at the little airstrip, one that wasn't much more than a flat spot in a desolate piece of desert. Satellite images showed a ramshackle pole building and a fuel pump and that was all the technology that existed at the so-called airstrip. It was exactly the kind of place that would accommodate a wanted criminal trying to avoid capture. The wait had begun in earnest.

Snake got off the plane and talked to the lone man who was at the airstrip. The two of them went into the building, and a few minutes later, Snake came out the back of the building and got into the beat-up old pickup truck that sat there. He took off in a cloud of dust, the engine spitting out a backfire, and left the airstrip behind. He also left the pilot slumped over the controls of his plane and the airstrip attendant lying on the floor of the building in a pool of blood. It could be weeks before they were discovered.

The clock ticked slowly by as the team waited and watched. Gunner kept an eye on the links Shadow had set up for him, paying close attention to Pyotr Baranov and Svetlana and her Russian protector. On Sunday, Pyotr received a phone call and Gunner was able to listen in.

"You got the package?" Pyotr asked. After listening, he said, "Good. I'll have the address for you in the morning as soon as I make the exchange. All right, goodbye."

Gunner watched him speak into the phone with a strange feeling of misgiving. Although he had no way of knowing who the man had been talking to, he was uneasy. He called Jax and told him what he'd seen. "You want me to have Pyotr picked up?"

Jax said, "No, Snake's going to need some help, a place to stay, transportation. Pyotr is the most likely person to give him a hand. He'll do anything for money. Keep watching him."

"All right. I'm going to put a man on him, so he'll be followed if he leaves his apartment."

"Good."

The team had reached the point in time where they believed that Snake could show up at any time. But nothing happened. Early Monday morning, Pyotr left his apartment and walked down the street to a coffeehouse. He went inside and ordered his brew at the counter before he went to find a seat. He joined another man at a small table in the back and the man following him snapped a few pictures. When the man across from Pyotr turned toward the camera, Gunner's man stiffened in shock. He called Gunner immediately.

"Pyotr is in a coffee shop, he met another man there and you're not going to believe who it is."

Gunner listened and then swore. "We've got to take them both. I'm sending men now. Don't let them get away."

It was a desperate race, but Gunner's men got there just as the two men in the coffee shop rose to leave. With a minimal struggle, the Russian and his companion were hustled into the black van that Gunner's men had arrived in. They raced to Gunner's headquarters and hauled them inside. Gunner was on the phone to Jax, and then he walked into the interrogation room and faced the man who had met Pyotr. He had been searched and was handcuffed to the table. An envelope fat with cash was lying on the table.

Gunner stared at him with contempt. "What the fuck did you do?"

The other man didn't meet his eyes. "I want a lawyer."

Gunner shook his head. "No. You know it's not going to go that way. The only thing you can do for yourself is tell me everything. And every second that goes by before you do that lowers your chances to get any kind of mercy. Now what did you do?"

The man sat silent.

"You've worked for us for how long? It's years, not weeks or months, isn't that right? So, you know what's going to happen if you don't cooperate, don't you?"

"I know what's going to happen if I *do* cooperate. I disappear, permanently."

"You piece of shit. You know Baranov's spilling everything right now; his only hope is to give us something before you have a chance to give it to us. You just signed a death warrant for a four-year-old little boy. You're not just going to disappear, you're going to spend the rest of your natural life suffering like you've never seen suffering. You know we have a place for people like you."

The man panicked. "You can't send me there! All I did was pass on an address."

Gunner looked at him with contempt. "Enjoy the next forty years." He turned and walked out, leaving the traitor begging and pleading in vain. He called Jax immediately. "Snake is a no-show, isn't he? He's on the way to your base. There was a second leaker and he just passed off the address to Baranov. We have to assume that he passed it to Snake before we got him. It's been almost two hours, but we don't know where Snake is starting from, so you're in a race."

Jax swore bitterly but he didn't have time for the explosion to happen then. "We're going to need a lot of answers, Gunner."

"I know. I've got men headed over to your location. They'll watch until it's all over, just in case we're wrong and Snake shows up, but go now. Get the son of a bitch."

In moments, Jax and his team were loaded up and speeding to the airstrip. Jax was sick with fear, knowing that Snake was on his way to the base they'd so carefully kept secret for so long. Snake would make sure the women suffered before they died and he would take Nicky to raise as his legacy, a fate that would be worse than death for the innocent little boy. They had to get there in time. He called Coop on their way to the airstrip and filled him in on the little that they knew.

"We'll batten down the hatches, boss, and set the emergency level alarms and defenses. We'll be as ready as we can be."

Jax said, "We don't know where he's coming from and we don't know how he's traveling, so you've got to be ready for anything. We'll be in the air in approximately twenty minutes."

"Will do. Be careful."

"You be careful."

Twenty minutes later, they settled back in the plane for the worst waiting of all.

Chapter 22

Coop and Chloe sat, heads together, talking tensely as Coop told her everything that had happened. "What do we do?" Chloe asked.

"We're going to set everything to emergency levels, the surveillance and the alarms and the automatic defense mechanisms that Joker and Shadow put in. He's not getting in here without a helluva fight. We're going to stay in the barn; it's a lot better equipped to launch a defense than the house is. We're going to have to keep the ladies calm. I want you to go to the house and get them to help you bring out anything you think you'll need to get through the next twenty-four hours. Do it as quickly as you can and then nobody will leave the barn again until this is all over."

"Okay. We'll get out here as quickly as we can."

"Chloe, just bring the bare necessities. We've got emergency supplies out here, so don't waste time trying to provide all the comforts of home. Just what we really need." Coop was dead serious and Chloe nodded at him.

"On it." She hurried to the house and set it in motion. To her credit, Galina took one look at her face and cooperated without a single question. Her calm was a huge help and the four of them gathered what they really needed and were back in the barn in less than twenty minutes.

Mary and Galina set about making a cozy little area away from the computers and weapons where they could sit with Nicky and keep him busy with books and movies on one of the laptops. Chloe filled a cooler with sandwich supplies and there were already plenty of drinks on ice. She went to check on the ladies and Nicky, and Galina waved her away.

"We're fine. Do what you need to do."

So, Chloe went back to Coop and followed his instructions as he reinforced their security. All the monitors were giving them different views from the surveillance cameras and Chloe was impressed all over again at the genius of Shadow.

Coop said, "There's only one clear way in, as you know. It would be possible to try to pick their way in through the woods, but it'd be really tough. The underbrush is thick and there are also the wires and booby traps that Joker set. There are alarms along the drive in and there's no way Snake can get in without setting one off. He'd have to know the whole setup and that's just not possible. With a little luck, he'll blow himself up trying to get in. But if he manages to make it up the drive-way, he's a long way from finding a way into the barn."

"How do Jax and the team get in?"

"Shadow can disable everything at once, or each alarm one at a time, then turn them back on. Hopefully, they'll get here before Snake does and we'll be set up and ready."

"And if they don't?"

Coop said grimly, "Then we'll be set up and ready without them. If we end up having to defend ourselves here, you get the women and Nicky into the gun lanes and have them lock themselves in. We built them to be as safe as a panic room. You get in there with them and keep them calm."

"And leave you out here alone? No, Coop, I don't think so.

I didn't do all that training just so I could go hide in a panic room while you defend us." Chloe was adamant.

He could see that there was no point in arguing with her. He'd cross that bridge when they came to it. "Okay, I'm going to go get us the weapons we might need. Yell if you see anything on the monitors."

He went to the weapons wall and opened doors, gathering what he wanted and then he hauled it all over to where Chloe was sitting. They loaded and checked their weapons and filled their vests with extra magazines for reloading. It remained quiet and the peaceful scenes on the monitors made their whole situation seem surreal. A couple of hours later, Mary offered to make sandwiches for all of them and Chloe grate-fully accepted. She brought food to Chloe and Coop and then carried lunch over to Galina and Nicky so the three of them could eat together without disturbing Coop and Chloe's concentration on the monitors.

The time dragged by, driving the tension up ever higher. "How do you stay so calm?" Chloe asked, tapping her fingers nervously on the tabletop.

Coop grinned and said, "Practice. Lots of practice." His phone vibrated and he looked at the message and gave her a wink. "They're on the ground. They should be here within the hour if I know who's driving."

Chloe sighed with relief. "Good, I can't wait until they get here."

"I'll second that one." Coop bit into his second sandwich, studying the monitors while he chewed. Nearly half an hour later, he stiffened and whispered, "Shit. We've got company."

Chloe looked where he pointed, at the monitor that covered where the driveway turned off the road. Nearly out of the camera's reach, she could see the back bumper of a vehicle that had been pulled into the bushes for cover. Straining to see more, she caught a glimpse of shadowy figures sticking close to the trees and underbrush at the side of the driveway. "There," she whispered shakily.

Coop nodded. "I see them. Looks like three, no, four of them. Get them into the gun lane."

Chloe nodded and went quickly but calmly over to the others. Galina clutched the bag they had filled with bottles of water, some snacks, and Nicky's books and movies. Nicky carried the laptop with him and Chloe led them back to the shooting area. She got them settled inside and Galina promised to keep the door locked up tight. Then Chloe left them, after testing the door, and hurried back to Coop. He took one look at her and knew it would be a waste of time to argue with her about staying in the blockaded room. They watched the monitors intently and saw the intruders making their slow, cautious way down the driveway. They huddled together and one of them pointed off into the woods. One of the figures went off that way and the rest of them huddled together, waiting.

A few long minutes passed, and then the quiet was inter-rupted by the sound of an explosion, powerful enough that Chloe and Coop could feel the building shake. The three figures in the driveway appeared to carry on an argument, and one of them, presumably Snake, pulled a gun out and gestured to the others to go on. They approached one of Shadow's alarms and suddenly a bright searchlight lit up and illuminated them clearly. Chloe and Coop could see all three of them as clearly as if they were standing before them; the man with the gun was indeed Snake. They retreated from the light until they were out of its range. A couple more minutes passed, and then one man was suddenly seen running straight at the light. He had nearly reached the light when a look of horror passed over his face, and just seconds later, the ground appeared to explode under his feet.

"Two down," Coop said grimly, "and we haven't even fired a weapon yet."

"God bless Shadow," Chloe responded.

The two remaining intruders proceeded cautiously forward, Snake keeping the other man in front of him. Coop was sending a text to Jax, who told him they were only minutes away. Chloe watched Snake and the man with him, inspecting the ground ahead of them before each step. They had made some progress when Snake suddenly grabbed the man in front of him and jerked him backward, flinging both of them to the ground. Bullets whizzed over them for a full minute before they stopped. The two men crept on, keeping to the ground until they got past the place where the bullets had come from.

"I can't believe they keep going," Chloe said softly.

"They're almost in the clear, at least as far as the driveway is concerned. The yard around the house and barn is not booby trapped that way; it's too risky with people out and about all the time. So, they'll be trying to breach the barn before long. The team is almost here, but they'll know what they're driving up on." Coop continued to watch and relay the progress to Jax.

Chloe sucked in a breath as she saw Snake and his man step into the barnyard. "Coop! There they are."

Snake surveyed the house and barn and sent his man to check out the house. He reappeared quickly, shaking his head at his boss. The two of them eased a little closer to the barn and began to circle it, checking it out all the way around. They spotted the cameras mounted on the outside of the barn quickly and began putting them out of commission.

"Son of a bitch," Coop muttered. "Okay, bring it on, boys."

The two of them had put on their vests and held their guns, ready to fire. Coop fired off another message to Jax and

Chloe strained her ears, trying to hear something from outside. Suddenly, there was a burst of automatic gunfire at the door as Snake tried to shoot his way in.

"Will it hold?" Chloe asked anxiously.

"Not for long," Coop said grimly. He turned a big, steel table on its side and said, "Get behind this; you can fire at them from here. Don't expose yourself, whatever you do. I'll do that when it's needed."

Chloe took cover behind the table and waited as Snake fired another burst at the door. The third round of gunfire took out the door, but the two men didn't immediately come rushing in. Coop could see the muzzles of their guns poked cautiously in at the sides of the doorway.

"Fire, Chloe, they're not in yet." They both fired at the edges of the doorway. When the gunfire died down, there was a movement and Snake's man rushed in, heading for cover behind a sturdy desk.

"Chloe, get down!" Coop showered the desk with gunfire, alternating between it and the doorway.

Then the man behind the desk opened fire, sweeping back and forth over the table they sheltered behind and Snake burst through the door, adding more gunfire. Mass confusion erupted with bullets flying and shattering computers, monitors, everything in the path of the gunfire. Snake was shouting at his man, urging him to move to another spot, and when he made a run for it, Coop shot him down. Snake peppered Chloe's end of the table with bullets and Coop made a move to get off a clear shot at him. As he rose to fire, Snake turned and sprayed bullets his way. Chloe screamed as she saw Coop fall and she fired frantically in Snake's direction. But she couldn't see him and her attention was on Coop as she crawled over to him and tried to find a pulse. She never heard Snake coming and he snatched her up off the floor, knocking her gun out of her hand with a vicious, chopping blow to her wrist.

Chloe struggled in mindless panic but Snake had her securely in his grasp and he snarled at her. "Where is the boy?"

Her head cleared a little and she gasped, "I don't know what you're talking about."

Snake gave a vicious laugh and said, "You little fool. I'm going to give you one more chance to answer my question and if you don't, I will shoot you."

"Then you'll never get an answer from me, will you?" she asked defiantly.

"Stupid bitch, how many times do you think I can shoot you without killing you? I assure you, I can do it many times. Now where is the boy?"

Chloe remained stubbornly silent and Snake shook his head at her. "You think I won't do it? Maybe you forget how much I enjoy hurting women." He dragged her over to a chair and forced her down into it, looking around for something to secure her. He found a roll of duct tape and taped her arms and legs to the chair.

Snake pulled a handgun out of his pocket and said, "One more chance. Where is the boy?"

Chloe knew that if she told him, he would most likely kill her immediately and she refused to say a word. He shook his head regretfully and then shot her through her left hand. She screamed in shock and pain, the agony so intense that her vision grayed and her hearing dimmed and she knew she was going to pass out. She prayed that she would; maybe it would buy her time, enough time for Jax and the team to get there. She let her head fall back, hoping that Snake would believe she was unconscious. But when Snake pressed a towel to her hand to stop the bleeding, she couldn't hold back the scream.

"There now; I can't have you bleeding to death before you tell me what I need to know. Again, where is the boy?"

"Wh-what are you going t-to do with him?" Chloe asked, trying to stall.

"That's none of your concern. But he is my grandson. He is my blood, my legacy. I'm going to raise him as if he was my own son, and I will pass everything down to him. He will carry on my blood."

"You don't have... anything to pass down to him. Russia has disowned you; they want you dead."

"They will understand once I have the opportunity to speak to them. I served my masters well; my operation was more successful than they ever knew. I will be restored to my position once again as soon as I have the chance to explain it to them."

Chloe stared at him. "You're crazy," she whispered.

"Never say that!" He roared the words at her, swiping a vicious, backhanded blow to her face that rocked her head back.

Chloe's vision dimmed again and she thought she heard something from outside, from a distance. *Hold on, Chloe, just hold on a little longer.* She moaned and let her head loll, tasting blood from where he had split her lip. There it was again; she was sure she heard something.

"Now, where is the boy?" He shouted the question, but she didn't respond, her head still hanging. Muttering, he stalked away and returned with a bottle of water. He poured out a glassful of it and tossed it in her face. Chloe's head jerked up reflexively and she coughed and sputtered at the shock of the cold water. "That's better," said Snake. "Now, where is the boy? I'm growing tired of asking you."

Chloe refused to speak and Snake heaved a great sigh. "Then you leave me no choice." He took the gun and pressed the muzzle against her knee.

"No, please!" Chloe let out a sob of fear and pain.

"This is your last chance to tell me; where is the boy?"

And then all hell broke loose. Men seemed to be running in from all directions, voices shouting. She heard Jax yelling, "Drop the gun, Snake. Drop it now!"

In that one moment of shock, Snake raised his eyes to see what was happening, and as he did, he lifted the gun away from Chloe's knee, starting to aim it at the man facing him. But he was too late, much too late, and Jax's bullet hit him directly between the eyes. The evil that was Viktor Vasiliev was gone forever, dead instantly. Jax was on his knees, cutting away the tape that held Chloe to the chair and gathering her into his arms, begging her to be all right. He carried her to one of the cots and laid her down, his touch gentle and his expression frantic.

"Coop." Chloe struggled to speak. "Help Coop, he's shot. Please, help him."

Finn was already kneeling beside Coop. "He's alive. But we need a bird, this one is going to require the hospital."

Shadow was already calling for help, and though it seemed like forever, the helicopter was there in record time. The medics had to work over him for several minutes before they loaded him in for the flight and Jax insisted that they take Chloe, too. Joker had gone to the gun lane to set the terrified women and boy free. Galina looked around the awful scene in the barn and looked up questioningly at Joker.

"It's over," he assured her. "Snake is gone forever."

A look of fierce joy swept over her face.

Joker said, "Why don't you and Mary take Nicky into the house? Coop and Chloe are going to the hospital and Jax is going with them. Nicky doesn't need to see any of this."

She nodded, struggling for words, and finally said simply, "Thank you. Thank all of you."

Chapter 23

C hloe had to have surgery on her hand to repair some of the damage caused by the bullet that tore through her palm, but it went well and she was able to leave the hospital after two days. Coop underwent surgery; he had taken four bullets that hit him in the shoulder, hip, and leg as well as three that hit his vest. His stay in the hospital was considerably longer than Chloe's, but he would make a full recovery. When he first came out of surgery, Chloe sat beside his bed and cried at the sight of the big, tough guy lying helpless in bed, hooked up to monitors and IVs. And when he came to and gave her a wan smile and a wink, she cried all over again. Jax firmly told her she'd had enough and wheeled her back to her room and hustled her into bed. He only left the hospital long enough to shower and then he was back, sitting in her room and keeping watch over her.

Jax drove her back to the house and she was greeted by the rest of the team as if she was a returning war hero. Galina and Mary were still there with Nicky, anxious to get back to their own homes, but refusing to leave until they could see

Chloe for themselves and thank her for everything she'd done. They had carefully explained to Nicky about his mother and the sacrifice she'd made to keep him safe and he hardly took more than three steps from her. He was awed by the fact that Chloe had been shot in the act of protecting him, his mom, and his Aunt Mary. He hugged her, careful not to bump her hand, and she promised him that she would tell Coop how thankful they all were to him. The next morning, Slade and Joker would drive them to the airstrip and put them on a plane back to New York. Gunner had heard from reliable sources that Russia had washed their hands of Viktor, and Galina, Nicky, and Mary were not to be touched.

Chloe gave them final hugs before they left the next morning and when she went back into the house, she looked around and tried to untangle her feelings about everything that had happened.

Jax walked in and put his arm around her. "Need to lie down?" he asked.

"No, I've had plenty of rest. It's just so quiet, and it's kind of weird that the danger is over."

Jax walked over to the window and looked moodily out at the barn. "Yeah, the danger is finally over. You and Coop were both almost killed, but it's over now. You can be free now; you can have your life back."

Chloe looked pensive. "What life is that, Jax? I've done more living in the past few months than I did in all the rest of my life."

"Now you have a chance to make a real life."

"So, what is it you're trying to tell me? Now that you've gotten your man, you're done with me? Did you really keep me to keep me safe, or was it to make sure that Snake would keep coming and you'd be able to get him?"

"I suppose I had that coming. But the fact is I was being

truthful when I told you that if I let you go, Snake would have killed you within hours."

"And what about when you told me that I was yours and you would never let me go?"

"That was before—"

"Before what, Jax?"

"B-before I really knew you. Before I... cared about you."

"So, let me get this right. You punished me, you fucked me, and you did it until I wanted it, until I craved it, until I couldn't get enough of you. Until I needed your touch, until *I* cared about *you*, so much that I don't want to go back to my old life. With you, I've seen things I never dreamed of seeing, I've felt things I never imagined I could feel. My old life was no life; it was just survival. I was just going through the days hoping to get through the next one. Life with you is rich with feeling, with companionship, with..." She stopped talking.

He turned to her with a trapped look on his face. "Chloe, I put your *life* in danger! I kept you so that I could keep Snake from killing you and I almost got you killed. And not just you; I almost botched the whole thing so badly that all of you could have been killed."

"No, Jax, you didn't! You trained Coop so well that he knew what to do. Shadow was a genius, with the traps and alarms that he rigged up. You provided everything we needed to protect ourselves. We survived because of you. And you made sure that Snake will never hurt that little boy and you did it without letting anything happen to Nicky."

"Chloe, you know what I am. I'm not a good man; I'm not a nice man. I'm a *killer*, for God's sake. I can't ask you to be part of that life. I'm never going to get away from it, not until I'm an old man. How could I put you through that? Danger is always going to be part of my life. You're too important to me to do that to you. You deserve better than me."

Chloe looked him straight in the eye. "That's a bunch of bullshit, Jax. You're not a bad man, and you're not evil. You're a good man, one who does things that nobody else can do, to stop truly evil people from hurting the innocent ones. You have to do hard things, damn hard ones, but they're things that bring good to people. And you're not asking me to be part of it. I'm telling you that I'm not going anywhere. Now that the hard part is done, you're not getting rid of me."

He stared at her for a long time and then he finally shook his head. "You are one helluva stubborn woman, Chloe Bennett. I should put you over my knee and spank some sense into you."

"You can't. I just had surgery."

"When you recover, I'm going to remember that you've got a spanking coming."

Her cheeks turned pink and she touched the tip of her tongue to her top lip. "Mm, well, just so you remember what comes after the spanking."

He reached for her, squeezing her butt with one hand and tipping her chin up with the other so he could capture her lips with his. "I'd never forget that part. Chloe, this isn't right."

"What isn't right?"

"Bringing you into this life, exposing you to all our ugliness. I can't have someone like you in my life. It's not right; it's not fair to you."

"Jax, I don't see your life that way. I see the good that you do. I see the people you save. How many people did Snake hurt or kill?"

Jax shrugged. "I don't have a number, but there were a lot."

"Do you think he would have stopped?"

"No, he never would have stopped. He liked it, he liked torturing people and killing them. He was never going to stop."

"So, thanks to you, people are being saved from him. I don't see that as something bad, I see it as something good, and I see you as you really are, a good man and an honorable one. I love you, Jax. I've loved you for a while now and I'm never going to stop. And I'm not walking away from you. You can't make me walk away from you. I've earned the right to be with you. So don't you try to make me walk away." Her voice was quivering with unshed tears and it stabbed him straight in the heart.

"You *love* me? Chloe, you know me, you really do, and you *love* me?" He was having trouble believing what he was hearing.

"Yes, Jax, I love you. With all my heart, I love you, and I intend to be with you."

"You know this doesn't change anything. You still have to obey me. It's still going to be a matter of keeping you safe."

She laughed, but her heart was beginning to sing. "And I'm still going to argue with you when it doesn't make sense to me."

"And I'm going to spank that gorgeous ass of yours when you don't listen."

"I wouldn't expect anything less." The little minx was laughing at him!

He wrapped her in his arms, careful not to bump her injured hand. He kissed her, long and hard. "And then I'm going to fuck you, until you scream and beg me for more."

She said smugly, "I wouldn't expect anything less. So, we have a deal?"

"Only under one condition."

"Mmm, what condition?"

He tipped her head up and looked directly into her eyes. "Under the condition that you marry me. I love you, Chloe Bennett. I think I've loved you since the first moment I looked into your eyes. Marry me."

Her eyes were full of joyful tears. "Yes. Yes, yes, you just try to stop me! God, I love you."

He kissed her again, and suddenly, his world looked like a much brighter place than it had for a very long time. "Not as much as I love you. You're mine. You're mine forever."

Kat Carrington

Hi! I'm Kat Carrington and I write romance; sweet, spicy romance with happy ever after endings. I'm a grandmother and I'm having the time of my life letting my imagination go and telling the kind of stories that I like to read. And it's been a wonderful bonus to find out that other people like to read them too.

I was born and raised in Indiana where I raised my kids and welcomed the most amazing people into my life, my grandchildren. Having grandchildren is my greatest blessing. I'm living now in South Carolina with my always supportive hubby.

From the time I learned to read, there was always a book in my hands. After I consumed all the fiction in my elementary school library I moved on to biographies, which I found to be endlessly fascinating. Once I retired and we moved south I discovered that I was ready for a new venture. I thought back to when I was in fifth grade and sat for hours at a time at my dad's big desk writing stories with a pencil on notebook paper. One day I opened my laptop and started a story.

That first book took nearly two years to write. I'd write for a while, then forget all about it for a while. Somewhere along the way it changed from a whim to a real story that I had to finish. And that's when Blushing Books changed my whole life. My book was accepted for publication and was released on May 29, 2019. Writing is now part of my life and I hope you all enjoy my stories and the characters I keep falling in love with.

Don't miss these exciting titles by Kat Carrington and
Blushing Books!

Elite 6 Assassins
Assassin's Captive

Birch Bend
Unspeakable Bonds

Dirty Politics
Crash and Burn

A Strong Man's Hand
Maggie's Match
Shelby's Secrets
Surviving Savannah
Boone Beginnings
Loving Leo

Dusty Dreams Ranch
Jessie's Dusty Dreams
A Dusty Dreams Wedding

Blushing Books

Blushing Books is the oldest eBook publisher on the web. We've been running websites that publish steamy romance and erotica since 1999, and we have been selling eBooks since 2003. We have free and promotional offerings that change weekly, so please do visit us at http://www.blushingbooks.com/free.

Blushing Books Newsletter

Please join the Blushing Books newsletter
to receive updates & special promotional offers.
You can also join by using your mobile phone:
Just text **BLUSHING** to 22828.

Every month, one new sign up via text messaging will receive
a $25.00 Amazon gift card, so sign up today!